ON GUARD

Emma knew that Sir Peter Dancy was the finest swordsman in all of England. But never in her wildest dreams did she imagine that she would have to try to parry the cuts and thrusts of his formidable foil.

Sir Peter's eyes gleamed with wicked amusement as he surveyed her, clad as she was in the all-too-revealing tights and flimsy, white ruffled shirt of a gentleman fencer. Emma was embarrassingly aware at this moment that her body was not that of a man's and that her soft curves might well be a tempting target for a different kind of sport than fencing.

Smiling, Sir Peter raised his weapon and told her to do the same. With a sinking feeling in her pounding heart, Emma watched him advance on her even as she strove to keep the tip of her foil between them. She knew that any time he wished, he could sweep aside her defenses . . .

. . . and then it would no longer be sword against sword, but heart against heart . . . .

Miss Cheney's Charade

Miss Cheney's Charade

by

Emily Hendrickson

A SIGNET BOOK

SIGNET
Published by the Penguin Group
Penguin Books USA Inc., 375 Hudson Street,
New York, New York 10014, U.S.A.
Penguin Books Ltd, 27 Wrights Lane,
London W8 5TZ, England
Penguin Books Australia Ltd, Ringwood,
Victoria, Australia
Penguin Books Canada Ltd, 10 Alcorn Avenue,
Toronto, Ontario, Canada M4V 3B2
Penguin Books (N.Z.) Ltd, 182–190 Wairau Road,
Auckland 10, New Zealand

Penguin Books Ltd, Registered Offices:
Harmondsworth, Middlesex, England

First published by Signet, an imprint of Dutton Signet,
a division of Penguin Books USA Inc.

First Printing, March, 1994
10 9 8 7 6 5 4 3 2 1

Chapter 1

EMMA paused at the top of the stairs, peeping over the banister while listening for any sign of Oldham, the portly and rather self-important Cheney butler. Hearing no sounds, other than the usual racket from the street beyond the front door, and seeing no sign of life, she quietly skimmed down the stairs until she reached her goal.

"Ah," she whispered in satisfaction. The mail had arrived and Oldham had placed the neat stack on the hall table. Ignoring the bills and other letters intended for her papa, she searched for and found the one she had hoped would come. After tucking it inside the reticule she had thought to bring along, she caught sight of a strange-looking missive addressed to her brother, George. Naturally curious and quite unable to resist such an intriguing missive, she hesitated.

With a furtive glance about her, she tucked this peculiar letter in her reticule as well. After all, George had been gone for two months and wasn't expected back any time soon. The letter might be important, for a message printed on sand-colored paper with blue and green stripes along the edge was certainly out of the ordinary.

Once in the safety of her room, Emma locked her door then pulled out the two letters. Sinking onto the pretty, if somewhat worn, chair near her window, she opened hers.

"Oh, thank goodness," she cried softly in relief. She hadn't realized how much she had counted upon the *Lady's Magazine* to buy her embroidery designs. Her pattern for a cap had been purchased for more than she expected, and they would be pleased to accept additional patterns from the talented hand of Miss Cheney. Since the magazine didn't publish the name of the designer, Emma felt there was no reason to be secretive over her identity. However, she did not wish her parents to know that she sought a source of extra pin money. While Cheney was a proud old name, the family had seen better days. Hopes for the future were fastened on both George and Emma contracting good marriages.

Emma thought—based on what she had seen of Society so far—that that particular hope grew dimmer by the day.

The other letter slid down her lap. Emma hastily grabbed it up, then slit the red wax seal with growing curiosity. Unfolding it, she gasped at what she saw.

Sir Peter Dancy, At Home, Monday 5th June, 1815 . . . A mummy from Thebes to be unrolled at Half-past Two.

"A mummy! How utterly marvelous! Lucky George. He always has the fun, while I am stuck with teas and routs and every manner of dull things," Emma said wistfully.

She leaned back on the chair, allowing herself to dream of the exotic collection she had heard about from several of the *ton*. Of course, Sir Peter was often spoken of with derision, for he appeared to scorn the dictates of Society. He set his own rules and lived to his own pleasing. But what a man he must be.

Emma hadn't met the elusive gentleman. He was reputed to be the finest swordsman in all of England, in addition to owning an amazing collection of Egyptian artifacts. She'd heard he was tall and slender with thick sandy hair and strange green eyes. Apparently he didn't care for the tiresome parties of the *ton* any more than did Emma.

London had been a bitter disappointment to her. She had hoped for so much. She soon realized that without a fat dowry the Cheney name counted for little. Had her father been a peer it might have helped. But he was merely gentry of fine and distinguished background. Emma knew no great expectations.

Turning her gaze to the letter once again, she wished with all her heart that she might change places with George, just for a day. Mind you, she wasn't an improper girl, falling into scrapes and whatnot. But . . . it would be wonderful to see a mummy from Thebes unrolled. Imagine. If only . . .

A rap at her door brought a halt to her musings. Swiftly crossing the room, she turned the key and let in her maid.

"Letters, Miss Emma?" Fanny said, studying the papers in Emma's hand with prying eyes.

Quickly refolding the two pages, Emma walked to her desk to tuck them into her writing folio for the moment. "One for me and one for George," she replied, truthful as ever. Emma never lied, although she sometimes neglected to reveal all of a matter.

"When will Mr. George come home?" the maid asked. "He's a nice, quiet young man, never chasing maids like some young gentlemen do."

Amused at this assessment of her rather unusual brother, Emma shook her head. "He remains off somewhere in the wilds of Suffolk, digging for ruins or something of the sort. Heaven knows when he will remember to return."

"Your dear mama wishes you to join her in the morning room. I 'most forgot to tell you." Fanny set to work at making up the bed, then putting away Emma's pretty bed gown of sheer cambric and her dainty nightcap.

Glancing at the clock, Emma found she had daydreamed for an hour. Her mother rose promptly at noon and sought the warmth to be found in the south-facing morning room. She expected her only daughter to bear her company.

Knowing she would be in for a scolding if she dawdled, Emma hurried down the stairs. Her thoughts remained in her room, however. Sir Peter Dancy and the mummy from Thebes seemed far more alluring than planning which rout or party to attend.

Her mother and two of her friends were sitting in the morning room, gossiping over tea and dainty biscuits.

"Emma, my dear. How nice to see you have kept yourself busy this morning." Matilda Cheney gestured to the pretty bowl of flowers Emma had placed on the low table near her mother's favorite chair. One of the few luxuries allowed, fresh flowers were a great favorite of the fragile Mrs. Cheney.

"You are fortunate to have such a dutiful daughter. Pity she has not found some nice gentleman who appreciates her," Mrs. Bascomb intoned in her pompous manner.

Emma glanced at the quizzing glass leveled in her direction by the overbearing Mrs. Bascomb and managed a smile.

"Emma never puts a foot wrong," Mrs. Cheney replied with complacency.

"Now, Mama," Emma demurred, knowing that if any of them were privy to her thoughts, they would be scandalized.

"Do you go to the Titheridge affair this evening?" Lady Hamley inquired, blinking like a nervous cat.

"That woman?" Mrs. Cheney said in a wondering voice.

"I know she is a trifle eccentric, but 'tis hoped her nephew might attend," Lady Hamley concluded with a significant glance at Emma.

"I trust you refer to Sir Peter Dancy," Mrs. Bascomb boomed out, startling Emma who had drifted off into a daydream again.

At hearing the very name that figured in her dreams, Emma straightened in her chair, listening attentively for once.

"I doubt if even she can persuade him to attend her gathering, no matter how select it might be," Mrs. Cheney replied with a hopeful look at her pretty daughter.

Knowing full well what she had seen in the looking glass this morning, Emma smiled back, resigned to her fate. There was nothing unusual in gray eyes and dark curly hair, certainly nothing to capture the eye of a notable like Sir Peter.

"Her chin is a trifle too pointed, my dear, but her eyes are quite pretty," Lady Hamley said in what she no doubt perceived as an effort to be comforting.

"Pretty is as pretty does. Now, if George would just marry a fortune, we might have a chance to find Emma a husband worthy of her." Mrs. Cheney compressed her lips in annoyance at her neglectful son.

Emma longed to explode in whoops of laughter. Worthy of her? And who did her dear mother think fit that bill?

"There are not so many fortunes to be had this Season," Mrs. Bascomb reflected.

"But most of the girls are bran-faced and lacking wit," Lady Hamley added with a smile at Emma.

Knowing she didn't fit this description, Emma smiled back.

It was settled that the trio of ladies with Emma in tow would grace the Titheridge affair this evening. Once this decision was reached, the matter of clothes became the topic of earnest discussion.

Emma went back to her daydreams, for she knew full well that she would be consigned to her best white muslin with the two flounces and low white-embroidered bodice. She thought she looked insipid in it, for her face was not fashionably pale nor was she properly petite. Perhaps her carnelian brooch and earrings would add a nice bit of color?

Lightly tanned from her many sketching walks and taller than average, Emma did not fit the current mode of fashion. She did not delude herself that merely because her dark hair was in crisp curls about her face and her eyes gazed out in a dreamy haze of gray that she might sweep any man, much less a wealthy man, off his feet.

But Sir Peter was supposed to be tall, very tall. And Emma bet her pin money that even if he hovered over a mummy and other exotic things, he wasn't pale and languid either.

"If Sir Peter does attend this evening, you must be sure to let him know how talented Emma is with her drawing pencil and watercolors," Lady Hamley said, blinking her eyes in her usual fashion.

"But," Emma protested, "many young ladies draw and paint. I am nothing out of the ordinary."

The three women studied Emma until she shifted uncomfortably on her straight-backed chair.

Lady Hamley sighed with regret, blinking over her teacup.

Mrs. Bascomb frowned, then brightened. "But you do very detailed and accurate drawings, my dear. Sir Peter might appreciate that."

Emma smiled wryly, wondering what difference that could make.

At long last she was released when the callers left and her mother went to inspect her gown for the evening.

Back in her room Emma sank down on her favorite chair and stared out of the window. Placing her elbows on the sill, she put her unfashionably pointed chin on her hands. What was she to do? No great beauty, how could she hope to catch his interest? Would he permit George's little sister to view the unrolling? No thought of capturing him as a husband entered her mind. She merely wanted to see his mummy.

She didn't need to take the invitation to Sir Peter's unrolling out again for study. She knew it by heart. She also suspected that no women were invited, it being deemed a scandalous thing for a female to see. But why? What would be revealed when the linen wrappings were removed? Just a body.

She paled at that actuality, then grew more thoughtful. Surely a body—after all those years and preserved with some sort of substance—would bear little resemblance to a living person. She had glimpsed a skeleton once when George had dug up an unmarked grave while hunting for Roman treasure. It was not so terrible, and it could not hurt you.

If Sir Peter attended the party this evening and *if* she had a chance to speak with him, she fully intended to ask him if she might make use of George's invitation. With that decision made, she settled into a daydream that involved Sir Peter, who strongly resembled the knight in her childhood book of fairy tales.

It was with nervous anticipation that Emma entered the Titheridge establishment that evening. Dressed with more than her usual care and listening for once to her mother's admonitions, she hunted through the throng of people for a tall, sandy-haired man with green eyes.

He was not there.

Not giving up quite yet, she followed in her mother's wake, entering the main room where the concert of foreign music was to be held.

Lady Titheridge had traveled over the world, collecting peculiar objects wherever she went. Emma longed to examine the items she saw more closely. Perhaps during the intermission she might slip away.

Then the music began. While her mother tried to conceal a pained expression, Emma thought the sounds exquisite, if out of the common way. Flutes and other strange instruments played music such as polite Society had never heard before. Emma felt it came from jungles and dark exotic places, creeping about and twining through one's mind.

When the intermission came, Emma tried again to find Sir Peter. She thought she had espied him in the rear of the room, but by the time she reached that spot, he had gone.

So she wandered about, heedless of her mother's little nods and motions, fascinated with the exotic jade statues and Ming bowls, the wood carvings, and intriguing jewelry displayed in glass cases and on shelves set into the walls.

"You are interested in unusual things, my dear?" Lady Titheridge asked, popping up at Emma's elbow.

"I find these fascinating," Emma replied truthfully. "I could study them for hours."

"Allow me to introduce you to a gentleman who shares your taste for the beautiful and unusual." She turned to a man who stood a few feet away and said in a quietly commanding voice, "Mr. Brummell, do come here."

Emma felt her heart sinking to her toes. It was not Sir Peter as she had hoped, but the notable Mr. George Brummell, the man who rivaled the Prince Regent himself for leadership of the *ton*. She had heard of his famous set-downs and dreaded meeting the man. Her gray eyes worriedly sought his, wondering at the twinkle she found in the depths of his gray orbs. He was dressed in his usual dark blue coat, its tails modestly long. Black pantaloons added to his somber garb, and his white waistcoat was unpretentious. Only his neckcloth was a miracle of perfection, drawing the eye to its quiet elegance.

Once introductions were made, Lady Titheridge drifted away, and Emma was on her own.

"You admire the objects our hostess has collected in her journeys?" he gently queried.

"Indeed," Emma replied with enthusiasm, returning her gaze to the far safer Ming vase on the shelf before them. "I could spend hours here, sketching the beautiful pieces she owns," Emma concluded wistfully, unmindful of the sharp gaze directed at her.

"I see you are not in the common way, Miss Cheney. Most young ladies prefer to draw a pretty scene if they must. Most choose to spend time flirting."

Suspecting she had somehow provoked him, Emma tilted her somewhat pointed chin and gazed back with what amounted to a touch of defiance. "I do not wish to draw what others do, unless it happens to be what *I* enjoy. I like to see remarkable things. In fact, I would like nothing more than to view Sir Peter's mummy. . . . " Then realizing what she had admitted, she hastily added, "Or something equally interesting."

Mr. Brummell's eyes gleamed with amusement. "You are

not busily hunting a husband, as most young ladies making their come-out do?"

"Mr. Brummell, what a shocking question," she chided, laughing and wondering why this man had acquired such a reputation for being snobbish. Emma found him utterly delightful. "As you pointed out, I am not in the common way." She sighed. "Most men do not desire a wife who is other than dutiful and dull, I fear."

"You would be dutiful, but hardly dull, Miss Cheney," Mr. Brummell replied gallantly, his eyes sparkling with his diversion in this unassuming, candid young lady.

"Mama says I never put a foot wrong, but she does not know what goes on in my mind, you see," Emma confided in a rash moment of revelation.

Mr. Brummell chuckled at this droll observation. "Miss Cheney, I predict you will make a wildly successful marriage. I almost envy the man, for you are most tempting in your ingenuous way."

"Mr. Brummell, I believe you are a monstrous tease." Emma gazed happily up at the man she had feared to meet. Gray eyes sparkling, she concluded, "I suppose I must rejoin my mama now, for it seems the music is to resume."

"You enjoy it?" he queried while edging around her in the direction of the door, obviously intent upon making his escape.

"I told you I like the unusual. Although I suspect that Mama finds it a trifle confusing." Emma flashed a smile at the imposing gentleman before her.

He smiled, then bowed over her hand in his farewell. "I shall make a point to find you a gentleman worthy of your unusual charms, Miss Cheney. They are too rare to go unappreciated." With that final comment he deftly made his way to his hostess, then disappeared.

"Emma, whatever did you say to that man?" Mrs. Cheney demanded behind the security of her fan after Emma slid onto the seat beside her. "I do hope you made a good impression on him. Everyone must have noticed that he singled you out for conversation, a most unlikely thing for *him* to do. It could be the making of you, girl."

"Mr. Brummell is very nice, Mama, not at all lofty as I've been told. We discussed the pretty things Lady Titheridge has collected." Of Mr. Brummell's promise to find Emma a man who was worthy of her, Emma said nothing. She discounted that bit of nonsense for precisely what it was . . . vague foolishness.

"I see Sir Peter finally showed his face," Mrs. Cheney observed from behind her fan, then wafted that lace-and-ivory item languidly before her.

Dismayed that by chatting with Mr. Brummell she had missed meeting the man she most desired to encounter, Emma searched the room until she spotted him.

He was most definitely tall, and that thatch of sandy hair made her long to run her fingers through it, merely to smooth it down, of course. She detected a gleam of impatience in those green eyes. How she wished she could defy convention and leave her seat to cross the room to his side. She would like to find out why people claimed his eyes were so uncommon. And . . . she would ask to see his mummy unrolled.

He had an interesting face she decided while a flute began a plaintive melody. A second flute joined in a haunting counterpoint while Emma speculated on that intelligent, lean face, the aristocratic nose, and those eyes. If she could but see them most closely. Sir Peter Dancy fascinated her to the point of impropriety.

"Emma," Mrs. Cheney whispered in a shocked voice.

Emma attended her mama and lowered her gaze to the fan tightly clasped in one properly gloved hand. When she turned again to find the man who intrigued her so, he was gone. Disappointment flooded through her. How she had counted on talking with him about the mummy and persuading him to allow her to view it. Her latest pin money had gone to buy a book on Egyptian discoveries, with drawings executed by the French artist, Vivant Denon. Wildly exotic, madly fascinating, they made her long even more to see the Dancy collection.

She must see it. But how? She worried her lower lip while contemplating various ways in which to accomplish her heart's desire.

If only she might trade places with George for an hour or so. What a silly notion. Why, even if some of his clothing might fit her, she would not dare to put it on. Not even to view the mummy.

Or could she?

That thought was so disturbing that she put it from her mind at once. Instead, she concentrated on the strange music drifting about the room and daydreamed about meeting Sir Peter. What a fascinating man he must be, she concluded dreamily.

Once the concert ended, she dutifully followed her mother to make her farewells to Lady Titheridge.

"Pity my nephew could not stay," her ladyship said to Emma. "I particularly wanted him to meet you. Any young woman who can captivate George Brummell for as long as you did is of more than passing interest. Mr. Brummell has impeccable taste, and I always heed his direction. Would you care to come alone one day to view my precious collection, my dear?"

Emma beamed in gratitude. "I should love above all to be allowed to sketch a number of the beautiful items I have viewed this evening."

"There is more, you know," her ladyship murmured in reply. "Come on Monday next. In the morning?"

With a glance at her mama, who couldn't possibly object to the time or the place, Emma nodded her pleasure, murmuring her thanks in a subdued and proper way.

"Well," Mrs. Bascomb said when in the carriage on the way home, "you have made a notable conquest this evening, my girl."

Mrs. Hamley blinked and nodded. "Yes, indeed. Lady Titheridge is of the highest *ton*, and as for catching the eye of Mr. Brummell, well . . . "

"Wait until word of this gets around, Matilda," Mrs. Bascomb said to Mrs. Cheney, who was sitting in amazed silence.

"Listening to that horrid music was well worth the pain," Mrs. Cheney concluded before bidding her two friends good evening.

Once inside their modest home, Emma paused at the bottom of the stairs. "Did you think the music so painful?"

"I should have been far more pleased were you to have met Sir Peter," her mother grumbled softly.

Emma just smiled and dreamily escorted her dear mama up the stairs to her room. Them Emma wandered down the hall to her own bedroom.

Lighting a candle from the small fire in the grate, she then sought her favorite chair and sank down to contemplate her strange evening. She could not see *how* it would happen, but she sensed that somehow the course of her entire life had altered because of what had occurred tonight. Or was she merely being fanciful?

She toyed with her fan while considering Sir Peter. She was *not* interested in him as a prospective husband. Marriage to a man like him might be rather overwhelming. But she was determined to see that mummy.

Then the idea that had flashed into her mind while at the concert returned. Suppose she borrowed a few clothes from her brother? And suppose she wore them to Sir Peter's house for the unrolling of the mummy? If she were to stay well to the back of the room and not chat with anyone, just keep quiet and unnoticed, could she achieve her aim?

"Monday, 5th June," the invitation had read. She sat up straighter. Suppose she gathered up her brother's clothing and put it into a small valise, then took it along to Lady Titheridge's on Monday morning. Then she could send a note to Mama that she was remaining for luncheon and the afternoon to view some more antiquities. It might work.

Her mama would be pleased to think that Emma was attracting the notice of an eminent person of the *ton*. As to what Lady Titheridge might construe from Emma's change, well, that was a problem.

Emma rose from her chair and began to undress. Fanny had not made an appearance, for she knew Emma preferred to be alone in the evening. It did not take her long to undress, don her night things, and pop under the covers to contemplate her grand scheme at greater length.

She would do it, she finally decided. Sliding from under the covers, she took a candle and peeked around her door to the empty hall. Not a soul around. Taking a deep breath, Emma tiptoed along to the next room where her brother resided when at home, which wasn't very often these days.

Once inside, she swiftly sought dove gray pantaloons, a couple of waistcoats, and a cambric shirt. A darker gray coat looked too big, but perhaps if she wore both waistcoats at once it might work. Then she hunted for a neckcloth. Knowing how difficult they could be, she decided to take several, just in case she made a botch of her efforts. Her last items were a pair of plain black hose and shoes.

She spirited her booty back to her room and wondered where to conceal it all until Monday. Finally she found a valise large enough to hold the clothing and settled under her covers with a wildly fluttering heart.

She would do it. All she had to do was manage to slip out of the house with her little valise, plus her drawing pad and pencils, without detection. That meant evading the pompous Oldham, who guarded the front door with gimlet-eyed fervor.

The following day when she was able to lock her door without suspicion from Fanny, Emma pulled the valise out and tried on the garb filched from her brother's wardrobe and chest. She studied her reflection in the looking glass and grimaced.

She and George resembled each other as siblings often do, but was it enough? George slouched just a bit, which was fortunate for Emma. Even though it went against her grain not to stand properly straight, the slight difference in height could be excused that way.

Then she wondered just how well Sir Peter knew George. She plunked down on the edge of her bed, staring at her reflection across the room.

That might prove to be a problem. She couldn't recall her brother mentioning Sir Peter, but that was hardly surprising, for George was uncommunicative at best. Witness his dreadful lack of letters while away. Poor Mama sighed every day when the mail did not bring a letter from him.

Well, she wouldn't say a word to anyone while inside the Dancy house. She would keep to the rear and be as inconspicuous as possible.

It would work. She would make it work.

The next few days dragged for Emma. She daydreamed more than usual, and her drawing pad acquired several well-done sketches of the elusive Sir Peter—done admittedly from a distance and memory. But Emma was very good at what she did. She possessed an uncanny eye for detail, as Mrs. Bascomb had observed. And she had caught the impatient gleam in Sir Peter's eyes, the tousled sandy hair.

Emma was pleased she had purchased a set of colored pencils with her latest pin money from Papa. She added the color to her drawing and felt it most lifelike.

On Monday she dressed with great care for her visit to Lady Titheridge's house. She escaped with the valise, slipping from the house when Oldham was otherwise occupied.

It proved to be wonderful. Her ladyship ushered Emma into one room after another, explaining where she had found her precious treasures and promising Emma she could come again to record more of her things.

When she viewed Emma's first drawing, she gasped with delight. "My dear, you are extremely talented. Oh, why could not Peter have stayed to meet you the other evening. You are precisely what he has been looking for—a talented pencil."

Emma had never thought of herself in that light, but merely murmured something vague in reply.

When it came time to leave, Emma sought out her ladyship, hesitantly placing her valise on the floor at her side. The sparkle of amusement lurking in Lady Titheridge's eyes encouraged Emma to speak.

"If you please, ma'am, I would like to change my clothes before I leave if I might." Emma stopped, hesitating before revealing more. Her ladyship's mouth curved into a delightful smile, and Emma plunged ahead. Gazing confidingly at her ladyship and feeling as though she'd made a splendid friend, Emma continued, "You see, I plan a little trick on a friend"— Well, he might have been a friend had he stayed to meet her— "and wish to wear some clothes belonging to my brother."

"A charade? What fun," replied the adventuresome Lady Titheridge. "Of course. *I* shall help you."

Chapter 2

EVELYN, Lady Titheridge, had spent years traveling the world and possessed a wonderful sense of adventure. That she was not in the common way became even more evident when Emma saw what enjoyment her elegant ladyship found in assisting Emma to rig herself out in George's clothing.

"Now, my dear, let me see how you look. Hm, you will most assuredly require a bit of padding, and those shoes are not at all the thing with your slender feet. It would never do for them to fall off while you mount the stairs! I shall see if my abigail can find something more fitting." Her conspiratorial smile gleamed a moment before she flitted from the room.

Emma studied herself in the cheval glass and had to agree with Lady Titheridge. She definitely needed padding here and there.

Within moments Braddon followed her mistress into the small bedroom where Emma anxiously awaited them. The sturdy maid studied Emma, then set to work. She deftly inserted sheets of cotton wool into Emma's shirt front, then tied the neckcloth over that into a most elegant and simple shape after helping Emma into the two vests. These contributed to the bulk and added just enough to Emma's girth.

Braddon whipped out a pair of gentleman's shoes from a small satchel she'd brought with her, then motioned Emma to a bench before a dressing table. She proceeded to slightly darken Emma's skin with a cream from a pot that had been concealed in an apron pocket. Then she brushed Emma's hair into a tousled effect. When the maid finally finished her efforts, Emma stared back at an unfamiliar young gentleman. Before her appeared a slim young man with a light tan, a fashionable hair style, and a neckcloth tied in the latest mode, and who looked remarkably like her brother, George, newly returned from one of his digs. She hoped.

"I do believe I shall fool everyone," Emma declared with dawning assurance.

"It is quite possible you shall pass," her ladyship observed.

"Tell me, ma'am, just how observant is Sir Peter?" Emma then inquired absently while checking the fall of her coat in the back.

"Aha! You are going to see his mummy unrolled this afternoon," the astute Lady Titheridge cried. "Well, I suppose he is like most people; he sees what he expects to see."

"Oh, dear," Emma said in dismay, placing one hand over her mouth. "I truly had not intended to tell you that. I fear I require practice in telling fabrications. You see, I do so want to see that mummy. When I espied George's invitation, it seemed like an answer to all my wishes. You are not too terribly horrified?" Emma gazed at Sir Peter's aunt with hopeful eyes.

"Not at all, well, at least not much. You will find I am the best of accomplices. Braddon will be silent as the grave as well. I hope you will take your drawing pad along and do a sketch or two?" her ladyship suggested slyly. "I am keenly interested, and the wretched boy did not invite me to his unrolling."

"I shall be happy to make a sketch if you think he will not be displeased. I intend to stay in the background. After all, I do not know how well my brother knows Sir Peter. While I resemble George, I may have trouble if Sir Peter recalls something I know nothing about." Emma wondered that her ladyship could call one as distinguished as Sir Peter a boy, then turned her concerns toward whether or not she might actually dare to sketch.

"Worry about that if it happens," Lady Titheridge replied with a smile. She checked the timepiece pinned to her gown and gasped. "You had best hurry if you do not wish to be late. I believe he intends to unroll the mummy shortly after half-past two. It is rising two now, and you will need a bit of time to go from here to his house."

Braddon walked to the door, then paused. "I shall have Leland summon a hackney for you, miss—or should I say Mr. Cheney?"

"I had best become accustomed to that name if only for the afternoon," Emma replied.

"You are a very brave girl, my dear. Not many young women would dare to pursue their heart's desire in such a fashion. You must exercise great caution and not allow anyone to guess your identity. *That* would bring your ruination!" Lady Titheridge admonished.

"I am aware of that, but I really wish to see the mummy. Since George is never in London save on rare occasions, I doubt if any of those in attendance will know him well." Then Emma declared with her endearing honesty, "I fear I have not made much of a splash in Society, ma'am. I doubt if any there will recognize me even if they might suspect I am not who I pretend to be."

"See that you remain as silent as possible and do keep to the rear." Lady Titheridge watched as her young guest left the room, then peered from the window while Emma entered the hackney. The amused gleam in her ladyship's eyes might have given Emma pause had she seen it. Evelyn, Lady Titheridge, decided then and there to see that Emma made her "splash," beginning with the much-desired vouchers to the Wednesday evening affairs at Almack's. Evelyn frequently attended and had never seen Emma present. Lady Titheridge left the room to make her way to her own dressing chamber with the intent of then paying a call on Lady Sefton, that favorite of the patronesses.

Emma was on edge. She was well aware of the dangers that lurked in her path, the least of which was that Sir Peter find her out. She nervously clenched and unclenched her gloved hands all the way across Mayfair.

After paying the jarvey from the little purse she had remembered to place in her pocket, Emma made her way up the steps to the front door. The sound of the knocker echoed within the house. She hoped that its resemblance to a sound of doom was merely her imagination.

The door opened and a jolly-looking man ushered her in with deference once Emma had extended her invitation—that is, George's invitation.

"Right this way, Mr. Cheney," the butler urged, having quickly perused the name on the card.

Emma followed him up the stairs, thankful that Lady Titheridge had insisted upon better-fitting shoes. Really, the pantaloons were most comfortable, and Emma wondered why young ladies might not wear something that offered such ease and freedom.

The drawing room was blessedly full of men. They were gathered in small clusters and were all deep in earnest conversation. Across the room the mummy reposed on an oak table, its bandaged contents waiting to be unrolled. Emma scarcely took note of the unusual and exotic furniture about her. Chairs with scroll curving arms and backs and rounded X-frame front legs were decorated with designs of lotus leaves, scarabs, and sphinxes all done in gold and black.

Emma slipped off to one side and around to a point where she thought she might see fairly well, making sure not to meet the eyes of anyone near her. She really ought not have attempted such a dangerous exploit. Sir Peter—or someone— was certain to catch her out, and then where would she be? In the soup, that's where. Her mouth was dry and she wished she dared to sip some of the wine she detected on a tray not far from where she stood. That was a sure way to disaster, and she dare not request water. Then she sensed someone had come up to her.

"George, how good of you to come. I had feared you would be off in Sussex," said a cultured voice to Emma's left. It had to be Sir Peter.

Heart pounding madly, she turned slowly, hoping she might manage to scrape by his scrutiny. "Wouldn't miss it for the world," Emma replied in the voice that she had been practicing in the privacy of her room. She hoped that she managed to sound like George. She chanced to look in Sir Peter's eyes to see if he accepted her disguise.

Not by a flicker of an eyelash did Peter reveal his shock at what he saw when the young man before him turned around. While there was a superficial resemblance to his casual friend, it was not George! And if it was not George, who was it? He pretended to countenance the impostor and chatted briefly before excusing himself to check on something with Radley. His butler had eyes as astute as Peter's, and it would be interesting to see what Radley made of this astounding development.

"Our last guest has arrived," Peter began.

"Indeed," Radley responded in his correct manner with only a slight elevation of his eyebrows to indicate he found anything out of the ordinary in the circumstances.

"Did you notice something unusual about him?" Peter turned so he might casually inspect this somewhat nervous newcomer who appeared to shun contact with the others.

"He had the proper invitation, and we often see young gentlemen who are somewhat slender, do we not?" Radley replied with a narrow gaze at this particular guest. As usual, his perception went beyond what might be expected, briefly observed, when his expression shifted to one of suspicion.

Peter couldn't prevent a grin from momentarily flashing across his face. He hastily wiped it away, but continued to dart glances at the young person who had pulled a drawing pad from beneath a coat and begun to sketch the mummy in all its wrappings.

Then Peter stilled for a moment. He knew bones very well, and those bones were not masculine in the least. Those long slender legs and the curvaceous hips did *not* belong to a young man. When he scrutinized the person further, the hands proved far too delicate in appearance. It was a woman! But who? She was tall for a woman, but shapely nonetheless, unless she had more padding than he suspected. She certainly resembled his friend, enough to fool nearly all who were not well acquainted with the elusive George Cheney.

Then he remembered. George had a younger sister who must be of an age to be making her come-out in London about now. She could have had access to the invitation and penned an acceptance with ease. How she thought she might perform such a charade was beyond Peter. She definitely presented a riddle and certainly was dramatic in presentation. But it was obvious she did *not* wish her identity to be guessed.

He observed that the other men in the room appeared not to notice a thing wrong with the young chap who so properly took a place off to one side. It showed a fitting respect to the older men, and they looked on the newcomer with benign disregard.

Deciding he had best attend to business before someone

looked more closely and precipitated a scandal, Peter strode to the front of the room to stand by the mummy.

"And now, gentlemen, the thing that has brought you here this afternoon . . . the mummy from Thebes." Peter began to weave the tale of how the mummy had been removed from Egypt and shipped home along with a great deal of other treasure his father had appropriated in the name of scholarship.

It had reposed in a dim corner of one of the storerooms until recently. Peter had decided to investigate the identity if possible. And that required unwrapping the body.

He noted that the young woman off to one side flinched when he mentioned the body encased in the yards of wrappings. He repressed a smile that longed to sneak out and continued with his intent.

With a flourish worthy of a showman, he began with the end of the linen strip and carefully, slowly, unrolled it, taking care to keep that roll sung so that the linen wrapping would not become an unmanageable tangle.

From where she stood, Emma watched Sir Peter commence the unrolling of the mummy. She had captured an excellent likeness of the wrapped body before he began, and she waited, pencil poised, for him to conclude. She concentrated on the details, the peculiar smell that drifted across the room to tease her nostrils, the coarse texture of the linen, and the small objects that came to light as the wrappings proceeded.

A scarab, large and faded blue, came to sight. Emma edged closer so she might draw it. Another amulet came to view, and Emma felt her excitement rise. She again edged closer to the table upon which the mummy rested.

Peter took note of the young woman's interest and lack of vapors. Whatever her name might be, she was indeed a plucky thing. He glanced at Radley, who assisted him with the delicate task of winding up the yards and yards of linen bandages, when he handed him another neat roll. At the end of each strip that roll was carefully numbered and placed aside on a nearby table. It seemed his butler also had watched the young woman and appeared to be impressed.

Peter took all the amulets and bits of jewelry he came upon and put them to the front of the table. The look of total absorption on the face of the strange young woman caught his curiosity. She continued to sketch each little amulet, and her eyes grew round with excitement when she viewed the pieces of jewelry. Just like a woman, he thought—captivated by jewelry even if it is old stuff removed from a mummy.

Yet he had to admit he found each item exquisitely beautiful. He wondered if there was any order or reason to where the amulets had been placed on the wrappings, or were they perhaps included at random. He'd likely never guess, but he found himself pleased that the young artist was recording them in order of removal.

Really, she proved to be a godsend, did she but know it. He had looked in vain for a man who would consent to draw his findings and had found not a soul. Apparently, the artists of the day considered it beneath them to do such a thing as sketch scarabs and necklaces, much less a mummy.

Peter's eyes gleamed at the sight that met his eyes when he lifted up the bandages close to the body. He held up a necklace that came to light as the piles of bandages had reached amazing proportions. The necklace was incredibly beautiful to his eyes.

In the middle of the center portion a pale green quartz scarab seemed to have odd wings sprouting from each side of it. These had carnelians and lapis lazuli set in narrow rows. A design he recognized as stylized lotus buds made a row of decoration that dangled from the lower edge of the design, which consisted of carnelian and lapis lazuli, gold, and a few other stones.

He reverently lifted up the necklace so that all might see. His little artist's gasp of delight would normally have given her away, but there was such a widespread reaction by the gentlemen in attendance that she went unnoticed. Murmurs went through the group, sounding like the hum from a hive.

"I say, Sir Peter, you have found a real treasure there," Mr. Reginald Swinburne declared in a hearty voice. "Fancy it lurking about your storeroom all these years. Good joke, what?"

Peter gave the man—a guest of a friend who had received an invitation and not someone he knew well—an annoyed glance.

"The gold alone must be worth a tidy fortune," added Peter's good friend Edward, Lord Worcester. He moved closer to the table to have a better look at the beautiful necklace, worthy of a queen.

"What a lucky chap, to have a father who brought home trinkets such as that," Lord Petersham said, envy clear in his voice. Since all knew his perpetual lack of ready funds, laughter drifted through the room, breaking some of the tension that had built up as the unrolling proceeded.

"I say, old fellow, you will have to hire a guard if you intend to keep all these things in the house," Mr. Swinburne advised.

Peter gave him a thoughtful glance, then reverently placed the necklace on the table so that his young artist might draw it next.

No one paid the least attention to the young man who so diligently drew each item. Peter figured that the others must have decided that he had hired an artist. No one spoke to the lad, nor did that artist receive more than the most casual of glances—fortunately. The last thing Peter wanted was a scandal on his hands.

At last the dark brown, leathery-looking body came to view. The skin was tautly drawn across the skull. Arms had been placed in a protective position across the chest. A rare and beautifully shaped beetlelike heart scarab had been put on the last bit of bandaging that covered the chest of the body.

"I think this must have been a princess from the wealth wrapped herein. Note the smaller size of the head and the structure of the body. She does not reveal any sign of injury, and note, gentlemen, how perfectly formed she is."

"Even her teeth look good," one of the men observed.

"Must not have been fond of sweets," another joked.

Emma wished they would all go away and leave her alone with the princess. She did not doubt for a moment that Sir Peter was correct in his assumptions. The body seemed so regal, and the scarabs and jewelry had been so wonderfully made that Emma had found it hard to contain her astonishment.

"What do you plan to do with the body now that you have it unwrapped?" Mr. Swinburne inquired as he hovered over the table holding the body and all the artifacts included with it.

"That shall require some thought. I may begin a sort of museum of my own . . . with the items my father brought as the foundation for it. I should need some help, but I believe I have found just the person to assist me." He glanced at the young artist to see the effect of his words on her. She had paled, but said nothing.

Instead, Emma began to sketch the body, carefully making a detailed drawing of the dear little scarab that had been placed directly over the heart. What a precious little thing it was. Emma intended to do full justice to the princess.

Gradually the voices faded away, although Emma took no notice. At last the room was empty, save for Emma and the Princess.

Peter reentered the room, pausing by the door to watch his little artist at work. He approached her, wondering just how capable she might be in her work. He did not have high hopes, but since he had no one else, he would make do with her efforts.

"I see you have been diligently at work. May I ask to see what you have done, old fellow?" Peter had decided he would not call her bluff, but treat her as though she had succeeded with her masquerade.

"Of course," she replied, looking about her with surprise when she offered him her drawing pad. "Where is everyone? Have I stayed so very late?" She looked horrified. Peter wondered if her mother would ask uncomfortable questions were she not to arrive home shortly.

He didn't answer at once, he was so captivated by the excellent drawings. She combined the skill of a draftsman with the delicacy of an artist. He could not have been more pleased.

"These are truly wonderful. May I have them? I'll gladly pay you anything you ask, for I had intended to hire a professional. Couldn't find one that would stomach the notion of drawing a mummy."

"I had intended to take these home and work on them a bit more. I have colored pencils that would enhance them, particularly the jewelry," she began.

"Bring them here, instead," Peter said with the urgency he felt. He could not allow these drawings out of his hands to be possibly lost or destroyed. "Could you come tomorrow morning—work with me? I know how interested you are in antiquities. And I suspect you would not be averse to a bit of the ready, for I know full well what it can cost to be involved in a digging . . . hiring all those chaps to muck about in the soil while you hunt for bits and pieces of Roman antiquities."

She stiffened, then appeared to ponder his suggestion. Peter held his breath while she seemed to have a debate with herself. Did she need a bit of money? Most girls must, and he knew the Cheney fortune was not great.

"I would be most indebted to you if you could see your way to helping me out. I have a secretary who is a fine chap such as he can manage, but he cannot draw worth a fig."

"I will have to think it over. May I take one of the sketches with me? I did two of the necklace. And then I really must fly. I will send you a note later if I may."

There was nothing he could do short of keeping her captive, and one hardly did that sort of thing anymore.

"I trust you will think kindly on my offer and need of help—considering that you are someone who has similar interests. It would not be for so very long, I think."

She merely nodded her head, while edging toward the door. Within minutes she had made her way down the stairs and out of the front door, clutching that one drawing of the necklace in her gloved hand. Radley had foreseen that she would need to leave soon and had summoned a hackney from the stand around the corner.

Peter stood by a window to watch the vehicle disappear down the street. He turned to face his butler and grimaced.

"She has gone, and I don't know if she will come back or not. Dash it all, I'm not even certain who she is."

"I wonder if your aunt might be of assistance? She might know which of the young ladies of the *ton* could do such a thing. It might be no bad thing were you to frequent a few of the balls and parties for a time. You might find her there," Radley suggested in an offhand manner.

"Hah!" Peter declared with affection, "I believe you are trying to find me a wife, old fellow."

"Now, Sir Peter, would I do such a thing?"

The two men, opponents of long standing, chuckled.

Peter turned again to consider the suggestion made by his butler, who actually was something closer to a friend, considering all they had gone through over the years. He had an excellent point. Peter decided he would take himself off and shock the *ton* by appearing at a few of the parties. His good aunt would know which ones to attend.

Emma exited the hackney in front of Lady Titheridge's with more haste than grace. Dashing up the steps, she smiled with relief when Leland opened the door for her, spiriting her up the stairs to the small bedroom where Braddon awaited her.

While the abigail removed the paint and eased Emma from her brother's garments, Emma pleaded with her to hurry.

"Calm down, my dear," Lady Titheridge urged as she entered the room. "I feel certain your dear mama will be mollified when you hand her these."

She held up coveted vouchers for Almack's in one hand, while smiling at Emma, secure in the knowledge that with the sight of these esteemed slips of paper all queries would be forgotten by Mrs. Cheney.

"Oh, my. Mama will surely be pleased," Emma said in a most subdued manner, awed at the turn in her circumstances.

"Now, tell me all about it. What was it like? Was it very grisly to see the skeleton? Were you able to make sketches?" Lady Titheridge inquired in a rush.

"It was utterly fascinating, ma'am. The body was not the least frightening. Your nephew believes it to be that of a princess. Fancy that! And I made some sketches." Emma reached for the one she had managed to take along with her. "He kept all the others, but I brought you this one to see."

"And this is a necklace that had been placed on her body? How curious. Not unlike what we do, I suppose," her ladyship mused.

"Oh, but ma'am," Emma interrupted in her hurry to be gone, "he wants me to come tomorrow to draw some more, color what I have done. What shall I do?"

"He said nothing about your disguise?" her ladyship inquired with a sharp look at Emma.

Emma shook her head. "Not a word. But he was much occupied with the mummy and all the important gentlemen who were there. I doubt if he paid me much attention."

Lady Titheridge looked a trifle doubtful at that, but said nothing.

Emma repeated, "What shall I do?"

"Why, I believe you ought to go. Goodness knows he has been hunting for someone to assist him for an age. He has an able secretary, although I believe he broke an arm not too long ago. At any rate, I recall Peter telling me that the man was not the least help in working with the Egyptian research." Lady Titheridge sank down upon a pretty little chair close to the window, holding out the vouchers for Almack's to Emma.

"I do not know if I can continue the disguise, this charade," Emma said in a whisper, looking to her ladyship with worried eyes.

"Nonsense, my dear. Leave the clothes here with us for the time being. Braddon will work a few miracles with them and perhaps increase your wardrobe a trifle. It is very important to my nephew that he is able to accomplish this task. I will do anything I may to help him in this effort." Her ladyship gave Emma an assessing look. "You are a godsend, my dear. You have the daring and the talent to carry this off, I am convinced. It will only be for a brief time. Surely you can do it? Try," her ladyship pleaded.

"I do not know, ma'am. I take such a risk."

"But what a wonderful risk! Think of it! No ordinary young woman would be permitted to handle such antiquities, or even see them, for that matter. You would be drawing the precious artifacts from a long-dead princess. That could happen but once in a lifetime. Would it not be worth everything?" her ladyship coaxed.

"Everything?" Emma whispered, echoing her ladyship. Emma considered what was at stake. Were she uncovered, her disguise revealed, she risked her entire future. The scandal didn't bear thinking about. Dare she spend a few days in close proximity to Sir Peter to draw those fabulous jewels and scarabs, the other things he wished recorded? She set aside the image of a tall, handsome gentleman for the moment.

She would be paid a sum of money to do this drawing, and that enticed her more than anything else, which said a great deal for her desire for a bit of income. If she were to attend Almack's, her best white muslin must be replaced at once.

The sight of the slips of paper—and such powerful persuasions they were—resolved her dilemma.

"I will try my best to please him," Emma said at last.

"Good," her ladyship said with great satisfaction clear in her voice.

Emma placed the vouchers carefully in her reticule, caught up her pelisse, then begged a hurried leave from Lady Titheridge before dashing down the stairs to the carriage awaiting her. It was not a hackney but her ladyship's personal vehicle.

At Emma's look of surprise, Leland unbent enough to explain, "Her ladyship is that taken with you, miss. I believe you remind her of herself when she was a girl." Looking as though he might have said more than he ought, he assisted Emma into the carriage.

Her thoughts were in a tumbled whirl on the drive back to the Cheney residence. How was she to handle this affair? Her ladyship had suggested she inform her mother that Lady Titheridge had begged Emma to assist her with a project. Emma concluded that her ladyship had the right of it. Mrs. Cheney would not care what it was as long as her daughter would be able to attend Almack's. Morning visits while Mrs. Cheney was still abed were nothing to be worried about.

"Emma, my dear, you are very late. We are to attend the opera with Mrs. Bascomb this evening. Where *have* you been" Mrs. Cheney demanded in her refined way when Emma slipped into the morning room.

"Lady Titheridge seems to have taken a fancy to me, Mother. Just look what she gave me before I left to come home." Emma pulled the coveted slips from her reticule to hand them to her mother.

"Vouchers!" Mrs. Cheney fluttered a handkerchief to her brow, then groped for her vinaigrette. "You will need a new dress immediately, for we must attend this coming Wednesday, naturally. Oh, bless Mrs. Bascomb for persuading us to attend the musical program at Lady Titheridge's. I have hopes for you yet, my dear."

Her hopes were nothing as compared to Emma's.

Chapter 3

EMMA watched the footman depart with her note to Sir Peter. "Be firm," she admonished herself. It was too late to turn faint of heart. She had agreed, as she promised Lady Titheridge, to do her best to assist Sir Peter.

Her mother, as usual, was still abed when Emma slipped from the house. This time Emma calmly informed Oldham that she was off to Lady Titheridge's—which was true as far as it went. No one need know that from there she whisked herself over to Sir Peter's establishment once she changed into her disguise.

She looked forward to seeing more of his house. What she had glimpsed yesterday afternoon, when she could tear her eyes from the mummy and the amulets, was fascinating.

Sir Peter had elected to decorate his house in the Egyptian style; unusual friezes had been painted on the walls. The furniture, such as the chairs she had observed, reflected the motif as well, and Emma wondered just how comfortable it might be. Or was he so busy that he never took time to lounge about? He did not fit the image of a dandy, for not one of them would admit to being interested in anything so scholarly as antiquities.

No, he was unique. He dressed in the height of fashion, albeit in a restrained elegance. Yet he clearly was totally absorbed in his specialty. From what Lady Titheridge said, Sir Peter had not paid the least attention to acquiring a wife. Emma found that tidbit of information most interesting—and curious.

She approached the house on Bruton Street with some trepidation. After sending off the note, she had taken time to color in the necklace from memory, and she wondered how close she had come to the original.

The same jolly-looking man let her into the house, and Emma envied Sir Peter his butler. He was not the least starched-up and looked as though he might actually have sympathies. When he smiled at her, Emma somehow felt secure.

"I am here to assist Sir Peter," Emma said in her pretending-to-be-George voice.

"Right this way, sir." The butler led Emma down a long hall. To one side she caught sight of a room painted pale green and decorated in white with Egyptian motifs. She wondered if that settee might possibly be comfortable, with its curved back and quite Egyptian style.

They entered into a large, well-lit workroom. Glass cases filled with Egyptian artifacts stood around the walls with a few cases in the center of the room next to a large mahogany table of simple design. Spread out on the table were all the drawings that Emma had done the day before.

She wrinkled her nose at the smell of the room, which seemed faintly acrid. Somehow the scent of ages permeated the air. She resolved to bring some cinnamon-spiced potpourri with her next time she came.

"Ah, George, good of you to come. You don't know how I appreciate your help. I suppose you developed that wonderful talent for sketching while in the field—all those Roman remains, you know." Sir Peter strolled into the room, joining Emma by the table. "Do you intend to return to Sussex when the weather improves?"

To Emma's knowledge George never allowed a little thing like inclement weather to stop him. Even if it poured rain or dusted snow, he found something to do. She avoided meeting Sir Peter's green eyes and nodded. The less she said, the better.

"You are looking a trifle peaked, if you forgive me saying so," Sir Peter continued without waiting for Emma to speak, squinting at her through narrowed eyes. "Best have a mind for your health. You know what they say . . . if you do not have a care, no one else will, either." He chuckled at his little *bon mot*, then turned his attention to the drawings.

"This is what I propose. You work at the coloring of these

drawings today. Ought to be able to do a few this morning. I shall catalog—or try to catalog—each of the amulets uncovered yesterday."

Emma found George's voice. "You have a difficulty with cataloging?"

"My handwriting is barely readable. Never one of my strong points, y'know," Sir Peter confessed with a twinkle in his eyes that Emma found rather endearing when she ventured to meet his gaze. "I say . . . you might be of help there. My secretary broke his arm last week. I sent him home to recover—not the least use to me. I could not help but notice *your* handwriting in the note you sent round this morning. Neat. Nice. I'd pay you the same amount. It would help you out with those digging chaps. I don't expect my friends to put themselves out to great effort without recompense, you know. Think on it if you will."

He affected a morose sigh, then went to a small adjacent room where Emma could see him bend over a desk piled high with papers. Poor man. Without a secretary to assist him, he truly needed help. But not hers, she reminded herself. She was not quite *that* desperate for money to take that sort of risk.

She resolutely turned her attention to her drawings and began to delicately color the first of the collection. Soon she was totally lost to the world, utterly absorbed in creating a perfect likeness of the first of the blue scarabs. This was followed by another amulet, and she sighed with satisfaction at the effect she achieved.

When next she glanced at the pocket watch Lady Titheridge had urged her to slip into her fob pocket, Emma was horrified to find the morning had flown. She popped up from her stool and marched to the door where Sir Peter sat in unhappy silence. Well, she amended, he was not exactly silent, for he kept muttering things under his breath that she most likely would be better off not knowing.

"I must leave for now, Sir Peter. I believe I may be able to return tomorrow morning if you like." Emma hovered near the door, wondering if she ought to persuade her mama to flee the country and away from danger. Yet, Emma ardently desired to sketch and color the artifacts arranged about the room. She would brazen it out as long as she might. That she felt an attraction to the sandy-haired man was completely disregarded.

"Since when have we been so formal?" Sir Peter grinned at Emma, and she felt an odd pang in her heart. "Plain Peter to you, George. And tomorrow will be fine. By the bye, how is that sister of yours doing? She come to London for her come-out as yet?" Sir Peter bent his head, seeming to examine the paper close to his nose.

Emma gulped and thought if Sir Peter was anything, it was *not* plain. "Emma is in Town. Mama's in a dither. You know how it can be."

"I expect Emma dances at Almack's by now?" he said with a casual air, glancing back up at her.

Emma decided that the reason his eyes had been described as strange was that they were changeable. One minute they seemed a translucent sea green, glowing like sunlight through ocean water. The next moment they were the unfathomable color of a deep forest glade. Either way, they were extraordinary.

"I do not know," Emma said. She had no idea what Wednesday evening would bring. "She'll attend this week," she stupidly admitted, then wondered if her brains had taken leave of her. Her only comfort was that Sir Peter was not likely to attend; she had heard he never did.

"That's nice," Sir Peter murmured in reply, returning his attention to the stack of papers. "See you tomorrow. And George, I do appreciate all you are doing for me."

Emma glowed inside at the thought that she was helping in so scholarly a venture. She whisked herself down the hall with a hurried smile at the butler as she sailed out the front door.

Behind her Radley gently closed the door, then bustled down the hall to pause before the desk where his employer worked. "Learn anything of interest, sir?"

"Her name is Emma Cheney. And she will be at Almack's come this Wednesday evening. I shall take your advice, I believe. Come Wednesday I will also attend Almack's."

"Lady Titheridge may acquire a few ideas, sir," Radley ventured.

"Let her," Peter murmured as he reapplied himself to his work.

Radley bowed, then bustled off to the kitchen for a pot of coffee and a few small buns that were favorites of his employer. He placed the tray close to hand, poured a cup of steaming coffee, then quietly slipped from the room.

At Lady Titheridge's establishment Emma found herself petted and fussed over. "What a wonderful girl you are," her ladyship declared when the last of the makeup had been removed and Emma's pretty face was back to its natural quiet beauty.

Emma grimaced. "Thank you. My dear mama would be pleased were some gentleman to think so. I believe it worries her that I have received so little interest. I understand she was a belle in her day."

"And so she was. And you shall be as well, mark my words." She turned to her maid. "Braddon, can you think of anything Emma might do to improve her looks by tomorrow evening?"

"What do you intend to wear?" Braddon inquired while studying Emma from all angles.

Emma gave the maid a confused look, turning to watch her expression. Judging from that, Emma must be hopeless.

"Mama hoped to order me a new dress in time, but the mantuamaker was inundated with orders. With everyone rushing from one ball and party to another, it is scarcely to be wondered."

"So you will wear . . . ?" Lady Titheridge said.

"The same dress I wore to your musical evening, I fear. What Mr. Brummell will say when he sees I have nothing else to put on does not bear thinking." Emma did not even consider fibbing to her ladyship. Why bother? Everyone in London had a pretty fair notion of what everyone else's prospects might be.

"Bring it with you tomorrow. Braddon is a miracle when it comes to altering a pretty dress. And as I recall, you looked quite pretty that evening."

Emma gave her ladyship an appreciative smile. Perhaps if her own mama would say a few kind words instead of nagging Emma to stand thus and sit so and countless little items, she would not be so nervous.

Tuesday evening was to be devoted to learning the waltz in case Emma be granted the privilege of performing that somewhat scandalous dance.

Mr. Cheney was pressed into service, for although he rarely attended parties, he truly enjoyed a whirl about the floor with his pretty wife once in a while.

"Now attend, Emma. It goes like this." He held her mama in his arms, and they began twirling about the floor in a delightful swaying rhythm that set Emma to tapping her foot. She watched carefully and then rose from her chair to attempt to duplicate the steps. With her natural grace it was not long before she caught on to the relatively simple steps. It was not like the quadrille or cotillion in the least. When her dear papa changed partners, drilling the steps, he found Emma a ready follower.

"You learn quite fast, my dear."

"If only she would take," Mrs. Cheney murmured into her handkerchief. "Although I cannot say I agree that unmarried ladies should be allowed to waltz. I should think *that* dance would put all manner of notions into their heads," she grumbled.

"I suspect those notions are already in place, my dear," Mr. Cheney softly said before escaping from the drawing room before his wife could think of something else for him to do.

The following morning, when Emma slipped from the house, she carried her best white muslin over her arms as well as the jar of cinnamon-spiced potpourri. Fanny had been that curious about the dress being removed from the house on the very day that Emma would wear it to Almack's. However, she could scarcely make an issue of it, a circumstance for which Emma was devoutly grateful.

Braddon looked over the dress, inspecting the flounces and the prettily embroidered bodice with a knowing eye. Then she assisted Emma into her disguise and sent her off.

Once Emma had left the house, her ladyship summoned her abigail to her side. "What can be done with the dress?"

The maid shook her head. "Not a great deal, my lady. 'Tis a comely dress, but would not take to alteration."

"I was afraid of that. Come, we will take it along with us to Madame Clotilde's. She has known my patronage for an age and will find something proper for Emma or I shall know why."

Braddon nodded and the two of them set off across town at an ungodly hour of the morning when they were certain to find the mantuamaker in her shop and no others around to possibly eavesdrop. Lady Titheridge had no intention of allowing anyone else to know her business.

Emma entered the lovely house on Bruton Street just off Berkeley Square with even more trepidation than before. Would she survive unscathed this morning? Or would he unmask her disguise? In her nervousness she scarcely took notice of the rooms they passed. All she knew was a sort of cold fear in her heart. She enjoyed yesterday morning more than anything ever, and she longed for another like it.

Radley ushered her along the hall with his seeming customary good will. "Sir Peter is busy at the moment, sir. However, your materials are right where you left them. Is there anything you require? A pot of coffee? Tea? Perhaps a glass of wine?"

"A pot of tea would be welcome. That misty rain coming down is rather nasty," Emma murmured while slipping onto the stool where she had worked the day before. She placed the small blue jar holding the cinnamon-spiced potpourri on the table and undid the lid, allowing the fragrance to permeate the air, thus canceling out the stuffy, acrid smell.

When Radley returned with a small tray bearing a pot of tea and a plate of ginger biscuits, she scarcely looked up.

Sometime later she heard a noise and gave a startled glance at the doorway. Sir Peter stood just inside it with a frazzled look on his face.

"Dash it all, I do not know why my secretary had to break his arm just now when I need him. I cannot write a decent hand—manage to blot my copy every time, y'know—and there is a letter that must go out today. You don't suppose . . . ?" He gave Emma a beseeching look that would have melted a heart of lead.

"I could try, I imagine. It will take me longer to do the drawings, of course."

"No matter," Sir Peter said, waving his hand as though to dismiss everything that might get in his way.

Emma found the letter fascinating. Sir Peter was writing to an official of the Egyptian government, such as it was, for permission to explore an area along the Nile River. Oh, how enticing it sounded. She sighed when she finished copying his scribble in her neat hand.

He looked over her shoulder, standing far too close for her comfort. "Excellent! My good fellow, you have a better hand than my secretary." He held the letter close up, examining it with a pleased look.

Emma smiled, nodded, then returned to her work. Something had assailed her when she was close to Sir Peter. Whatever it was left her oddly breathless. She was most likely better off keeping her distance from him.

She checked her watch often after that and left the house promptly at noon, dashing to Lady Titheridge's house with the greatest of speed.

Leland again ushered her to the little bedroom where the other conspirators awaited her. While Braddon eased her from George's garments, Lady Titheridge fidgeted about the room before coming to a halt in front of a redressed Emma.

"I trust you will not take it amiss when I tell you that we decided there was nothing that could be done to your pretty dress. We did not wish to spoil so lovely a thing."

Emma gave a wry nod. "I quite understand, my lady. I shall wear it and tilt my nose at anyone who dares to snub me for it."

"That's my girl," Lady Titheridge said with approval. "However, I have a suggestion. I have another gown that should fit you. Show it to her, Braddon."

Whereupon the maid brought forth a positively breathtaking gown. It had an elegant white crepe skirt trimmed with silver and point lace, with a richly embroidered border at the bottom. The top of the bodice duplicated that intricate design in miniature, and delicate wisps of silver looped over the tiny puffed sleeves. It was utterly simple, yet grand.

"You cannot mean this for me," Emma declared in faltering tones. "Why, it looks as though it has never been worn."

"To tell the truth it has not. I fear it is too young for me, and I cannot bring myself to return it." Lady Titheridge exchanged a look with her maid.

The words had the ring of truth; still Emma gave her ladyship a thoughtful look. Then her youthful desire to appear special at her induction to the delights to be found at the esteemed dancing establishment of Almack's overcame any reluctance.

"I shall take great care of it, to be sure," Emma said with reverence.

"Oh, it is yours. It is of no use to me in the least."

Emma overcame her shyness with this great lady so far as to place a demure kiss on her cheek and offer blushing thanks.

"The morning went well?" her ladyship said while walking with Emma to the top of the stairs. "I expected it would. Now, be gone with you. You must rest for this evening."

Emma took both dresses and went home in a daze. She continued more or less in this state until it was time to dress for the evening. Fanny had a hundred questions about the beautiful dress, none of which Emma bothered to answer.

"My dear girl, wherever did you get that gown?" her mother exclaimed when her daughter drifted down the stairs to stand before her. The vinaigrette bottle was produced, and Mrs. Cheney plumped herself down on a hall chair, unable to imagine what Emma had done to warrant such a fashionable gown without any money.

"Lady Titheridge insisted I wear it this evening. She said she had ordered it and then decided it was too young for her. I am to keep it . . . if you approve, of course."

There was no way to deny this generosity, and Mrs. Cheney babbled all the way to Almack's about how glad she was that her dearest friend, Mrs. Bascomb, had persuaded her to attend that delightful evening of music at Lady Titheridge's house.

Emma ignored the transformation of the painful sounds to that of delightful music. To tell the truth, Emma was uneasy.

Once they had arrived, presented their tickets to the gentleman who ruled the entry, then walked up the stairs, Emma found she was past caring about her impression on those dragons of Society. Come what may, she intended to have a wonderful time, insipid refreshments notwithstanding.

There were but three of the patronesses in attendance this evening. Lady Sefton gave Emma a particularly sweet smile and studied her when presented. "So you are Evelyn's little friend. I have promised her that you shall have a waltz this evening. Later on?" Lady Sefton gave Emma an encouraging smile, then turned to the next in line.

Emma nodded, too overwhelmed to speak intelligently.

Mrs. Cheney, as dazed as Emma had been earlier, guided her daughter over to where she recognized a few of the matrons. Emma was introduced to two young women she had not yet met and greeted several others she had encountered at parties so far attended. Then she saw Lady Amelia Littleton, her school-days friend, and joined her in nervous chatter.

She could scarcely believe that she was actually where so many craved to be. Attending the dance assemblies at Almack's was the utter peak of social standing, topped only by a presentation at the Queen's Drawing Room—and even that was debatable as to priority.

"I believe I shall swoon before the evening is over," Amelia whispered, echoing Emma's fears.

However, the evening proceeded tolerably well, for Emma at least. Then Mr. Brummell entered the rooms, and Emma could almost feel a thrill of apprehension flow through the air.

Not fearing him in the least, Emma smiled at him when she caught his eye. She repressed a grin at his answering look of surprise. When he came to her side and gave her a look of inquiry, she almost giggled. "Well, and here I am. Did you ever?" she whispered to him from behind her white lace fan.

"I vow you are quite the most refreshing sight in the rooms, my dear. However did you accomplish the transformation? You look ravishing." His gaze swept her gorgeous gown, taking note of every detail.

"Lady Titheridge. I cannot explain all, but she has become like a fairy godmother, I believe." Emma twinkled a look at Mr. Brummell, rather liking his wry reserve.

"Interesting. I see her nephew is gracing us with his presence this evening. Unusual. I must say hello to the chap. One is required to be *au courant* with the latest gossip, you know."

The dandy sauntered off toward Sir Peter while Emma sank down upon the straight-backed chair providentially behind her. Double drat! What if he came near her? Worse yet, what if he asked her to dance with him? Oh, mercy me, she wailed inwardly. Her heart fluttered like a frightened bird, and she felt as close to fainting as ever in her life.

"You are amazing," Amelia said, quite awed at Emma's acquaintance with Mr. Brummell, before she drifted off to dance.

"At last you may meet Sir Peter, my dear," Mrs. Cheney whispered. "I do believe he is coming in this direction."

Emma rose and blindly accepted the first request that came her way, a spotty young man who had dashed over to find out what it was that drew George Brummell to this relatively unknown girl.

Peter came to a halt just short of where Emma Cheney took the hand of a young chap for a country dance. He was stunned at the sight of her. Why, she was beautiful! Her skin was creamy and begged to be stroked. Her dark hair now rioted in saucy curls about her head. She danced with grace and charm. And under that gorgeous creation she wore was a pair of the finest legs he had seen on any woman or opera dancer. And only *he* knew, with the exception of her dresser, of course. He suspected his expression might be a trifle smug.

When Emma returned to her mother's side, she found Sir Peter approaching with Lady Sefton. The countess had a twinkle in her eyes.

"My dear Miss Cheney, may I present Sir Peter Dancy as an acceptable partner for the next waltz. He informs me that as a friend of his aunt's he feels certain you will be kind enough to accept him."

Emma placed her gloved hand in his and murmured something in reply. When they twirled out onto the floor, she felt as one awaiting an execution must feel . . . sort of numb, terrified, and wishing it would all be over soon.

The magic of the music and the dance began to overcome her fears, and she relaxed a trifle. He had not said a word, other than some nonsense about the waltz. She ventured a glance at him, then paled at his next words.

"You look a great deal like your brother, although I suppose you know that. Except George is not half so pretty as you, of course." He chuckled at his bit of wit.

Emma smiled weakly and longed for the dance—which seemed to go on forever—to be over. That odd sensation of breathlessness had returned. The room seemed to diminish to a tiny area that surrounded just the two of them. It had to be his closeness. The warmth of his hand on her back, even through his gloves, and her hand as well, appeared to radiate outward. A glance at those remarkable green eyes nearly undid her.

"George comes and goes. I seldom see him. He is so busy with his interests, you know," she finally said, figuring it was better to get it out in the open than wait for the axe to fall on her neck.

"Well, I can tell you that I am jolly glad for his assistance. Don't know what I would do without the help he is giving me. Worth a fortune, his talent is." Sir Peter bestowed a heart-melting smile on Emma that dazzled her. She wished he would not smile at her like that. It made her heart flutter at an alarming rate. Yet, those green eyes sparkled with pleasure, it seemed, not censure as she had feared. "Why, do you know his handwriting is superb, and as for his drawing, I feel quite lucky to have talked him into helping me."

Emma flashed a look at Sir Peter, almost a disbelieving one. Had she heard aright? "That's lovely," she murmured in reply, not quite up to something witty.

The dance finally concluded, and Sir Peter properly escorted Emma to where her mother sat in stunned happiness.

He bowed to Mrs. Cheney, then turned to Emma with a warm look. "I suppose your card is filled, but if not, may I beg another dance from you?"

Emma did not have the presence of mind to keep her card from his hands. She watched, quite numb with apprehension, while he deftly caught it up, then signed his name opposite a later waltz. She thought his smile a trifle wicked, but what could she say with her mother sitting there all ears?

If she could just manage to leave this place without disgracing herself, Emma thought she might die happy.

Lord Worcester appeared and requested his dance. Emma threw a helpless look at her mother, wondering if this gentleman would blurt out the truth. Her mother made little shooing motions. Emma could imagine her formulating a tale to share with Mrs. Bascomb come tomorrow afternoon.

Fortunately the dance proved to be a Scottish reel, which was not only lively but kept partners separated much of the dance. If Lord Worcester had any queries, he did not have a chance to ask them, which suited Emma to a tee.

She was confused when Amelia glared at her, but had no time to dwell on the matter.

It was a shock to see Mr. Reginald Swinburne approach her

for a dance. She somehow had not expected to see him at Almack's. While he wore the form-fitting black tights that showed a modest amount of black-striped silk stocking worn by many other men as an alternate to the black knee-britches also allowed at the assemblies, his coattails were excessively long—almost to the ankles—and his cravat had not the simplicity that Mr. Brummell espoused. Indeed, that length of linen immobilized his neck, rising so high he could not turn his head in the least. But then his coat was padded so much, Emma doubted if he could bend, either. She thought he looked a bit silly, like a pouter pigeon about to strut.

"Miss Cheney, may I request a dance?" he said, bowing slightly before her, thus confirming her suspicions about his inability to bend.

Seeing that Sir Peter approached, Emma desired to move as far away from him as she might. Also, it would be rude to refuse Mr. Swinburne.

She gracefully agreed and permitted him to escort her to the center of the dance floor. The dandy was stiff in his movements, yet appeared light on his feet. When the pattern of the dance permitted a few words, he spoke.

"I am well acquainted with your brother, Miss Cheney. You resemble him, as you must know. Fine fellow, George," he concluded with a solemn nod.

Emma whirled down the line of the country dance with a wild desire to giggle. George? Well acquainted with this foppish dandy? Absurd. Fortunately for her, she kept her countenance, for proper decorum at Almack's assemblies was strictly observed.

At least no one had accused her of trading places with her brother, and for that she was humbly grateful. Then it came time for the second waltz with Sir Peter. Butterflies took wing in her stomach, and a strange desire to giggle over nothing assailed her. Nerves, she decided, steeling herself for the coming ordeal.

One gloved hand touched another. It was when his gloved hand slipped around her slender waist that she felt faint. Oh, she must not reveal her inner sensibilities. His effect on her became more pronounced each time he neared. She had best strive for distance!

Firming her resolve, she met his gaze with resignation. "I am surprised to see you here this evening. Someone chanced to mention that you never grace the assemblies with your presence." She wished it had proven true.

"I wanted to please my aunt," he lazily replied while expertly twirling Emma through a breathless turn. He looked off to his left. When Emma glanced in that direction, she saw Lady Titheridge standing by Lady Sefton. Emma returned a nod of recognition, then again looked at Sir Peter.

"You are much attached to your aunt? She is a very dear lady," Emma concluded with genuine pleasure.

"There is nothing I would not do to please her," he said, but looked at Emma with a peculiar light in his eyes that made her very curious.

When Emma and her mother finally took leave of the dancing assembly, they were both exhausted. Mrs. Cheney was nearly beside herself with happiness for her dear girl.

Emma was merely relieved that she had survived unscathed. How she was to rise at an early hour to present herself at Sir Peter's house was beyond her. But she would do it. She had a strange urge to see if he would recognize her. It was like a death wish, she supposed.

Chapter 4

WHEN Emma opened her eyes the next morning, she peered at her clock on the chimneypiece through a fog of fatigue. Then the time registered, and she slid from her bed with groggy haste.

Fanny slipped into her room with a tray of hot chocolate. "La, miss, I thought you would still be abed. You did come home a bit late last evening."

Emma sipped the chocolate with gratitude for a sustaining liquid, then began her preparations for the day. It mattered little what she wore to Lady Titheridge's house, for she changed immediately. So she pointed to the simple green sprigged muslin and commenced dressing.

"You ain't goin' out this morning?" a scandalized Fanny cried in alarm when she saw Emma grab for the reticule that held her little purse.

"Lady Titheridge depends on me," Emma murmured vaguely. She left Fanny muttering dire remarks about young ladies who ventured out into the mists of the morning before it was proper. Emma was glad she might slip out without the garrulous Fanny tagging along with her as would be deemed proper under most circumstances. While the maid did her work well enough, she was a tattler, make no mistake. Emma didn't need any complications at this point.

Lady Titheridge was still in bed when Emma walked up to the little bedroom. She whispered to Braddon that it wasn't necessary to disturb her ladyship, and the maid fully agreed.

In a shorter time than Emma would have believed, she was again on the street and on her way to Sir Peter's house.

His cheerful butler let her in and ushered her back toward the workroom with dispatch. She checked the timepiece in her pocket to discover that it was now one hour since she had climbed from her bed—a record to be sure.

"A pot of tea and perhaps a few biscuits, sir?" the butler inquired.

Emma's empty stomach gurgled, and the butler raised his brows in dismay.

"I suspect you neglected to eat a proper breakfast. Why do you not join Sir Peter in his breakfast room, for he has not left the table as yet." The butler paused, waiting expectantly at her side.

She didn't know whether to agree and appease her appetite or remain and be safely away from Sir Peter. Her decision was taken from her hands when the butler patted her on the shoulder and urged, "Come along, sir, there is plenty of everything, and Sir Peter will enjoy your company."

She thought he exhibited a high degree of familiarity with his employer, but on reflection decided it must be nice for a lonely bachelor to have someone who was friendly.

"Well," Sir Peter declared while placing his fork on his plate and rising from the table, "I certainly didn't expect you to be so early this morning."

Emma stared at him in puzzlement. George had not left the house last night so far as Sir Peter knew.

"Ah, your sister must have created a bit of a fuss when she came home so late. Hard to sleep through that," Sir Peter said in a rush.

"You met my sister?" Emma said cautiously.

He nodded in reply while helping himself to a slice of ham and another spoon of buttered eggs. "Dig in, do. Don't stand on ceremony here. Radley, fetch another pot of coffee. Or do you prefer tea?" he asked Emma.

"Tea, if you please."

Radley disappeared while Sir Peter studied Emma. "I gather you didn't sleep any better than I did last night. You look fagged to death."

Emma took an affronted breath, then firmed her lips, refusing to rise to what might be deemed bait. She merely nodded. "London is dreadfully noisy, even at night. I much prefer the country."

"Ruins are quiet, true. Tell me, what do you hope to find

down in Sussex?" He buttered his toast, heaped a spoon of marmalade on top, then resumed eating.

Here Emma stood on firmer ground. She followed suit, relishing the flavor of the ham and eggs mixed with a nibble of marmalade. Oh, was anything ever as good as an English breakfast? At last, when she had mulled over how to say what she thought George might say, she replied, "Treasure. I'm convinced that there must be a lot of coins and other things like jewelry left behind when the Romans departed. Bound to be. People were killed, and ofttimes hoards were forgotten in a rush."

"Not like the deliberate placement of articles in a burial chamber such as the Egyptians did." Sir Peter said in somewhat of an agreement.

Emma racked her brain for all she could remember of Roman burial practices—which wasn't much—and shared that with Sir Peter. By the end of the morning meal she felt remarkably at ease with the man she hoaxed.

When they entered the workroom, she discovered the body of the long-dead Egyptian princess had been placed on her worktable. Emma halted just inside the door before taking a hesitant step toward the table and the skeleton.

"Come, have a look. I am debating whether or not to try to restore the wrappings. What do you think?" Sir Peter strolled across to survey the skeleton.

Emma caught sight of the neat stacks of bandages off to one side and shook her head. "I do not see how you could hope to duplicate what was done so long ago with those wrappings. Best leave the princess be, I suspect." She joined Sir Peter at the table, touching one of the princess's hands with a tentative finger.

"I suppose you are right. After all, you have a good deal more experience at this than I do," Sir Peter replied thoughtfully with a glance at Emma.

She nearly laughed at the very notion. Not but what she wouldn't have liked to join George in his explorations. He wouldn't have her along for anything.

"Radley and I placed her on a sort of pallet. Give me a hand with it, will you? I intend to put her under glass; the bones will be more protected that way." Sir Peter gestured to the other end of what Emma now perceived as a padded bit of wood.

Emma willingly took the other end, finding the burden to be slight. It was a novel experience to be treated as a man and not a helpless female. She found she rather liked it.

"What about the necklace you found? Is it safe?" Of all the things found, the beautiful necklace had not been brought forth for Emma to draw. "Did someone not suggest you hire a guard for these treasures?" she asked while helping Sir Peter place a glass lid on the case.

"The only item worth stealing is the necklace, and I keep it quite safe," he reassured her.

Before Emma could ask if he wanted her to draw it, he added, "I will bring it out the next day you come, but I believe I should like a representation done in either watercolors or oils. Do you use either of those mediums?"

"I can manage watercolors," Emma replied, remembering in time to use her George voice.

With the body carefully beneath glass, Emma studied the woman's face again. "She looks peaceful, somehow. I do not think she was murdered."

"Ah, yes, you would know about the great number of times that murder was a way to secure power, for the Romans were not above using the same method."

Sir Peter drew companionably close to Emma. His arm brushed against hers as he pointed out the little things she had missed, the holes punched in the ear lobes for earrings, for example.

Emma's tingling response to that casual touch shocked her a bit. Could he possibly guess that she reacted to him in such a foolish manner? This would never do, she scolded.

It was close to noon whey they finished the examination, and Emma gasped when she checked her pocket watch.

"Must you go so soon? We could have a bite of nuncheon if you liked. I intend to see your sister later on, although do not tell her so."

"My sister?" Emma feared that her voice sounded a trifle squeaky.

"Well, I enjoyed dancing with her last night. Charming girl, Miss Cheney. Will you be at home this afternoon?"

"Me? No. No, I must visit the British Museum, talk with a chap there," Emma mumbled in a frantic effort to think of an excuse to be away.

"Before you go . . . what sort of flowers does Emma like?" Sir Peter inquired lazily.

"Um, oh, most anything," Emma murmured, thinking that in this she knew she sounded just like George, who scarcely knew a daisy from a rose.

With great haste Emma excused herself and dashed out the front door and down the front steps into a waiting hackney. It didn't even occur to her to wonder about the convenient appearance of the vehicle, figuring the efficient Radley had summoned it. Emma changed as usual at Lady Titheridge's. Braddon was her customary efficient self, helping Emma to hurry her switch.

Oldham opened the front door with his usual stately grace when Emma hurried up the steps. Inside the front hall she discovered a flattering number of flower tributes.

Fanny appeared from the shadows of the hall and offered her help. "May I carry a few of these to your room, miss?"

"I expect we had best arrange them in the drawing room," Emma replied with an astute knowledge of her dear mama. "Mama will want to point them out to Mrs. Bascomb when she comes."

With a pleased flounce, for any attention to her mistress reflected upon her as well, Fanny gathered three bouquets in her arms, then followed Emma up the stairs.

Emma scarcely knew what she did. All she could think was that Sir Peter was coming to call this afternoon. Oh, was there ever such a muddle? Her curls had been restored to their normal arrangement and her face returned to its normal hue. But inwardly she seethed with anxiety.

"Help me, Fanny. I must dress in a very feminine way for this afternoon." Emma searched the contents of her wardrobe for the most frilly garment she owned. This wasn't easy, as she tended to simple clothes.

Fanny pulled out a pretty blue jaconet muslin. The long sleeves were finished with a puff at the top drawn up by a narrow tape in a casing. The narrow skirt was trimmed with a great many rows of corded tucks and hemmed in scallops. The neckline dipped rather low, creating a minuscule bodice that fit snugly to Emma's nicely firm bosom. She quickly slipped the dress on, then fingered the delicate lace that edged the neckline.

"I look quite ladylike in this, do I not, Fanny?"

The maid gave Emma a quizzical look, for Emma seldom seemed overly concerned about her appearance. "Yes, miss. Be there a special gentleman calling today?" the wily maid inquired.

"Perhaps," was all Emma would allow.

Downstairs in the drawing room Mrs. Cheney sat in pleased conversation with her dearest friend. Mrs. Bascomb had gazed at all the floral tributes Emma received and gasped with amazement.

"Emma took, then?" Mrs. Bascomb cried.

"I would say that she created a favorable impression on quite a few gentlemen. Mr. Brummell came over to chat with her. Lord Worcester asked her to dance. And Sir Peter Dancy asked her to waltz with him *twice*. Lady Sefton herself presented him to Emma as an agreeable partner. He was most attentive," Mrs. Cheney concluded with justifiable satisfaction.

"I suppose that even her pretty white muslin appeared new at Almack's, her not having been there before," Mrs. Bascomb ventured to say.

"As to that, Lady Titheridge presented Emma with a lovely gown from the finest mantuamaker. My abigail told me that her ladyship always goes to Madame Clotilde." Mrs. Cheney sat back with an expectant air, awaiting her friend's reaction to this exceptional news.

Before Mrs. Bascomb could come forth with an answer, Emma entered the room, having listened and decided she had best halt the crowing.

"Well," Mrs. Bascomb declared, "you look as fine as fivepence this afternoon, my girl. Your mama tells me you were a great triumph last evening."

Emma bowed her head in what she hoped was a modest response and said, "Mama had best not refine upon it too much. Only time will tell how I get on."

Oldham entered behind Emma to announce, "Mr. Reginald Swinburne, ma'am."

Close on his heels the splendid dandy came into the room and made a most elegant leg to Mrs. Cheney and Mrs. Bascomb before turning to Emma. "You look even more charming today than last evening, a feat I had not thought possible." He waved a handkerchief in the air, the scent of violets drifting across to tease Emma's nose.

Emma stifled a giggle that longed to escape and meekly curtsied to the astonishing sight before her.

The dandy had dressed like most of his group—pale buff pantaloons with black silk hose discreetly revealed above black patent shoes. His cravat was a miracle of starched linen, rising high enough to choke him, she thought. His shirt points were in danger of putting out his eyes, dare he turn too quickly. And his dark blue coat, well, that excessively padded and boned creation hugged his waist and helped to puff out his chest. A pigeon, she thought again, a huge, blue-and-buff pigeon. More than anything, she wanted to laugh and knew she must not.

Only the sight of his waistcoat prevented her, for it was a hideously gorgeous creation made from puce satin embroidered with gold and silver threads. It took her breath away just thinking of what if must have cost. Of course, most of the dandies neglected to pay their bills—or so she had heard—so he probably didn't worry about such mundane matters.

He brought forth a dainty bouquet of violets to present to Emma, and after thanking him politely, she sniffed the charming arrangement nestled in white paper lace.

"I am pleased you like them. Violets are my signature, you see." He tilted his head in an attitude that revealed its noble shape and gestured with one arm. Why, Emma couldn't imagine.

It brought another wave of French violet scent to her nose, stronger than the flowers in her hand. Emma couldn't hold back the smile that burst forth. "How clever," she managed.

Mr. Swinburne preened, sneaking a glance in the looking glass above the fireplace to assure himself that all was in place, no doubt.

"You have a very fine looking glasses, Mrs. Cheney," he pronounced to his hostess. "Excellent quality. I have one tinted a delicate pink, for it makes me cheerful, not to mention look my very best."

"What a splendid notion," Mrs. Cheney said with a quick look at Mrs. Bascomb. "I shall have to avail myself of such an item, for there are days when one feels quite blue, you know."

Mr. Swinburne laughed appreciatively at this little sally, then turned to face the door when Oldham again entered.

"Sir Peter Dancy, ma'am," he intoned in his best manner. Emma thought Oldham looked like more a stuffed cod than usual, if possible.

Sir Peter greeted the ladies with unaffected good manners, then scowled at Mr. Swinburne.

Emma nervously licked her lips, then held her breath a moment. Would he recognize her as the George he had seen but this morning? She advanced to where he stood near the fireplace.

"Thank you so much for the lovely flowers. I am fond of roses, especially pink ones," she said quietly so not to offend Mr. Swinburne and his modest offering of violets.

"I thought they suited you, for you have such a comely pink in your cheeks," he replied gallantly.

Emma couldn't help but contrast his compliment to her with the self-serving words from Mr. Swinburne. That gentleman had presented his violets because they reflected him. Sir Peter offered roses because they reminded him of Emma, or so he claimed.

"Tea or coffee, gentlemen?" Mrs. Cheney inquired, quite as though she were accustomed to such lofty visitors every day. "Perhaps a glass of canary?"

Oldham had caught the significant glance from his employer and shortly brought in a heavily laden tray to place before her.

"Tea," Sir Peter declared at the same time that Mr. Swinburne requested coffee.

Emma poured at her dear mama's request and watched Sir Peter with uneasy vigilance when not so occupied. What went on in his mind? Had he detected her disguise and only waited to expose her charade? She was in agony of suspense, scarcely aware of what she did or said. Since she did not pour tea or coffee on her gown or the floor, and the dainty slices of buttered bread remained unspilled, she gathered she didn't give herself away.

Why, oh why, had she attended Almack's last evening? She had been so happy with sketching at Sir Peter's house. Now it all might be ruined, for no unmarried lady could possibly enter the house of a bachelor gentleman. Not even to sketch antiquities could she cross the threshold, unless accompanied by her mother . . . or his aunt, she reflected. If worse came to worst and she dare not continue with the disguise, she might prevail upon Lady Titheridge to chaperon her a few mornings.

This settled in her mind, she relaxed just a shade, then stiffened as Oldham again entered the drawing room. He looked impossibly starched up as he announced, "Lord Worcester, ma'am."

"Ma'am, I should have guessed the others would be before me." He bowed correctly to Mrs. Cheney, then turned to Emma. "I enjoyed our dance of last evening and thought to see you again. These fellows"—he gestured to Sir Peter and Mr. Swinburne—"are a plague."

"Really, sir." Emma gurgled a delighted laugh. Lord Worcester did not seem half so intimidating this afternoon as he had in the hallowed halls of Almack's. The memory of Amelia's unhappy face came to her, and she wondered what there might be about Lord Worcester that brought such a reaction.

Although the allotted time for Mr. Swinburne's call had passed, he improperly remained, contrary to most dandies' behavior. It seemed he did not wish to yield the field to his friends, although Emma suspected that the friendship was of the most distant sort.

She had begun to relax when Sir Peter spoke into one of those momentary silences that occur. "I fancy you are quite proud of your son. George has been such a help . . . " he began.

Emma hastily broke into his flow of words—something she normally would never do—and said, "Sir Peter believes dear George to be an authority on Roman antiquities, Mama. Imagine my brother advising anyone on anything." Her tinkling laugh sounded false to her ears. Her mother glared at her before smoothing that expression from her face.

"George is rarely at home anymore. He insists he will find a treasure, but I declare, I doubt it." She sipped at her tea and gave Emma a questioning look regarding her daughter's unseemly behavior.

Mrs. Bascomb came to an unknowing rescue when she turned the conversation to Sir Peter. "And your antiquities are to be rated superior, we understand. It is so rare that a gentleman shows interest in such elevating matters," Mrs. Bascomb concluded with a nod of condescension.

Sir Peter bowed in her direction, acknowledging the tribute with a gracious smile.

Emma thought his smile held a gleam of amusement, but that might have been for Mrs. Bascomb's tribute, pretentious as it was.

The conversation turned to more general topics like the weather—dreadfully cloudy yet not too chilly for this time of year—and the various entertainments abounding in London during the high Season.

The gentlemen were about to take their leave when Sir Peter paused after rising from his chair and bowed to Mrs. Cheney. "I wonder, kind madam, if I might persuade you to join me this evening, with Miss Cheney, of course, and perhaps your husband. There is to be a grand opening of Vauxhall for the Season. I understand the Prince Regent himself is to attend. The owners have promised all manner of innovations."

"I had heard a rumor they were to close, for they did not do at all well last year," Mrs. Bascomb murmured.

"Well, it appears that Vauxhall will be even greater and grander *this* season," Sir Peter said persuasively.

Emma was torn. She had read the account of the grand reopening at Vauxhall. It promised to be wonderful entertainment, and she wanted more than anything in the world to attend this festive occasion. On the other hand, it would mean a close proximity to Sir Peter Dancy for several hours, and that she dare not risk.

Then she glanced at him again. Unless he was for some peculiar reason of his own pretending to go along with her disguise, he had not to this point recognized her as both George and Emma. She continued her debate for only a few moments, for her wish to attend proved a trifle stronger than her fears of detection.

"Oh, Mama," she cried softly, "do let us go. I have read of all the promised entertainments to be introduced and they sound prodigiously wonderful."

Mrs. Cheney, looking delightfully affected, nodded her agreement. "I have also read the accounts. You are most kind to offer this treat, Sir Peter." A cat with a bowl of cream could not have looked more smug then when Mrs. Cheney exchanged a glance with Mrs. Bascomb.

Sir Peter turned to the other gentlemen, his brows raised in inquiry.

"I regret that I am otherwise occupied this evening," announced the dandy Mr. Swinburne.

"I should like to join you if I may," Edward, Lord Worcester replied to the unspoken invitation.

"Good enough, Worcester," Sir Peter said by way of confirmation.

"Emma knows a charming girl she might invite to join us if you wish," Mrs. Cheney offered hesitantly. "Lady Amelia Littleton."

"Fine," Sir Peter said with good humor.

Lord Worcester had given a start at the mentioned name, but said nothing. Emma wondered at the expression on his face.

"It will be a wonderful treat," Emma declared, deciding that she would send a note to Sir Peter explaining that George would be unable to come in the morning. She didn't wish to risk Sir Peter's scrutiny immediately. And besides, if they remained at Vauxhall until the wee hours, she had no desire to drag herself from her bed to stagger over to Sir Peter's at some ungodly hour of the morning while pretending to be George, who must have had more sleep.

The gentlemen departed, and at the urging of her dear mama, Emma went to her room to compose a note to Lady Amelia.

Not having seen a great deal of Lady Amelia since their school days, Emma wasn't certain how she would view a near-last-minute invitation. She needn't have worried. Within a brief time an acceptance was returned with the footman to the affect that Lady Amelia had been longing to attend the grand opening and was most pleased to accept.

"Mind you, Emma, I was most displeased when you interrupted Sir Peter while he was here. Not good breeding, my girl," Mrs. Cheney scolded when she recalled the event some hours later.

"I am sorry, Mama," Emma replied with all due humility. "I found the notion of George assisting someone like Sir Peter to be a bit humorous, you see."

"George is a sad scamp, I fear," his loving but sorely tried mother replied.

Emma hurried up to her room in order to dress for the evening. She thought scamp an odd appellation for the absent-minded and serious George, but would never argue with her mother.

In a gown of silver gauze over pink taffeta, newly come from the mantuamakers, Emma felt quite festive. It was more stylish than most of her gowns, and she blessed her papa for insisting she visit the same mantuamaker who had made the gown from Lady Titheridge. So Emma had slipped out and been graced with a pretty gown that fortunately had not been claimed.

For all that he remained silent, Mr. Cheney was most observant. He knew quality when he saw it, and he wanted the best for his Emma. He looked pleased with the results of her shopping trip.

The three were joined by Lady Amelia some time before the gentlemen were to arrive. It had been arranged that they all meet early at the Cheney house before proceeding to the Vauxhall Gardens.

Sir Peter had declared before he left, "It is bound to be crowded this evening. We had best start early, or the bridge will be impassable, and as to the wherries, well, they are a dangerous mode of transport in the event of a throng of people."

Emma had observed to herself that nothing could be half so dangerous as Sir Peter. The whipcord leanness of his handsome person frightened her even as it thrilled her. Now she awaited his appearance with trembling. Why he had chosen to take them up, she couldn't imagine. If only *he* had not been the one to possess the Egyptian objects she longed to draw!

Lady Amelia looked charming in apple green silk trimmed with peach rosebuds. Peach silk rosebuds wound through her fair hair. Emma envied her polish.

When the gentlemen arrived, Emma observed that Lord Worcester glared at Lady Amelia and she returned a look perfectly as odious. What a dilemma.

"We have met, I believe, Lady Amelia," Lord Worcester drawled hatefully, most unlike his previous charming self.

"Edward, you have known me since I was in pigtails and you in short coats. Don't you come over the lordly lord with me. I know you far too well," Amelia replied with a snap.

His lordship looked annoyed, but said nothing to this accusation. He offered his arm, which Amelia accepted with good grace.

Mr. and Mrs. Cheney elected to travel in their own coach, having brought Mrs. Bascomb and the widowed Lady Hamley along at their expense.

Lady Amelia settled opposite Lord Worcester while Emma sat next to her and watched Sir Peter sit opposite herself.

"I understand you had an unrolling of a mummy at your home this past Monday," Lady Amelia said with a nod to Sir Peter.

Emma almost gasped. Had it only been last Monday? Today was Thursday, and it certainly seemed more like a month than a few days.

"That is true. It proved most successful."

Lord Worcester peered out of the window and exclaimed, "Look at the carriages! I vow we will be fortunate if we ever make it."

Emma looked to Sir Peter and decided that if the circumstances were different, she would not mind in the least being shut in a carriage with him.

But she was more or less trapped in her deceit. How agonizing to desire to record those priceless antiquities and yet also be drawn to the man who owned them, and who would no doubt be scandalized at her charade. Could she, dare she continue with her deception? She knew she ought to halt her subterfuge. There were many reasons for sanity to reign—her reputation, to mention one. Yet—and she turned a thoughtful gaze on Sir Peter—she would, she *must* risk all just to be near him for a little longer. Whatever happened, she would have this.

And of course she wished to please his aunt, she reminded herself in an effort to add to the outrageous justification of her acts. As if *that* truly was sufficient.

Chapter 5

IN spite of the throng of carriages the coachman soon worked his way into the line of vehicles crossing Westminster Bridge to Vauxhall Gardens.

Emma solved the dilemma of *not* looking at Sir Peter by admiring the interior of the coach. Dark brown leather panels were offset by beige silk curtains. The seats and squabs were the softest brown velvet and most comfortable. In fact, it was by far the nicest coach Emma had ever had the good fortune to ride in, even if one of the occupants made her decidedly uneasy.

At last the coach halted and the steps were let down. Sir Peter assisted Emma from the coach rather than allowing the groom to help her. She was surprised at that, giving him a quizzical look.

However, he had sent the groom ahead to purchase the tickets and took charge of those when the fellow returned. Emma's parents and guests arrived before too long. Within less time than any of them could have believed, they were entering the Gardens and strolling along the Great Walk.

Since the Cheneys wished to stroll along at a slower pace, arrangements were made to meet later for supper.

Emma had longed to come to this fascinating place for some time, but her parents had thought of one excuse after another. Now that she was actually here, she felt a rush of pleasure. As much as Sir Peter unnerved her, she would ever be grateful that he was responsible for her visit.

She attended to his explanation of the plan of the Gardens with one ear while looking about her with undisguised delight.

"The Italian Walk is off to the right along with the South Walk and is a trifle more splendid than this. To the left of us is the Hermit's Walk. There is a transparency of a hermit seated before his hut toward the upper end of it. It is lit from behind and surprisingly lifelike." Sir Peter gestured in that direction, and Emma turned her head to look.

Emma gazed along the walk and said, "It looks exceedingly dim along there, not the least like where we walk now. I vow, there must be hundreds of lights along this avenue. And," she said with amazement, "how bright they are. Why do they not have the same sort of lights in the city?" She gestured to the bell-shaped lamps on brackets attached to each tree along the walk.

He gave her a thoughtful look and said, "Some people are not inclined to haste in these sort of matters."

"The Hermit's Walk is almost as notorious as the Lover's Walk, or so I have been told," Lady Amelia inserted at this point. She had politely placed her hand on her escort's arm, but looked as though she would gladly box his ears instead. "And what Sir Peter called the Italian Walk is what less proper people call Lover's Walk." She bestowed a vexed look on Lord Worcester and then pretended to study something in the opposite direction.

Emma wondered what had been said between the two in their quiet conversation. Lady Amelia was no milk and water miss, and Emma rather admired her for it.

"Do you wish to explore?" Sir Peter said softly for Emma's ears alone.

"Gracious, no," Emma whispered back. "I am not that improper." And then she almost laughed when she remembered how she had dressed in George's breeches and hose, his coat and cravat, and permitted Sir Peter to see her in such. And when she recalled how her legs were revealed, she blushed.

"I feared as such," Sir Peter said with such a doleful face that Emma had to laugh. She could feel the heat leave her cheeks and hoped her face had not totally given her away.

"What does that sign say?" she then asked him to change the subject.

"Can't say. I'm a bit nearsighted, and unless the printing is large and clear, I cannot make it out at this distance." He frowned in an apparent attempt to read the sign, but did not reveal what it was for Emma's benefit.

Hope rose within Emma. If he did not see all that well, per-haps that explained why he failed to make the connection be-tween George and herself. It also explained why he frowned at papers so often. Much cheered by this conclusion, Emma brightened and felt immeasurably better.

Sir Peter gestured to a number of pavilions that served as supper boxes and said in a very offhand manner, "We shall have our supper there later on, but first I thought you would enjoy exploring a bit."

"Indeed," inserted Lady Amelia, "Edward is excellent at ex-ploring. Why, one time he had me so lost I thought I would never see home again."

"You would persist in tagging along," he grumbled.

"Beast," Lady Amelia hissed back.

"I do believe those two have known each other for an age. They remind me of George and me when we get together," Emma whispered to Sir Peter.

"Pity your brother couldn't come along this evening."

Emma pretended not to hear this comment, turning her head to stare at the approach of a gentleman who was playing what appeared to be several instruments at once.

"Senor Rivolta, I believe," Sir Peter murmured.

Since Emma had read of the senor's capabilities in the newspaper, she knew who it was, but found the sight amazing. "I scarce think it is something one would wish to see more than once," she observed after a bit of the noise. "But he is most amusing."

They watched him for a few minutes, Lady Amelia keeping time by tapping a toe.

When they strolled on, Emma stumbled on the brick walk and found Sir Peter's arm swiftly around her lest she fall. Her reaction to this treatment shocked her. Oddly enough, she found a peculiar sort of comfort and warm sense of security when held close to his side. Naturally, this could not be, and he soon released her. To her chagrin she discovered she rather missed his closeness.

"What is that lovely building over there?" Emma nodded to a rotunda facing the Great Walk. Lady Amelia and Lord Worcester lagged behind, exclaiming over a new diversion.

"Come, I shall show you. 'Tis the New Music Room, where

concerts are held during inclement weather." He began to guide her in that direction when they encountered a group of jolly fellows intent on something else.

A rude fellow jostled Emma, and she shrank back against Sir Peter. It was most likely lucky for the man that Sir Peter felt obliged to care for Emma and not press the man for his rudeness, for the dark look he gave the man made her shiver.

Inside the building Emma came to a halt, thus bringing Sir Peter to a standstill as well. Elaborate carvings and niches were everywhere, painted white and bloom color. Portraits of their Majesties were to either side of the entrance. There seemed no end to the elaboration of decoration, and Emma whispered—the place had that effect on one—to Sir Peter, "I do believe he became a bit carried away in here," referring to the creator of the place.

The orchestra sat to the left, and there was a sort of desk for the musical performers behind which Emma could see an impressive organ. A chandelier at least eleven feet in diameter held an incredible number of lamps in three rows. Beyond it the ceiling was painted as a shell with a picture in the center, and Emma thought it the prettiest room she could ever recall seeing.

She tilted her face up to inspect the carved plumes that crowned the windows, and Sir Peter drew closer. "Emma, there is something I should discuss with you."

She immediately turned her attention to him, meeting those strange green eyes with wary regard.

Before he could open his mouth to tell her what it might be that appeared so important, Lady Amelia and Lord Worcester burst through the door.

"So, here you are. My heavens, what a place this is," Lady Amelia cried. "Look, Edward, did you ever see so much carving in your life? Although I must say, that painting of Venus and the Loves is a trifle revealing for my taste."

"As it is on the ceiling, you can easily avoid looking at it," his lordship said with a sniff.

"It is too fine an evening to remain in here," Emma urged, hoping a change would bring a stop to the petty quarreling of those two. She tugged at Sir Peter's arm, and they led the way from the rotunda.

Emma thought he gave a resigned sigh, but she was not sure. Then she wondered if he planned to tell her that he knew of her disguise. She decided she would just as soon leave the unmasking until later—much later.

"I should like to see the ballet theater," Lady Amelia begged prettily.

Her escort murmured, "You would."

"Why, Edward, I have it on good authority that you are quite fond of the ballet . . . or the dancers at any rate. I was told you are a frequent visitor—a most successful one, in fact—to the green room after a performance." She gave him a saucy look, then led him along to the door of the ballet theater.

Emma admired her daring while deploring her lack of tact. If, as Emma suspected, Lady Amelia truly liked Lord Worcester, Emma thought she would be better off by not sniping at him.

"Do you wish to view the ballet?" Sir Peter inquired while keeping her close to his side in the throng. His action enabled him to speak quietly. Shouting was so rude.

Emma found it difficult to answer. She knew she had best not be alone with Sir Peter again for many reasons. Yet she found his company very agreeable. It was a dilemma she had not expected to face.

"I believe I should like to see the marionette theater. I have ever known a fondness for the little puppets—they are usually so silly and agreeable. Would you mind if we went there instead?"

She was pleased that she had made the request when he turned a slow, amused smile at her. "Charming, I'm sure."

After informing Lord Worcester of their intent, Sir Peter and Emma strolled along until they came to where the puppet show was being held.

They entered, then sat on a bench where Emma thought they might have a good view.

It proved to be delightful; far better, Emma suspected, than the ballet. And if Amelia and Lord Worcester quarreled, she did not wish to be near them.

The puppets were dressed in elaborate costumes, and the plot of the little play was unexpectedly good. She laughed and scarcely noticed when Sir Peter placed his arm at her back.

She eventually gave him a questioning glance when at last she became aware of his action.

"No backs on these benches," he said by way of explanation. "Thought I'd give you a bit of bracing."

Emma turned a thoughtful countenance back to the little stage, but said nothing in reply. Were her mama to see this, Emma would receive a lecture on repulsing advances. Yet . . . was this truly an advance, or thoughtfulness?

At last the villain had been conquered, and the princess in the story fell neatly into the arms of the handsome prince, who had been in disguise for some time. Emma shrank a trifle when the disguise was stressed. Would it not be lovely if—when her disguise became known by Sir Peter—she could tumble into his arms? She rather suspected she might meet with a horrified stare and contempt. Life was not like a fairy tale.

They applauded, then rose and made their way slowly from the little theater.

Once outside, they walked back to the ballet theater, where they found Lord Worcester pacing back and forth. When he spotted them, he rushed forward, hands extended.

"Have you seen her?" He seemed quite frantic.

"No," Sir Peter replied, having the sense to know his friend meant Lady Amelia.

"She made another of her little wicked remarks, and we had a few words. Then she flounced off, saying something about seeking better company. I thought she was teasing. In a few minutes, when I decided that perhaps she meant what she said, I came out here and she had disappeared. I was dashed glad to see you two come up, I can tell you."

"We must search for her. But we can scarcely make a fuss, for it would destroy her reputation," Sir Peter said with due consideration for the impulsive, peppery young lady.

"Split into three directions," Emma said bravely. "I shall stay on the Great Walk while you two can explore the more poorly lit areas. I feel certain I will be all right in such a well-lit walk."

"I do not believe that to be the case," Sir Peter began when he was interrupted by his friend.

"That is an excellent notion. There are so many people about, you will be as safe as though you were at home."

Emma was not convinced, but she felt it was imperative for three rather than two to hunt for Lady Amelia.

Sir Peter agreed with obvious reluctance, and the three set off in different directions. Sir Peter headed toward The Grand Cross Walk, while Lord Worcester indicated he intended to inspect the Lover's Walk.

"Lady Amelia would likely go there just to spoil things for lovers," he declared with a sour expression.

Emma grew very conscious of being alone and unprotected when she proceeded along the Great Walk all by herself. She could not see her parents, nor could she espy Lady Amelia. She thought it best to move slowly, to scrutinize every grotto, every statue, every little thing of interest placed along the bricked avenue for amusement. If she carefully avoided meeting anyone's eyes, she might succeed in not being accosted. No sight of Lady Amelia could be found. At the far end of the walk Emma turned to retrace her steps.

So far she had managed to ignore the knowing looks and murmured invitations. The evening had not yet reached the point where drunken revelry became the norm of behavior.

At the entrance to the Hermit's Walk she paused. Frowning, she stared more intently. Was that not Lady Amelia's gown in the distance? Earlier she had said—in jest, Emma believed— that she wanted to see the hermit for herself.

Surely Lady Amelia was not so foolish as to traverse the dark walk alone!

Then Emma stiffened, for it seemed that not only was Lady Amelia in the Hermit's Walk, but another person stood next to her. It also seemed to Emma that Lady Amelia backed away. A man was forcing his attentions upon her pretty young friend. Mercy!

Emma searched the throng of people who drifted along the central walk. Not a soul was around that she dared to ask for help. Surely it was too risky to wait.

Darting along the Hermit's Walk, Emma thought herself a great fool to stupidly rush off by herself. Yet, something had to be done before Lady Amelia was harmed . . . or worse.

Catching sight of a fallen limb, Emma stooped to pick it up, then stealthily slipped up behind the two who were in heated argument. The man had clasped Lady Amelia by her arm and apparently refused to free her.

"Well, my fancy leddy, you'll give me a kiss or rue the day you came 'ere. Anyone off by herself is askin' for the likes of me. I'll take care of you good and proper." He laughed and then made an offer that made Lady Amelia cry out in fright.

Incensed at his crude talk and his insult to a Lady of Quality, Emma raised the limb and brought it down over the cursed fellow's head.

He crumpled to a heap at their feet with a groan.

Emma dropped the limb, backing away even as Lady Amelia turned with a cry.

Lady Amelia hurled herself at Emma, weeping on her shoulder with abandon. At last she dried her tears on a scrap of linen.

"What a wretch he is. I merely wanted to stroll along to see the hermit. This creature"—Lady Amelia touched the still form with the tip of her slipper—"insisted I must go off with him. As though I would ever do anything so stupid." She sniffed into the handkerchief again.

"Perhaps you ought to have waited for all of us. I should have liked to see the hermit as well, I believe. Lord Worcester is beside himself with worry for you."

Lady Amelia brightened. "Truly?"

"You are very unkind to him, I believe."

"He deserves every bit of it. You have no notion what I have suffered at his hands over the years."

"Well, I doubt if you endear yourself to him with harsh words or teasing," Emma observed while edging away from the man on the ground who showed signs of recovering from the blow to his head.

"We had best return to face their anger, I suppose," Lady Amelia said, following this observation with a deep sigh.

"Let us hurry. I should not like to be here when that odious man comes to, I believe," Emma muttered, urging her friend along the walk toward the central area at a faster pace.

They passed couples along the way, the girls giggling, the men persuasive. Lady Amelia sniffed in disdain.

"What silly geese those girls are."

"Happy, however, I suspect," Emma replied, now almost running in her eagerness to reach the more well-lit area.

They were breathless when they came to the Great Walk.

Lady Amelia looked about for a bench upon which to sink down.

She explained, "Edward will crown me, and not with jewels, either. I believe I'd rather be seated when he does." She plumped herself down on the first bench she saw.

"I think you are a trifle cruel to him," Emma said while repressing a smile.

Sir Peter came up to them with a rush. "Wherever did you find her? We have looked everywhere." He bestowed a disgusted look on the unhappy Lady Amelia.

Just behind him Lord Worcester came hurrying along, his face contorted in wrath. He marched up to where Lady Amelia perched on the edge of the stone bench and stopped, staring down at her.

Then, while Emma gasped in alarm, he hauled her up. He clasped her firmly with his two hands and looked as though he were merely assisting her. Emma suspected the gentleman longed to shake Lady Amelia. He gazed down at her face.

"Amelia," he began, then halted. A rather odd expression crept over his features as he held his nemesis close to him, his hands clasping her slender arms so tightly.

"Edward?" she replied hesitantly. She sounded curious and breathless at the same time.

They might have stood that way for some time, but were interrupted.

"Ah, so here you are," Lady Titheridge cried with seeming pleasure from off to their right. She was accompanied by several elegant ladies and gentlemen, none of whom Emma knew.

"You could not miss this affair, either?" Sir Peter said with a fond look at his aunt.

"I am pleased you bring Miss Cheney. She has been a great help to me lately," her ladyship said with an affectionate smile at Emma.

Sir Peter gave Emma a quizzical look while she prayed that Lady Titheridge would hold her tongue. Precisely what Emma could have been helping with was beyond her at the moment. It seemed to her that just when she began to relax, another pitfall opened before her, ready to entrap her. She wished she had not begun this pretence.

If her ladyship told Sir Peter that Emma had been drawing her precious treasures collected during her many travels, Sir Peter might acquire ideas he did not already have regarding the identity of George.

Yet . . . she recalled the emotions that came over her when she had studied the mummy with Sir Peter at her side, explaining numerous details to her. She would not have missed that for anything.

"I say, His Royal Highness has arrived," one of Lady Titheridge's party announced much to Emma's relief.

Emma had only viewed the Prince Regent at a distance, and she looked forward to seeing him closer up.

The first gentleman of Europe, as some called him, made his way along the walk. Numerous lords and ladies attended him, clustering about him as he strolled along.

He exchanged casual greetings with many, and when he came to Sir Peter, he paused to greet him, commenting, "How goes the Egyptian business? One of these days I should like a viewing if I may."

"I would be honored, Your Highness," Sir Peter replied. "I hope to have all the things arranged in order before too long."

Then he introduced Emma, and she thought she might expire with nervousness. Even if he was grossly fat, there was something about the Prince that commanded one's respect. She dipped a proper curtsy, then peeped up at him.

The Prince looked at Emma, then back to Sir Peter and winked. "Carry on," he murmured as he strolled along down the avenue.

"I should like to," Sir Peter said under his breath.

At least Emma would have sworn that was what he said. The words were softly spoken and with intensity. She wondered what he meant.

There was a fanfare, and Lady Amelia cried, "It is time for one of the new acts."

"Madame Saqui, you mean?" Emma answered while looking about to discover where the tightrope event might be held. People began to push and shove all about them, and she wondered if she would be trampled in the rush.

Sir Peter placed a protective arm about Emma's shoulders and led her through the throng to a safer place from which to observe the spectacle. "Over here. This is where the Cascade used to be. It has been replaced by this woman. I hope she is worth it."

"It's a pity to miss the waterfall, for I understand it was lovely. But from the advertisement, Madame Saqui sounds spectacular."

And she was.

While absently leaning against Sir Peter, Emma watched the lady appear at the top of a high platform. Dressed in a tinseled and spangled white short dress over white pantaloons with a headdress of white plumes, she descended in a shower of Chinese fire. Lights flashed; wheels, rockets, and stars burst in the air while she ran lightly down the rope, pausing only for a few moments in the center. This was for effect, Emma decided after taking a breath when she realized she had been holding hers.

"Amazing," Emma cried to Sir Peter over the enthusiastic applause.

"She's not much to look at, but most daring," he allowed.

And with another look Emma had to agree, for Madame was most masculine in appearance. Once the clouds of smoke had dissipated, Emma could see that she was no beauty and possessed remarkably muscular legs. Before Sir Peter could conclude that George lacked those sort of muscles, Emma turned and took a few steps away from the scene. Sir Peter dutifully followed along.

After this performance they encountered the rest of the Cheney party. Mrs. Bascomb and Lady Hamley looked somewhat dazed. It seemed they had seen His Royal Highness quite close and had yet to recover.

"This has been quite a gala reopening," Mrs. Bascomb declared fervently.

Lady Hamley blinked in her usual way, nodding all the while.

"Sir Peter introduced me to the Prince," Emma informed them with a touch of pride. After all, a girl in her position did not often have this occasion.

"I should enjoy the marionette show, and this new act by

Fantoccini sounded appealing," Lady Amelia exclaimed, nudging Lord Worcester in the side.

"Had we gone with Miss Cheney and Sir Peter, we would have viewed it, minx. You cannot have everything your way."

Emma had the sudden notion that Lord Worcester had more on his mind than the marionette show.

Lady Amelia took a deep breath, then said nothing.

"Now, I believe we are all together at last," Sir Peter said with a glance at Lady Amelia. "Why do we not repair to the pavilions?" He addressed the group as a whole, but turned to look at Emma.

Emma gazed back into his eyes and wished again that she could do away with George once and for all.

"Time for our supper," Sir Peter proclaimed after clearing his throat, leading them back to where the little pavilions sat.

Emma decided that the ham was not sliced quite as thin as she had been told, although her mama whispered that the sum demanded for the food was most shocking.

"Delicious, Sir Peter," Emma pronounced and wondered how in the world she could ever go back to being George again.

As though he sensed the direction of her thoughts, he said, "I received a note from your brother. He is occupied tomorrow morning. I wonder if he could come in the afternoon? I am eager to have that painting completed."

"No," Emma replied bluntly. At his look of surprise she temporized, "George said something about being busy all day." It was one thing to slip from the house in the morning while her mama was asleep. It was quite another to explain her absence in the afternoon when Mama was about.

"I see." Sir Peter frowned, but did not explain what it was he understood.

Emma could not help but wonder what he saw. Was she imagining things in her guilt? Did she fancy every word to have a second meaning? Silly girl, she tried to reassure herself. Delusions? She prayed not.

They were about finished with the charming meal when Emma recognized one of the young footmen from Sir Peter's household. She placed her glass of wine on the table, then touched Sir Peter on the arm to catch his attention.

"Look, is that not one of your servants?"

Sir Peter nodded, then rose from the table. Within minutes he had found the fellow and received his message.

When he returned to his party, he wore a greatly troubled expression.

"What is it?" Emma said with a frown. "Something is wrong."

"Someone has tried to break into the workroom where the princess mummy is located. He smashed a window. Radley was on guard, so prevented the fellow from entering the house. He fired a shot at him, but missed. At least it frightened him away."

At his words the group rose to their feet, troubled exclamations erupting.

"Do you fear he will return?" Emma inquired.

"He may," Sir Peter admitted.

"I say," Edward said, "that *is* a shock."

Mrs. Cheney wondered what the world was coming to that a person's home might be invaded so easily.

Mrs. Bascomb declared that she, for one, wished to leave and see if *her* home remained intact. Lady Hamley blinked and stuttered something about villains.

Somehow the life had gone from the party, and all agreed that perhaps it was time to leave.

Chapter 6

ADMIRABLY concealing his impatience, Peter saw to everyone's comfort in the carriages, then bided his time on the trip across the bridge and into Mayfair. When he caught Emma watching him, he realized he was drumming his fingers on his thigh, evidence of his worried state.

"Please, if you might put me down at our home, I should be grateful," Lady Amelia said into the silence of the carriage. "I feel certain you wish to discuss the attempted robbery, and I most likely would just be in the way."

"That's not true," Peter began courteously.

"Why, Lady Amelia," Lord Worcester drawled, "you show great sensitivity. I almost believe there is hope for you yet."

"Edward, if you do not cease bedeviling me, you will not live to know if you are right or no." Lady Amelia glared at him with an intensity that Peter could almost feel.

Whatever feelings had occurred between those two in the few moments at the gardens had vanished. They were back at daggers-drawn once again.

Peter gave the altered instructions to the groom, then settled back again. It was a relief to have the carriage halt before Lady Amelia's home, for the silence was becoming far too intense.

Lord Worcester correctly escorted Lady Amelia to her front door, then declined whatever she suggested. In the light from a flambeau they could see him shake his head.

"It would seem that your friend does not care overmuch for mine," Miss Cheney said with resignation.

"Not to worry. One of these days they may wake up to realize they are ideal for one another," Peter said with more optimism than he really felt. *That* situation would only occur if they didn't kill each other first.

Miss Cheney shook her head in disagreement. Peter could see her amused smile from where he sat.

It wasn't long before they arrived before the Cheney home. Lord Worcester paused outside.

"I do not know if I can be of assistance to you, but you have only to ask, old chap." He gave Peter a somewhat uncertain look, not taking one step toward the front door.

"Come in, come in," Peter said with a glance at Miss Cheney. He hoped he concealed his impatience, but suspected she knew. "Edward, keep the tabbies at bay while I have a brief chat with Miss Cheney."

"That I can do easily enough." Edward gave his good friend a cheerful smile and joined them.

The three entered the house, and Lord Worcester went up to the drawing room immediately. Emma stood at the bottom of the stairs awaiting whatever Peter had to say to her.

Peter felt devilishly absurd. He wondered if she suspected that he knew her dual identity. He had taken great pains to convince her otherwise. He had no trouble with his eyesight, but hoped she would tumble for his ruse. Now he needed her to work with him. With her keen vision and knowledge of what he was attempting, she would be of immeasurable assistance to him. Her artistic ability was precisely what was required at the moment.

"I truly need George's help," he said at last. "Could you possibly persuade him to come to my house in the morning? Perhaps he could postpone whatever he needed to do? Tell him that it is deuced important."

"Such language, Sir Peter," Emma scolded gently with a twinkle in her fine gray eyes. If she had not been confident that Sir Peter had not caught on to her disguise, she would have been suspicious of the sparkle that lurked in the depths of his green gaze.

"But will you try?"

"You are most persuasive. I will ask him," she said at last, wondering what on earth George could do that would help . . . and that *she* might perform!

"He *must* agree. Two heads are better than one, they say, and I cannot trust just anyone with my plans." He shifted from one foot to the other, looking tense and uneasy.

Her curiosity piqued at this snippet of information, Emma added, "I feel certain that George will be there if I tell him that you rely on his assistance."

"Well, that puts me at some ease, then. I have no doubt that you can be most persuasive when you choose."

He smiled down into her eyes, and Emma wondered whatever had come over her. Her knees felt distinctly wobbly, and her heart was fluttering like a wild bird caught in a net. When he casually picked up her hand to tuck it next to his firm, muscular body, she wondered if she would be able to walk up the stairs without tripping.

Catching her skirt up slightly in her free hand, she stood at the bottom of the stairs, staring into his eyes. She bestowed an uncertain smile on him, becoming lost in those green eyes for a moment before her common sense returned.

"Shall we join the others?" he gently queried.

"Oh! Of course, how silly of me." Emma wrenched her gaze from his and resolutely trod each step with care as they slowly made their way up to the drawing room.

She stood on the threshold with Sir Peter, exceedingly conscious that every eye in the room had turned in their direction.

"What a perfectly dreadful ending to a lovely evening," Mrs. Bascomb declared.

"Indeed, it was." Emma sighed with relief that no one intended to make some witty remark about her and Sir Peter. "I enjoyed the gardens enormously. Then to learn that some robber had attempted to enter Sir Peter's home, most likely with the intent of stealing something from his famous Egyptian collection, well . . . " She turned an indignant gaze to her father, who had always solved her problems. "Papa, what do you think?"

"Indeed, sir. I should appreciate your counsel," Sir Peter said with gracious courtesy.

"This city becomes more lawless by the day," Mr. Cheney complained, strolling over to stand by the fireplace. "Thieves enter any home they please with impunity. It seems they neither fear the gallows nor transportation. It is so now that a man takes his life in his hands if he so much as steps from his house to take a walk once evening has come. I thought when the Mohawks were past, we might have it better. It would seem not. I remember when those nasty bullies roamed the streets at night."

"What is to be done, Papa?" Emma demanded with the faith of a loving daughter.

"As to that, Sir Peter had best hire a guard. You said your butler is armed. Excuse me, young man, but is he of an age to do battle? I have dealt with criminals in my day. They can be fiendishly powerful when motivated." Mr. Cheney directed a steely gaze at Sir Peter.

"I intend to seek professional assistance. Perhaps a burly fighter at night with a Bow Street man by day would do the thing." Sir Peter looked about the room, adding, "I would hope my servants have remained silent about this matter. I presume that none of you will discuss it with others. It will be a trust between us."

Lady Hamley and Mrs. Bascomb appeared much struck with the magnitude of his faith in them, and they eagerly nodded their compliance with suppression of gossip. When he turned to Mrs. Cheney, she also nodded. He noted her glance at Emma, but he left that young woman until last.

"Sir, I appreciate your advice." Then he turned back to the ladies. "I trust that this little business has not totally ruined your evening?"

The ladies burst forth in raptures over the many treats they had experienced while at Vauxhall. Lady Hamley blinked while assuring Sir Peter it was a treat to be always remembered with pleasure. At her side Mrs. Bascomb nodded her agreement.

Emma caught the look exchanged between Sir Peter and Lord Worcester and wondered even more what it was that George might help Sir Peter with that Edward, Lord Worcester couldn't do just as well.

The younger gentlemen excused themselves shortly following this. It was clear Sir Peter was anxious to see for himself what the damage might be. She walked with the guests to the bottom of the stairs.

"You will not forget to speak with George first thing in the morning?" Sir Peter said so softly that she doubted if Lord Worcester could hear the words while listening to Oldham's offer to fetch a hackney.

"I promise that unless he has something desperately pressing, he will be there." Emma avoided meeting his eyes when she said this, for she wasn't certain but that she might betray her masquerade.

"I depend upon you," Sir Peter replied, then picked up one of the hands Emma had clasped before her to bestow a gentle kiss on the palm.

She swallowed carefully while trying to ignore the thrill that had shot through her with his gesture, then bravely said. "Good-bye, sir."

"Not good-bye, Emma. Just good night," he said with a dashing smile that cut straight to her heart.

She managed a reproving look at his improper use of her given name, but didn't scold him. It would call attention to something best ignored for the moment.

While marching purposefully up the stairs, she ignored the tumult of emotions what whirled through her. Hoping to avoid a discussion of Sir Peter's intentions with his particular notice of her, she went directly to her room.

"Laws, miss," the irrepressible Fanny said when Emma entered, "you look as though you had quite a time of it this evening."

Emma glanced down at her gown to see a slight tear near the hem. She supposed the limb with which she struck the villain must have damaged it.

"Well, could it be repaired, for I dearly like this gown."

Fanny gave the silk a dubious look. "Best give it to Hocknell, then."

While exasperated with Fanny and her considerable efforts to escape extra work, Emma acknowledged that her mother's abigail was a better seamstress and nodded her head in reluctant agreement.

Fortunately, Fanny quickly helped Emma into her bed gown and took herself off. That was one blessing with Fanny. . . she never lingered to chat, so eager to head for bed was she. Which was why Emma preferred her not to wait up.

Once under the covers Emma debated her dilemma. Dare she go to Sir Peter's in the morning? She had truly intended to send George off to Sussex and then offer her own services, taking Fanny along for propriety. Were she very careful, it might work.

"No, it would never do," she confessed to the moonbeams that peeped through her window. "I'd be found out, and that would put paid to a respectable marriage for me. And *that* would break Mama's heart. Not to mention put Papa into a fit of the dismals." She sighed. "No, George will have to go in the morning. I can only pray that Sir Peter continues to see what he is supposed to see," she whispered in desperation.

Oldham scarcely blinked when Emma marched out the front door the following day. She bravely set forth in the hackney that now lurked in the vicinity every morning, hoping to see her emerge from the house, Emma suspected.

"The same address, miss?" he asked.

"The same," she replied, then sank back to contemplate what she needed to say to her ladyship.

By the time she arrived at Lady Titheridge's home, Emma was in a fine state. "Thank you, Leland," she murmured upon entering the quietly impressive hall.

Braddon caught sight of Emma in the upstairs hallway and hurried to meet her. "Just go in the usual room, and I'll fetch her ladyship."

Emma nodded in agreement and swiftly went into the pretty little room where her things were neatly hung. George's things, that is.

She was staring out of the window across the chimney pots when Lady Titheridge bustled into the room.

"What? You are off this morning in spite of what must have been late hours?" Her ladyship crossed to the fireplace where Braddon stirred a small fire into life, then sat down to await Emma's explanation.

"Someone tried to force entry into Sir Peter's house. From what I could tell, it must have been the workroom where most of his collection is housed. He means to obtain the services of guards. He also wants George to assist him with something. Oh, dear ma'am! What am I to do? I had so hoped to end this charade." Emma held out her hands in a plea for help.

"Hm. You do have a dilemma." Her ladyship rubbed her chin in reflection, then cleared her throat. "It is apparent he values your opinion, not to mention services. I believe it best if you proceed with a visit to his house. That is the only way you will know what he wishes George to do."

"I admit a longing to know what is going on. Is that so very dreadful of me, ma'am? A girl is usually left out of anything interesting. For once in my life I shall be a part of something exciting." Emma advanced to face her ladyship with a determined step. "I shall do it . . . for his sake, and I shall confess for my own as well. Of course this is our secret," she said with an appealing look at both women. "When I consider what might happen should my foolishness become known, I positively shudder."

"Rest easy on that score. You are certain that Peter has not guessed?" Her ladyship gave Emma a bland look.

"Well, if he had, would he invite me to share in the action he intends?" Emma replied, although not sure of her point.

"I suppose not," her ladyship agreed. She waved her hand at Braddon, and that good abigail hastily brought forth the second set of garments for Emma to wear. A bright vest was produced to put on over the pantaloons. There was not much variety, but as most gentlemen favored a dark blue coat and biscuit pantaloons, it would not be remarked were Emma to show up in the same garb for days on end, with an occasional switch to the gray set of garments for a change.

Emma stared back at her reflection after Braddon had completed her ministrations. "That does it, I suppose. I am not sure my own mama would be positive of my identity in this garb. I shall see you later and tell you all."

"It is our secret, rest assured," her ladyship said with a fond look at Emma's brave stance.

At the house on Bruton Street Emma found the rotund Radley in a dither most unlike his calm, smiling self.

"Sir Peter is expecting me, I believe," she said with a hesitant look at the butler.

"Oh, sir, we are so pleased you have come. My master was worried you might be called away to Sussex."

Emma gave a start and wondered how he had suspected she had considered such a flight for George. Then she gave a sniff of derision. He couldn't have known, for there would be no reason to suspect that George would rush away, particularly when Emma revealed Sir Peter needed him.

She followed Radley back to the workroom, then halted in her steps.

"What are you doing?" she cried, just barely remembering to use George's voice.

"I thought I might install bars on the inside of this window. Be a good chap and hand me the hammer." Sir Peter stood near the top of a decidedly wobbly ladder. In one hand he held an iron bar, the other hand leaned against the wall. He looked perplexed as to how he ought to proceed.

"I think you are batty," Emma murmured, but complied with his request.

"I suppose you can think of something better?" He turned around to glare at her, and the ladder gave an alarming lurch.

"Actually, I suppose bars are useful . . . for *this* room. Tell me, do you intend to place bars on every window in the house?" Emma put her hands on her hips in her amusement, standing as she had seen her brother stand countless times.

Sir Peter climbed down from the ladder placed against the wall and sank down upon the stool Emma used when drawing.

"Blast! I hadn't thought of that. I told Emma last night I needed your good head. Glad you could come." He rose from the stool to give Emma a firm handshake, not the lightly proper sort given to ladies.

"I am surprised you use her given name, Sir Peter," Emma said in attempted rebuke.

"Up in the boughs at that, are you? Never fear, my intentions are honorable." Sir Peter flashed a handsome grin at George and placed the iron rail back in a box on the floor.

Beyond that he said nothing, and Emma knew a strong desire to kick him in the shins or box his ears. Perhaps this was the feeling Lady Amelia knew when she glared at Lord Worcester? Exasperation.

"What I want at the moment," Sir Peter continued, "is to have you complete the drawing of the necklace. I have a hunch *that* is the item the thief was after last night. What I'd like to do is hang the drawing up in the room, then possibly take the actual necklace to the British Museum for temporary safekeeping."

"It seems to me that you would be better off bringing it to Rundle and Bridge for the time being. They must have an excellent safe to hold their jewels." Emma studied the window surround. It showed evidence of a prying bar having been used. How fortunate Radley had fired that shot to frighten the intruder away.

"Capital! What a good head you have on your shoulders. I hope you find that treasure you seek, for you certainly deserve it." Sir Peter rubbed his hands together, a pleased expression on his face. He strode to the concealed safe in his wall behind a representation of an Egyptian wall painting.

Emma devoutly hoped George would find his treasure, but for different reasons. She discreetly averted her eyes from Sir Peter's efforts to open the safe, then turned when she heard the sound of a box being placed on the table.

"Like to see it again?" Sir Peter gave her an inquiring look, and Emma observed that odd light was back in his eyes again.

"Yes, indeed," Emma said, almost breathless with anticipation.

He lifted the lid of the flat black box. Inside, reposing on a bed of velvet, was the necklace. Emma sighed at the exquisite simplicity of the design, the beauty of the color and workmanship. She hesitantly touched the center gem with one finger.

"Think Emma would like to wear this?" Sir Peter asked in a careless way with a casual gesture toward the elegant and priceless piece of jewelry.

Emma closed her eyes. He couldn't mean what he said, could he? "I should think any woman would be pleased to adorn herself with this creation."

"Funny, I had no idea you were so knowledgeable about women, George, old man." Sir Peter clapped Emma on the back with a vigor that nearly threw her off balance.

Yes, she mentally concluded, a kick in the shins ought to do nicely. However, she attained her balance and attempted a smile in reply.

"This is what I propose," Sir Peter began in a confiding way, and Emma felt a rising excitement.

"First, you shall finish the drawing you began, coloring it in with watercolors. Think you could make it more intense, brighter than usual?"

"If I put several layers of color down, the color deepens,"

Emma said, eyeing the valuable necklace with a feeling somewhere between awe and desire.

"By all means, deepen."

It wasn't so much what he said, it was the way he said it that
prompted Emma to glance up at him. His face was as bland
and devoid of insinuation as possible. She decided she was
being foolish and overly suspicious.

She climbed onto the stool, opened her drawing pad to the
first sketch she had done, then proceeded to concentrate on a
new one. She dimly perceived Sir Peter's retreating footsteps.

Radley disturbed her peace with a tray bearing tea and ginger biscuits. Emma murmured an absent word of thanks. She
didn't bother to wonder what Sir Peter was doing, for the
necklace captured her entire attention.

But the memory of his words lingered while she worked. He
had wondered if Emma would like to wear the necklace.
Would she? She turned her head to study the princess, so
neatly laid out on the pallet with her arms crossed over her
chest. The necklace had been placed on the wrappings not far
from the top, so it hadn't touched the skeleton. But even if it
had, Emma had no fears on that account, nor was she inclined
to be superstitious. She would don it in a flash, had she the
chance.

In several hours of intense effort she finished what she felt
was an accurate representation of the necklace. She had captured the highlights on the stones, the variations in color, even
the shadows that served to give the piece depth.

She looked across the little room where Sir Peter had
worked previously and found him watching her. It made her
uneasy to think he might have observed something in her
movements that could appear feminine. Oh, to be done with
this charade. And yet, she would never have had the rare opportunity that George had been given simply because he was a
male.

"Finished?" he said, rising from his desk.

"Done," Emma replied with satisfaction. She rubbed the
back of her neck while watching him cross the room to join
her. She hadn't realized how stiff she'd become. Her neck was
sore and her shoulders ached from bending over the table.

Sir Peter observed her distress and blandly suggested,

"What you need is a bit of activity. Do you fence? It is wonderful exercise and teaches balance and refinement of movement as well."

"No," she snapped back. Emma gave him a horrified glance, then hastily concealed her feelings behind an equally bland expression suitable for George.

"Pity." He considered this lack a moment, then continued, "I shall give you lessons. I'm no novice at the sport, as my friends will attest. It will be good for you. You have grown too pale at this work, and I blame myself. This will permit me to atone."

He picked up the finished painting and strode off with it while Emma sat in a daze. How was she to handle this matter? It was utterly dreadful. She could never appear in a fencing costume—whatever that might be—and risk exposing herself to Sir Peter and anyone else who lounged about the place. Where *did* one fence? What did they wear?

She rubbed her forehead, feeling a headache coming on with grim intensity.

It was some time later when Sir Peter reappeared, although it seemed but minutes to Emma.

"Let us be on our way, then," he said with a grin.

"Our way?" Emma echoed, feeling distinctly as though she had been asleep rather than awake.

"Rundle and Bridge. Remember? It was your excellent suggestion." His genial words struck alarm in Emma's heart.

"Oh." Emma searched her mind with frantic haste. "I cannot go with you! I did have that business to handle, you may recall. Take a stout footman with you. Perhaps Worcester will oblige?" She edged her way around the table and toward the door, intent upon making her escape. She grabbed her hat before slipping through the doorway. George would assuredly have to make his way down into Sussex.

"Very well," Sir Peter replied with good grace. "But I insist on the fencing lessons. You never know when it will come in handy, old chap. As your father said only last night, it is dangerous for a man to walk out after dark these days."

Emma struggled not to laugh. Dangerous outside? Nothing could be as *dangerous* as standing in this room with Sir Peter.

"Promise?" He walked at her side on the way to the front

door. When Radley opened the door for her, she could see the same hackney waiting at the curb. She longed to make a mad dash for it and flee.

What could she have said in reply to Sir Peter's offer? She knew enough to understand it was a great honor to be taught by the premier fencer in all of England. But what if he discovered she was a woman?

There was no way out. Emma bowed slightly, then said, "Fine. Perhaps next week?"

"You will enjoy it, I promise. I know I shall."

Emma left the house, wondering precisely what he meant by that remark. Or was she being foolish to read all manner of things into a simple statement?

Once Emma had departed, Peter turned to his butler and announced, "Mr. George Cheney has agreed to allow me to teach him to fence, Radley."

"But you never teach anyone, sir," the butler replied in astonishment.

Peter rubbed his hands together with a certain feeling of glee. "I shall now." A great deal hinged on Emma's ability to learn the skill of a fencer. A great deal. He had plans for Emma Cheney.

Across Mayfair, Emma ran up the stairs to where Lady Titheridge waited for her in the hall.

"Whatever has happened, dear girl? You are as white as a sheet!" Her ladyship placed an arm about Emma's shoulders and strolled into the little bedroom with her.

"Oh, dear ma'am, such a disaster has befallen me!" Emma cried while stripping off her brother's coat. Braddon hurried in and began to help Emma with the awkward clothing.

"I am all ears. Tell! You promised," she reminded Emma.

"Sir Peter insists upon teaching me to fence!" Emma placed her hands on her hips and exchanged a worried look with her ladyship.

"Oh, dear." Lady Titheridge sank down on the pretty little chair to contemplate the most recent catastrophe. "Does your brother not know how to fence?"

"George never had time to learn, as far as I recall. He always had his nose in books or was out digging for ancient objects, that sort of thing." Emma slipped on her petticoat, then permitted Braddon to help her with her dress.

"I believe you must do this thing . . . the fencing," Lady Titheridge reflected. "He has a reason, whatever it might be."

"Never say so, ma'am," Emma declared with dismay.

"You are in far too deep at this point to quit, my dear," her ladyship mused. "I fear you must see this thing through. You want above all to assist my nephew in saving his precious Egyptian collection. Such a sacrifice is nothing in comparison."

Emma sank down upon the edge of the bed in utter consternation. "But what about the costume for fencing? I fear it will prove dreadfully shocking."

"Not man to man, dear girl. Nothing shocks a man, or so I believe."

Emma gave her ladyship a dubious look. "You want me to proceed with fencing lessons? This, in order to help Sir Peter?" Emma didn't quite see the connection.

"If he needs assistance, you may find it useful . . . in repelling intruders or something of the sort," her ladyship replied with maddening vagueness. "It would not harm you to know a form of self-defense."

The image of herself clad in heaven-knew-what garb, fending off a burglar intent upon stealing the priceless Egyptian collection sounded pretty incredible to Emma.

"Remember Boadicea, Emma dear."

"Heavens," Emma murmured, thinking of the warrior queen of early Britain—the brave woman who had led a rebellion, nearly wiping out an entire Roman legion.

Chapter 7

"THIS is what I am to wear?" Emma did not remember to use her brother's voice when the shock of what her garments were to be when taking fencing lessons hit her. She brushed the clinging biscuit pantaloons off with a shaking hand. The white shirt was bad enough, but these . . . they were indecent. When partly concealed beneath the coat, the fit was not as noticeable; indeed the coat covered a great part of her legs and . . . posterior.

Fortunately, the frills on her shirt front helped to cover her right where she needed it most. There was no way one might disguise her legs when so exposed. No matter, the pantaloons were vastly comfortable, and the freedom of the shirt with its loose sleeves was marvelous. It was shocking. But for a young lady, *not* a man, she reminded herself. Only the leather face covering she wore tied about her head gave her any solace. If anyone was so rash as to enter the room while the lesson was in progress, he would never guess her identity.

"Perfectly respectable," Sir Peter replied.

"Oh, quite, of course," Emma said in a gruff voice, reminding herself that she must have no missish airs nor react to things as she might otherwise. Oh, she inwardly wailed, this was bound to be a disaster. The only good thing, if you could call it thus, was that Sir Peter did not permit anyone else in the room when he was teaching.

It sounded as though he must have had scores of pupils, and Emma knew she ought to be grateful that she would at last do something a man could do. What a pity she had to pretend every moment.

Her daydreams had never been like this. In them she had always been the fragile princess, cherished and adored, petted and loved. This fencing seemed a trifle too energetic, but then, Sir Peter was not the man of her dreams. He was odious, dictatorial . . . and dangerous to know.

"I suppose you could wear your waistcoat if you like. A good many fellows do," he added in an offhand way while strolling across to a case from which he drew a dueling sword, or épée.

Emma hastily donned her bright patterned waistcoat and felt a little better for it. Every layer of clothing offered her more protection.

He took another sword out, then turned to face Emma. He offered one sword to her. It was long, flexible, and had a button on the tip—to protect them from an accidental wound, she supposed.

"First we salute." He brought his sword into a perpendicular position, point uppermost and guard close to and on a level with his chin. "Thus so," he concluded.

Emma followed suit, feeling just a trifle silly. It looked so very serious, but then perhaps it was at times.

"Now, the first matter of importance is distance."

Emma wondered how anyone with a nearsighted problem could fence if any distance was involved.

He continued, ignoring her abstraction. "It is of the utmost importance to keep a proper distance from your opponent at all times, both in attack and defense. Also, I will teach you how to gain ground on your opponent without exposing yourself to great danger."

Emma could not refrain from a gasp of dismay. He ignored this.

"Now, you will shortly discover how to rectify this problem should you find yourself misjudging the distance. I will show you how to withdraw instantly to a safer position." He gave her that reassuring smile of his. Emma wondered if it was the sort of look a fox gave a hen just before eating her.

"It all sounds most dangerous to me," Emma muttered under her breath while positioning herself as he began to demonstrate.

"Your first position is the prime, or parry. It is called thus because of the sword being whipped out to defend oneself in the event of attack. It will protect the entire left side of the body from exposure to your opponent's sword." He made a slash through the air with his sword that looked like a dangerous action to Emma.

"If I stayed home, I'd not have to worry," Emma said quietly, mostly to herself.

"Attention," Sir Peter scolded.

Emma subsided immediately.

When she arose this morning, she had not guessed that she would be in a long narrow room, alone with Sir Peter, and garbed in just her pantaloons, waistcoat, and a ruffled shirt. She felt exposed and wondered if the leaping about that he began to demonstrate might not undo her carefully bound breasts. She decided she would not be terribly active.

"You position your arm thus," he said with a glance at her. "The hand should be in line with the left shoulder and on the same level."

Emma tried to duplicate his actions and failed.

"No, no," he scolded patiently after she made several attempts. "Allow me."

Her eyes grew large and most alarmed as Sir Peter placed his arms about her to correct her position.

"See here, the forearm should not be exactly at a right angle to the upper arm, but slightly in advance. The blade will be slanting forward, a trifle downward, never vertically. This is a common mistake for beginners, one I feel sure *you* will not make." He guided her arm into the correct position with a gentle touch.

She could not find her voice to reply. He stood close to her, one arm about her, and then the dratted man had the audacity to smile down at her with that bone-melting intensity. She would be undone, she knew it. At the moment she could only hope she did not dissolve.

"You drop the point of the sword toward the area just above your opponent's knee," he instructed in that patient way he had.

Emma smiled. There was nothing she would like better than to take a stab at Sir Peter. He was a fiend, insisting that she must take fencing instruction. Whatever could she do with that ability? Fight? She quelled a shudder and tried to pay attention to his words. This was difficult because he would look into her eyes and then she was lost again. Oh, why was he so dashing, so daring, so dangerously male!

"Now we shall practice."

Emma tried to duplicate his foot movements and tried holding her arm just so, remembering to keep her hand so high and positioned as he had demonstrated. It was not easy. She found herself repeating and repeating until she could have screamed with frustration.

And then she began to understand the intent of the positions. Little by little she made progress. Her feet began to dance lightly over the mat; her arms and hands obeyed her wishes.

At last he said, "Very good."

It would have been nice to wipe off that surprised look from his face. She was beginning to think a woman might do very well at this sport. It appeared to require light footwork and a deft touch . . . something women usually possessed.

Emma courageously thrust her sword precisely as he directed, hitting the dummy of holland cloth stuffed with feathers right above the knee. She leaped forward and back on the thin mat intended for the practice with what she hoped was grace—or at the very least agile footwork.

"Bravo," Sir Peter cried at last, leaping around to face her while nudging the dummy aside. "Now, again!"

And again and again Emma repeated the action until she thought she would drop with fatigue and strain.

Then he countered with a different thrust, and Emma backed away from him, wondering what she ought to do.

His eyes danced with that peculiar sparkle she had observed before, and she rather wondered at it. Perhaps it was his enjoyment of the situation, or maybe his pleasure with the fencing. Somehow she mistrusted it.

"Seconde!" he cried, then performed the same thrust once again to demonstrate it for her.

Emma concentrated on his action, then copied it precisely, if a bit clumsily.

"Excellent," Sir Peter shouted as he dashed about to confront her from another direction.

She spun as well, parrying his attacks as best she could. It was not long before she could almost anticipate how he would thrust at her. She grew more confident with her footwork, dancing and leaping lightly across the mat while swinging her sword in the correct manner. She had not forgotten her desire to hit him. Perhaps that was what impelled her to continue— her desire to best him.

"Enough," he cried at last. He brought his sword up before him once again to place a light kiss on the hilt, a sort of cere- monial salute.

Emma gulped at the image that sprang to her mind when he saluted the sword . . . and her in that manner. It had nothing to do with fencing in the least.

Placing his sword into its case, he joined her. She knew she must look bemused, and certainly felt so. He whipped off his face mask, then removed Emma's. "You did very well, George."

While mentally scolding herself for succumbing to missish airs for a few moments, Emma felt pride that she had done well in a man's sport . . . even were she never to use it again. She mopped her face with a towel, thinking it fortunate that men were allowed to sweat without censure.

"You must go now?" he said when Emma donned her coat in preparation to leaving.

"Oh, I must," Emma said with a shaken voice. He was doing it again, gazing down into her eyes, resulting in that pe- culiar effect on her nerves. She wondered if that odd light in his eyes might be due to his nearsightedness.

She backed toward the door, intent upon her escape.

"I had hoped we could go over the security measures I have taken," Sir Peter said while strolling along the hall at her side.

Emma thought weakly that if she did not find a place to plunk her body down, it would take matters into its own and she would find herself on the floor.

Striving to appear nonchalant, Emma in her best George voice said, "What have you done besides remove the necklace to Rundle and Bridge?"

"I have a chap from Bow Street coming over this afternoon. And he promised to locate a pugilist for me who would be an adequate guard for the night." Sir Peter paused before the front door. Radley lurked in the background, but Emma was only dimly conscious of his presence. Her entire being was focused on the gentleman before her.

"It sounds as though you are taking the correct direction," she managed to say while longing to lean against the door.

"I would beg your assistance again. We shall have another lesson when possible. I look forward to a good bit of exercise. Confess—do you not feel better?" He gave her an arch look, quite as though he knew how she yearned to collapse on a bed and sleep.

Emma nodded, then edged her way out the door. "Sorry old man, I really must depart. Meeting, and all that. Appreciate the lessons more than I can say," she mumbled. Then before he could delay her again, she dashed for the hackney, calling out, "Same address."

She collapsed against the cushions, utterly done in and wishing that she might take off for the country or somewhere.

When the door closed, Peter leaned back against the wall and looked at Radley. "She was quite magnificent, you know. Natural ability and grace. Splendid timing and thrust. Once she learns all the positions, we will have some excellent sport." He chuckled, a most elated sound. "I think she is badly confused at the moment, and I hope to keep her that way for some time."

"You do not worry about compromising her, sir?" Radley gave Peter a troubled look.

"No, no," Peter said softly. "She will be just fine." He strolled off down the hall, whistling a gay little tune.

Behind him Radley stood in perplexed silence a few minutes before securing the door and bustling off to his tasks.

Emma, however, did not feel the least fine at the moment. She stormed into Lady Titheridge's house in a highly irate mood.

"You did not warn me, dear ma'am, that I would wear this," she charged. She pulled off the coat and stood arrayed in the ruffled shirt, waistcoat, and biscuit pantaloons worn during the lesson. Her slim legs were revealed in shocking delineation. The curve of her hips led the eye to shapely calves and trim ankles. With a glance in the looking glass Emma flipped a finger at the ruffle along the front opening of the shirt.

"Thank goodness for this, or I would have been undone. I

do hope my bosom was not too pronounced. Never have I wished to be as flat as a board until today. It would have helped a bit, I think," she concluded without much conviction. "Shall I demonstrate what I went through?"

She thrust her arm out as though to manipulate an épée, dancing and leaping about as she had done during the lesson.

"Good grief!" her ladyship said in fading accents while she sank back upon the chair.

"Precisely," Emma agreed, wiping her brow with the back of her hand. She looked to Braddon, who immediately assisted Emma from George's shirt and pantaloons. She splashed herself quite liberally with lavender water, then dressed in her own modest gown.

"What am I to do, ma'am?" Emma appealed to her confederate while Braddon brushed out her curls.

"We are in a decided fix," Lady Titheridge admitted. "I believe you must brazen it out. To retreat at this point would be to admit failure. You cannot allow that. Besides, I think it your duty. I believe he needs you very much."

"Why?" Emma wondered aloud as she recalled those green eyes that looked at her in *such* a way. Yet she was attuned to duty and had always done her duty in the past. If Lady Titheridge was convinced that it was Emma's *duty* to spar with a sword, she would.

"Because my nephew seems to feel there is no one else he can trust, and you have skills important to him at this time. You simply cannot desert him now," Lady Titheridge said in a most pleading manner.

Not proof against her ladyship's plea, Emma nodded even as she sank on the bed with a sigh. She looked longingly at the pillow, then resolutely rose to leave.

"I had best return to the house before Mama asks too many questions. I will take a nap, then prepare to face the *ton* this evening as though I had not a care in the world but the color of my gown and the arrangement of my curls."

"And where do you plan to go this evening?" Lady Titheridge inquired with what seemed like proper courtesy.

"Mrs. Bascomb has persuaded my mama that Lady Sefton's little party will be the thing to attend. Little! If the house is not full to overflowing, I will miss my guess."

"A sad crush in other words. You know every hostess hopes for that, my dear." Lady Titheridge twinkled a smile at Emma, one of agreement with the absurdities of the *ton*.

Emma sighed. "Of course. I am just tired. I will feel better when I have rested some."

Lady Titheridge watched her young protégée quietly slip from the bedroom, then her ladyship crossed to the window, deep in thought. Before long she went to her desk and wrote a short letter. Once it was sealed, she summoned Leland.

"See to it that this note is sent to my nephew at once."

Leland exchanged a look with his mistress, then bowed. "Of course, milady. At once."

Emma dragged herself up to her room, thankful that her mama was deep in conference with Mrs. Bascomb at the moment. She could hear Mama extolling the benefits of Dr. Vernal's Tonic Pills For Nerves to her friend. Tonic pills? Emma wondered what they actually contained, for she had no great faith in the quacks her mother continually consulted.

However, Emma was grateful to Dr. Vernal at the moment, for the discussion permitted her to escape an inquisition. Mama did not consider it proper for a young lady to be present while health was discussed. And dear Mama would have wormed the details of Emma's supposed visit to Lady Titheridge in no time if she was in prime form.

At last in her room, Emma thankfully slipped her gown off, then crawled into bed. Her world had turned topsy-turvy from the moment she had met Sir Peter Dancy. She wished she had been prudent and not attended the unrolling of the mummy from Thebes. With that foolish deed all sorts of trouble had arisen. And now she was *fencing* for pity's sake. Scandalous.

The last thought she knew before drifting off to sleep was that his eyesight must indeed be terrible if he had not detected her disguise by now.

When she awoke, her natural optimism returned. As often the case, things looked better when one had enjoyed a refreshing sleep. In the looking glass she saw a sparkle in her gray eyes again. Her fatigue had vanished, and she was ready to face the evening with reasonable enthusiasm.

"La, miss, you will need a new dress at the rate you be

going about," Fanny said when she bustled into the room, carrying Emma's freshly ironed white silver gauze gown over her arms.

"I cannot ask Papa for another just now. Perhaps later on," Emma murmured, wondering just how much Sir Peter intended to pay George for his art work. She would never make a person of business, for she had taken one look into those green eyes and totally forgotten to inquire. And yet she must confess that while she had begun this work for a few needed pounds, she now treasured the adventure, not to mention the proximity of Sir Peter Dancy.

She hastily slipped into the gown, then allowed Fanny to fuss with her curls before rising from the dressing table, picking up her reticule.

A knock on the door alerted her to possible trouble. When her mother entered, Emma steeled herself for difficulty.

"I brought these up for you myself, dear." Mrs. Cheney held out a dainty posy of violets. "Mr. Swinburne begs the pleasure of a dance at the party this evening. I believe he must be more worthy than we first believed."

Emma shook her head. "I doubt it. But of course I will grant him a dance. I have observed he is everywhere accepted and the hostesses appear to like him—in spite of his dandyism."

"Young men like to embrace eccentricities. When he matures, he will find them all absurd and become a dutiful husband." Mrs. Cheney smiled with the knowledge of her unassailable wisdom.

While Emma had not the experience of her mama, she doubted that Mr. Swinburne would ever fall into that mold. He would more likely spend himself into bankruptcy and join those fleeing to Europe to escape their creditors. It seemed to Emma that the list of bankrupts published in the paper grew longer every day. Papa took the major papers, and *The Mirror of the Times* faithfully printed the bankrupts. How dreadful it must be to be without funds.

"Come now, I do not wish to be late. You will dazzle the gentlemen." Mrs. Cheney gently guided Emma out of the room and along to the stairs. "I am pleased to see that you are at last taking my advice. When Fanny informed me that you were napping, it did my heart much good, and yours too, I daresay."

"Yes, Mama," Emma replied dutifully. She could scarcely admit to her dear and fragile mama that the morning had been spent in exercise—dashing and jumping about on a mat while waving a sword in the air. Mama would most likely have a fatal attack of palpitations.

The crowd at Lady Sefton's was as predicted—a sad crush. While standing in line on the stairs, Emma observed that Lady Titheridge attended the party. Then Emma paled when she saw who was at her ladyship's side—none other than her nephew, Sir Peter Dancy. Drat the man. Why had Emma been told that he seldom went about in company? It seemed to her that every time she went somewhere, she found him as well.

If she were a vain creature, she might think he sought her out. She knew better than that. He showed a few signs of the dandy, and more than a few of the eccentric, not to mention a dangerous gleam in those eyes. He exhibited none of the signs of an enamored swain.

Lady Sefton greeted Emma with more than common courtesy. "I am pleased to see you, Miss Cheney," she said with a genuine smile. "When shall we have the pleasure of having you at our little assembly again?"

Emma glanced at her mama, then said, "I expect we shall attend come Wednesday evening, Ma'am." The nonsense of calling Almack's a little assembly was enough to send Emma into a state of terminal giggles.

"Lovely," replied her ladyship, then turned to the next in line.

"Emma," declared Lady Cheney from behind her fan, "I do believe there is a chance you may take. Oh, I do hope so."

"If I do, you may thank Lady Titheridge and Mr. Brummell. People have a tendency to follow where they lead."

"How wise you are becoming, my dear," Mrs. Cheney said with amazement and delight.

Emma was spared a reply when Mr. Swinburne glided up to her, bowing over her hand with consummate grace.

"How it pleases me that my humble tribute has found favor in your eyes," he gushed with a look at the violets.

"She is not an heiress, however, Swinburne," said a wry voice from behind Emma.

She turned sufficiently—although she really did not have to, for she knew that voice—to see Sir Peter at her shoulder with Lady Titheridge at his side.

"Naughty boy," her ladyship scolded affectionately. "You ought not say such things, you know."

"I believe it is true," he said again with a glance at Emma.

Emma gave him a speaking look, then turned her gaze to Mr. Swinburne. She really did not wish to encourage the man, but she detested Sir Peter for his wicked comment. She knew her financial status and he knew it, but he did not have to broadcast it. It was not the *done* thing.

"Will you grant me a dance?" Mr. Swinburne said to Emma, tossing a pitying look at Sir Peter. It was clear that the dandy believed his appearance to outshine Sir Peter's. Indeed, it did. Pale yellow knee breeches with a sky blue waistcoat embroidered in orange and puce flowers beneath a dove gray coat made him stand out. In spite of Brummell's dictum that one ought not attract undue attention, Mr. Swinburne caught the eye.

"I should be most pleased," Emma replied with her natural grace and charm.

"Not before you allow me to beg a waltz with you later on," Sir Peter declared most gallantly.

With Lady Titheridge looking on and wearing a benign smile, there was nothing for Emma to do but nod pleasantly and say, "I would be honored, Sir Peter."

His lazy grin down into her eyes forced her to stiffen her knees. If only she could dismiss this lamentable tendency to weak limbs when he smiled at her, things would improve; she just knew it.

Mr. Swinburne claimed her hand, and Emma found herself free of Sir Peter. Not but that she did not know where he stood or with whom he danced all the while. She particularly observed his cotillion with a beautiful blonde.

Miss Richenda de Lacey was an heiress, incredibly lovely and possessed with about as much brains as God gave a flea. Or so Emma had been told. She had never met the girl. It was most peculiar that Emma felt an odd urge to scratch the beauty's eyes out.

"Miss de Lacey is quite charming, I believe," Emma drawled to Mr. Swinburne at the conclusion of the dance.

"The heiress?" he replied, thus betraying an interest in her dowry more than her charms. "Indeed. I have heard tell she has devoted bachelors littering her drawing room every afternoon."

"And are you one of those?" Emma inquired with an arch lift of her brow. She really did not care if he was, but she longed to know who made up that coterie.

"At times." With a change from his usual dandy airs, he gave Emma a level look. "There comes a time when a chap must either settle or decamp. Like many other fellows, I have an internal debate on the subject. When I am with Miss de Lacey, I ask myself if I could."

Emma understood. He wondered if he might tolerate the little peagoose as a wife. An enormous dowry could go a long way to helping a man endure a silly wife. "There is always dinner at White's."

"True," he concluded with a second glance at Miss Richenda de Lacey. "Beauty is as beauty does," he commented obliquely and strolled off in her direction.

"You are looking exceedingly thoughtful. Are you not aware that such introspection is not permitted during a dancing party?" Sir Peter spoke softly into one of her ears. She could feel his breath on her neck, and she trembled at his nearness. Then she scolded herself. She was being as silly as Miss de Lacey.

"Well?" he said, turning her about by taking her hand and drawing her out to the dance floor.

"I had not realized this was to be a waltz," she said, rather than comment on his remarks.

"You promised it to me," he reminded. "It is the supper dance as well, so I shall enjoy the pleasure of your company. Unless you are of another mind?"

Emma knew it would be bad manners to refuse him, and no one else had asked her to supper. "I should be pleased to join you for supper."

"You say that with the enthusiasm of one going to the tooth-drawer," he complained.

Emma neither denied nor agreed with his accusation. Instead, she looked away from him—anywhere.

"Are you frightening the other gentlemen away?" she suddenly asked when she observed how the other men watched her with Sir Peter and retained their distance. "They seem to respect you a great deal. Do they fear to tread on what they perceive as your territory? If so, you must find a way to disabuse them of the notion. Perhaps a light flirtation with Miss de Lacey would do the trick?"

"Emma," he said in a quiet warning.

"I have never given you leave to use my Christian name," she charged. "You appear to be a very forward gentleman, I must say."

"Did your brother tell you he is learning to fence?" Sir Peter said, rather than argue with her.

"Yes," she managed to admit.

"Did he say if he liked it?"

"I believe he finds it fascinating," she replied with a strong element of the truth. She fastened her gaze upon the violets in her posy.

"Good. He shows a natural ability. It would be a shame were he not to develop it."

Emma could not think of a reply to this comment, so she remained silent. She did recall something one of her earlier partners had said about Sir Peter. He told Emma that he wished he might persuade Sir Peter to give him fencing lessons, but that the baronet never took pupils.

So where did that put Emma? Why was he offering to teach George? She wished she knew. She also wished she did not long to be with him at those lessons.

Chapter 8

THEY left the ballroom floor to proceed to the room set aside for supper, immediately after the waltz concluded.

Emma found respite in stepping away from Sir Peter's side—as much as the crowd allowed. Even the touch of his hand had an odd effect on her. It disturbed her hard-won calm.

"Oh, look!" she said with relief. "There is Lady Amelia, and she is with Lord Worcester. I do hope they will join us," Emma declared with more enthusiasm than she had shown at Sir Peter's invitation to supper.

She drifted across the room to embrace Lady Amelia lightly, then draw her along to an empty table that would hold six. They were chattering like a flock of magpies so Peter set off to find nourishment.

"Worcester," Peter said in acknowledgment when they met at the vast table spread with delectables.

Lord Worcester placed a savory on one of the plates in his hand and gave Sir Peter a resigned look. "I suppose you saw my supper partner. Be a good chap and join us."

"I believe my reluctant partner has already accomplished the matter." Peter gave his friend a wry grin and glanced over to where Emma sat in animated conversation with Lady Amelia. The girls were joined by Miss de Lacey while Mr. Swinburne crossed to fetch her a plate of food.

"Cat among the pigeons, I perceive," Peter muttered to Worcester. "The heiress has joined them."

"Really? What luck. I must find a way to keep from wringing Amelia's pretty neck. Perhaps I can take up a flirtation with Miss de Lacey?"

"Sorry. I have all ready been ordered to do just that."

"What? Ordered?" Edward nearly dropped the lobster patty he had been about to place on his plate.

"It seems that Emma is under the impression that the other men at the ball believe she is my particular lady. Emma thinks it is to her detriment. I am under orders to disabuse them of the notion."

"You don't say so," Edward said, pausing to stare at Peter with amazement. "Does she not know what a catch you are, old boy?"

"It would appear she neither knows nor cares," Peter admitted with chagrin.

"Well, I never," Edward muttered after a glance at the remarkable Miss Cheney.

"I couldn't agree more," Sir Peter said before leaving the table now less laden with food to return to his diffident partner.

"Have you heard anything from Henry Salt?" Lord Worcester quietly asked Peter while the women were chatting and Mr. Swinburne had gone to replenish his plate.

"The last I heard he was trying to get the best of the French consul, Drovetti. Every time Salt finds an antiquity he wants to remove from Egypt to the British Museum, Drovetti screams his objections. Of course Drovetti wants to haul everything back to France. I understand they squabble like a pair of fishwives. They must supply a good deal of amusement for the Egyptian authorities."

"Odd to think of the British consul-general behaving in that manner," Worcester replied. "Do you think there might be a connection between what is going on over there and the attempt to steal from your collection?"

"I doubt it, although one never knows. Perhaps I ought to investigate the local French to see if there is a likely possibility. I wonder if either Emma or George speaks French fluently?"

"You aren't contemplating involving *her* in this, are you?" Worcester looked aghast at the very idea.

"She already is involved. By the bye, did you know I'm giving lessons in fencing?" Peter said softly. "I have found a most excellent pupil."

"But you never do," Worcester replied, keeping his voice

down with effort for he was clearly dumbfounded at this bit of news.

Peter nodded, while carefully not looking at Emma. "I'm finding it quite a challenge. I believe I have missed something by not sharing my skill in the sport."

"Keep this to yourself, or you will have chaps lined up outside your door by the dozen," Worcester cautioned.

"Mum's the word," Peter agreed. Then he glanced around to observe that others had begun to drift back to the ballroom. "I believe I shall take Emma in hand and see what we can discover."

"You think she will go with you? When she isn't much interested in you as a catch?" Worcester grinned in amusement at his friend's discomfiture.

"Believe me, she will go along," Peter said with confidence.

Turning to face Sir Peter, Emma wondered what it was that had been said to bring that look of unholy glee to Lord Worcester's face. She was about to chastise Sir Peter for failing to flirt with Miss de Lacey when he turned to her with a serious expression on his face.

"Emma," Sir Peter began, then lowered his voice so she had to strain to hear him, "I need your help. Worcester wonders if a Frenchman might be involved in the attempt to steal the artifacts in my collection. Do you speak French?"

"I do," she replied. She frowned, wondering how on earth she might assist him.

"Stroll around the ballroom with me. It is possible we might hear something of interest." He rose, holding out his hand to assist her.

"Why, of course. Is it possible?" she whispered while rising from the table to join him.

"Anything is possible," he replied close to her ear while deftly placing her hand on his arm. If Emma thought him a trifle proprietary, at least he had ignored her during supper. She feared to be linked with him when she was quite certain he had no personal interest in her.

She gave him a quick look and wondered at that gleam in his eyes. It had to be brought on by the challenge of tracking down who it was that sought to steal the collection. What else could it be?

Lord Worcester claimed the beautiful Miss de Lacey as a partner for the next country dance. Lady Amelia flounced off to her mama's side where her next partner could solicit her hand for the dance. Mr. Swinburne disappeared in the direction of the card room.

"We are alone so I can explain a little. It is known that the French are eagerly trying to cheat the English out of the treasures found in Egypt. French Consul Drovetti is nothing more than a brigand, screaming at *our* consul-general with every find he makes. Worcester wondered if Drovetti had a Frenchman here in London, perhaps one of the sham refugees who have served as spies. My collection is well known; there is no difficulty in obtaining information on it, or where I reside."

"With Napoleon on the rampage again, how can the French even remotely think of such a matter as antiquities?" Emma demanded, looking about her with questing eyes. Could there be such a spy at work? Here? She well knew they had infiltrated the country into a great many positions and places. It shocked her to think how many English had aided the French in one way or another.

"Drovetti is in Egypt, far from home. Neither England nor France can spare men to stand guard on those two. Salt and Drovetti are as though they were in another world, for communications are difficult at best and take forever to reach home. It would be a matter of a man having been given orders and following them—even if his country is in dire straits at the moment. He may not learn of it for weeks. It is a matter of money."

Emma stared at him for a moment, then took a step forward. "I suspect we had better not wear such serious faces. People will either think we have been quarreling, or that we have received news of a death."

"True," he said with a grin while commencing their stroll about the vast room. "Or worse yet, that we have had bad news from the French battle front."

Emma shivered at the very thought. She hated the very notion of war, of young men dying. Yet England must be defended against the Corsican monster. How appalling that Napoleon had managed to escape from Elba while the Duke of Wellington was off in Vienna. Of course Wellington had left the Congress and was now headquartered in Brussels where he assembled an army from England's allies. Surely the duke would find a way to defeat Napoleon. To do otherwise was unthinkable.

"Do you think the duke will be able to destroy that brute Napoleon?" Emma asked while pretending to admire one of the floral arrangements.

"I have every confidence in the man," Sir Peter replied.

Emma paused, turning her head as though listening to something Sir Peter was saying to her, but in reality straining to hear a softly spoken conversation to her left—in French. While nearly all the gentry and aristocrats of England could speak passable French, this couple expressed their sentiments in flawless Parisian.

At a quizzical glance from Sir Peter, Emma quickly frowned, then faintly shook her head. At last she gestured they should continue their stroll.

"And what was that about?"

"I heard excellent French spoken and wondered what they found to say while at a ball. I fear it was nothing much of interest . . . unless they spoke in code. There I fear I am of no help to you in the least."

"Pity my cousin is not in town. Victoria and her husband are rather skilled in codes and the like."

"Are they indeed?" Emma said with a touch of awe. It seemed the Dancy family possessed a number of unusual females from what she had heard. A painter, a sculptress, an engraver—so many talented and creative women. "And your sister?"

"She once managed to fall into scrapes with distressing regularity. Now she is married and off my hands."

"Your poor sister." Emma paused again, ostensibly to adjust the fall of her elegant silk shawl, and gift from Lady Hamley.

"Another conversation?" Sir Peter immediately understood what she was about and attempted to assist her with the rearrangement of the white shawl.

"I am not certain," Emma whispered. "At times it is difficult to tell whether a person is merely attempting to use a dab of French to impress another, or if it is a genuine exchange."

"I am impressed with your many talents. My aunt tells me

that you sketch as well as your brother. She is very pleased with the colored drawings you have done for her." His smile invited her confidence.

Emma blushed; she could feel the heat stealing across her face and down her neck. Oh, what a wretched situation. She wanted nothing more than to reveal her complete identity to Sir Peter. Yet could she? What would happen?

Setting aside her worry for the moment, she gestured they should continue their lap about the room.

Nothing more reached their ears. When they reached Emma's mama, that dear lady looked up in surprise.

"Dear me, I wondered where you had disappeared. It is not the thing to go off like that," she scolded gently.

"We merely strolled about the room, Mama," Emma replied patiently.

Mrs. Bascomb directed a knowing gaze at Sir Peter, but blessedly said nothing.

At that moment a servant approached Sir Peter with a silver salver in hand. On it reposed a small letter.

"What on earth?" Sir Peter said with a deal of puzzlement. One did not normally receive messages while at a ball.

Begging the lady's permission, he broke the seal, then scanned the brief contents.

"Trouble?" inquired Emma astutely.

"Indeed," replied Sir Peter, holding the now refolded missive before him. "There has been another attempt on the house. Someone tried to enter through the upstairs window. One of the maids happened to be in the room, making up the fire. Her scream sent him across the rooftops in a hurry."

"How fortunate she was in there at the time," Emma said quietly, trying not to look alarmed.

"Tell your brother I shall be in need of his excellent help come morning, will you?" Sir Peter murmured so that Mrs. Cheney was not aware he addressed Emma.

"Oh, dear," Emma whispered. Then she firmed her spine and nodded. "I will."

"You will what, dear?" Mrs. Cheney inquired, her gaze darting back and forth between Emma and Sir Peter like a ferret on the prowl.

"I will be happy to assist his aunt tomorrow morning,"

Emma lied, feeling utterly awful that it was necessary. "She has been such a dear delight, and I do admire all the beautiful things she has collected."

"I stand to inherit the lot of them, you know," Sir Peter said with that twinkle back in his eyes.

"I see," Emma replied, trying to sound impressed. Actually, she was, but she didn't understand his purpose in telling her about it.

Since Mrs. Cheney had great hopes for Emma and she did not wish to harm the excellent connection with Lady Titheridge, she smilingly agreed it was wonderful that Emma could be of use to her dear ladyship.

Emma exchanged a rueful glance with Sir Peter, then watched him weave his way through the crowd. He had again placed a kiss on her hand before leaving, a light touch but felt even if she wore her gloves.

Then she was claimed for a Scots reel, and she had no time for reflections. When the gentleman brought her back to her mother, Emma was relieved to hear her express a wish to leave.

"I vow, all these late nights just do me in. As it is, I shall have to sleep until noon. I do not know where Emma finds the energy to rise so early." She smiled fondly at her dearest daughter and hope for the family future. She again looked to Mrs. Bascomb and continued, "Were it not for Dr. Vernal's pills, I should expire, I just know it."

"Of course we must leave at once," Emma said promptly, wanting to avoid a discussion of her mother's favorite topic. She gathered up her mama's shawl and her posy of violets.

A glance about the room to see if Mr. Swinburne remained did not find him, and she decided he had found the play in the card room to his liking. The dandy was not athletic and no doubt found dancing for very long to be exceedingly tiring.

Mrs. Bascomb and her mama discussed the ball all the way to the Bascomb residence. After that good lady had made her exit, Mrs. Cheney studied her daughter.

"You look worried, my dear."

Mrs. Cheney had an alarming tendency to be perceptive at times. Emma was sorry that this had to be one of them.

"It is nothing, Mama. So many parties, routs, and assemblies eventually become fatiguing. I shall welcome a good sleep."

Those words seemed to appease Mrs. Cheney, who sank back against the squabs with a satisfied expression. "I believe that Mr. Swinburne might be brought to scratch, you know."

"Reginald Swinburne?" Emma cried in dismay.

"He is a presentable gentleman and dresses in the highest of fashion. We have not discovered the source of his income as yet, but he must have deep pockets if he can afford so many luxuries." Mrs. Cheney nodded complacently.

"Mama, the first priority of a dandy is his dress. I have no doubt he owes his tailor yet for last year's bills. Besides, you did promise that I should at least like the man I marry, and I cannot like Mr. Swinburne."

"Try a bit harder, dear," was Mrs. Cheney's reply before leaving the carriage when it drew to a halt before their residence.

Emma said nothing to this, pretending not to hear the injunction.

Come morning, Emma crept from her bed and silently dressed herself before Fanny could enter. Her room was chilly, for the fire had gone out. However, it served to help her wake up.

She was about to slip from her room when Fanny opened the door. She entered the room, then stood there, mouth agape at the sight of Emma, up and dressed.

"Lauks, miss, what you be doin' at this hour of the day, all ready to go out?" the maid demanded—most impudently, Emma thought.

"Is that my chocolate I smell?" she said in a pleasant manner, ignoring the maid's inquisitiveness. "Oh, good, you brought me some rolls."

Emma took the tray and eagerly sipped the steaming chocolate and munched the rolls. She was hungrier than she had realized. But then, last evening she had been too troubled to enjoy her supper.

"You goin' out?" Fanny said while deftly making up the bed.

"You may remain here. I shan't require you this morning," Emma said by way of an answer.

Fanny looked resentful at this reply, but dared not sass her mistress.

As quickly as possible, Emma had donned her shawl and bonnet, caught up her reticule and gloves, and was running lightly down the stairs. Oldham was nowhere to be seen, so she slipped from the house with only Fanny the wiser.

She found a hackney at the stand around the corner. Emma gave him the order to proceed to her ladyship's address and then contemplated her coming day. Would she again have a fencing lesson? She had best be prepared. And how did Sir Peter expect George to help him?

Her absentminded brother had never been one to exert himself for another. Emma wondered what made Sir Peter think George had changed any.

Lady Titheridge was still abed when Emma presented herself at the front door. Leland ushered Emma to the little bedroom without the necessity of caution. The house was so silent that any sound would have disturbed those sleeping.

Braddon soon appeared to assist Emma from her sprigged muslin gown and into the biscuit pantaloons, white shirt, the bright waistcoat in alarming proportion. She helped with the tinted face cream, then altered Emma's curls.

Before she left the room, Emma smoothed a white stocking up her leg, wondering again if she would be required to have a fencing lesson. She still ached a bit from the last one. She had taken the precaution of binding up her bosom again, just in case, although anyone with half an eye should be able to tell that Emma was not George. Emma wondered—could Sir Peter really be so absentminded and nearsighted that he couldn't detect the difference? It was all very strange.

Lady Titheridge's carriage awaited Emma when she exited the front door. The coachman silently assisted her inside, then drove off to the house on Bruton Street without a word exchanged.

Radley was not in evidence. A footman ushered Emma into the workroom, where a much beleaguered Sir Peter studied his collection.

"What is wrong?" Emma said in George's voice. She might

as well ask anew, for it was certain that things had changed since the receipt of the letter last night.

"Radley was shot at this morning."

"Why, that's terrible! No idea as to who might have taken aim at him, I suppose?"

"He was in here, cleaning up, making certain all was in order. He is the only one other than myself who has a key to this room." Sir Peter turned to face Emma, and she was shocked at his expression. Deep distress could be seen in his eyes.

"You cannot blame yourself. How badly is he injured? How did it happen?" Emma was equally distressed over the shooting, for she liked the genial butler.

"Fortunately, it is a mere graze. The felon aimed from that opposite rooftop. Must be a crack shot to hit his target at that distance when Radley was moving about."

Sir Peter joined Emma at the window and pointed out the roof from where the villain must have shot in order to hit Radley.

"I am impressed with your concern for a servant," Emma said trying to sound sort of gruff.

"Been with us since I was a lad. He was around far more than my father."

Sir Peter said no more on the matter, but Emma guessed it was the oft-told tale of absent father and servant to hand.

"Look, old chap, the Bow Street man is coming at noon. There isn't a great deal we can do until he surveys the place," Sir Peter said in an abstracted way.

"My, they certainly take their time," Emma said wryly.

"Nothing was stolen; no one was murdered. A shot servant is not sufficient to cause a great reaction, I gather." Sir Peter began to pace back and forth in front of the princess.

"But you care," Emma replied softly, almost forgetting to sound like George in her sympathy.

"Do you suppose there is someone seeking the mummy? They are still in demand for medicine, you know. Believe it or not, there are people who are convinced that a mummy will cure a vast array of ailments."

Emma gasped, then bit back what would be a girlish chuckle. "How foolish some people are."

"I wonder if the chap will suggest I pack it all away."

"Where would you store it?" Emma wondered.

"I refuse to allow some villain to force me to such a position. I will fight," Sir Peter declared.

Emma drew back in alarm at his fierce expression. "You'll need your own army," she said without thinking.

"Ah, you have the right of it. That reminds me . . . we had best get on with your lessons. You are prepared to proceed?" Sir Peter grabbed Emma by the arm and led her away from the workroom, locking the door behind him.

Before she knew it, they were back in the narrow room with the mat. The dummy was nowhere in sight. Emma carefully removed the blue coat and hung it on a peg, then turned to face Sir Peter. Surely he must take one look at her and know the truth.

She tied on the molded leather mask he handed her, then marched onto the mat to wait. With long strides he crossed to the box with the swords, removed them—first assuring the buttons were secure—then offered one to Emma.

She remembered the salute from yesterday, but had forgotten her position just a trifle.

"No, no," he said with a returned patience. "Shift about this way and you will be fine."

Emma resigned herself to an hour or so of torture and raised her sword.

"We shall practice the positions, the mechanics of our movements today. Now, let us commence."

He immediately began, without warning and in fierce attack. Emma was on guard at once and attempted to parry his thrusts with what she had learned yesterday.

The going was difficult, for it seemed to her that he gave no quarter. She leaped forward, bounded back in retreat, then plunged at him again, recalling her desire to hit him.

He touched her again and again with the tip of his sword when she failed to evade his long reach. It was not enough to wound, and the button was safely in place, but Emma wondered how she would fare.

At last he paused, permitting Emma to blot her face.

"I believe we shall go over the footwork. You seem to have a natural instinct for this, but still, there are a number of steps or jumps it is good to know. If you are to be an acceptable partner, you must practice everything daily."

He had turned away from Emma when he said this, which was most fortunate, or he would have seen her place a hand to her bosom in dismay. He could *not* be serious, could he? Nonsense. Why, all Emma had to do was have George disappear.

Then Sir Peter turned again to face Emma, and she hoped none of her fears was revealed in her stance, for the mask protected her from his gaze, such as it was.

And that was another thing that bothered her. If he was so nearsighted, how could he detect the direction of the bullet? Or had Radley been able to see that man before he fled? There seemed to be more questions than answers. She wished she might ask, but to do so would definitely reveal who she was. Oh, was there ever such a conundrum?

"Pay attention now," Sir Peter said in a laughing voice. "What a daydreamer you are. And I thought I was bad."

He began to show Emma a series of steps and jumps that he insisted she learn to perfection. By the end of two hours she was ready to drop in her tracks. She ached with fatigue and worry.

Finally, he took her sword from her to place alongside his in the case. "Tomorrow we shall consider the tactics of fencing."

Emma just barely refrained from crying out that she would not be there ever again, that George was leaving for Rome or some distant spot.

When he turned to take her mask from hands that trembled ever so slightly, he said, "I am grateful you are willing to do this. I need someone I can trust and rely upon to assist me. If this thief is not caught soon, I may have to resort to depending upon my own resources. May I count upon you to help?"

Emma turned her head slightly so he could not see into her eyes, nor all of her expression. What could she do? She took her coat down and proceeded to slip it on.

"You show great promise as a swordsman," Sir Peter continued. "Before long I would be glad to have you at my side in a fight, were it necessary."

"A fight?" she echoed. Her blood chilled at the mere thought of it.

"Villains at times seem to exhibit a reluctance to merely

drop dead of their own account," he said in a derisive tone. When Emma glanced at him, she met that green gaze and saw a man who had fears, pains, inner doubts. That he would permit her to see them shook her greatly.

Without considering the ramifications of what she said, she held out her hand in a gesture of assurance. "Of course you may count on me. I will be here tomorrow."

She thought he seemed excessively relieved, but it served to point up how worried he had been. It must be dreadful to be so alone. Although Lord Worcester appeared to be a good friend, it was not to him Sir Peter turned when this trouble arose.

George had been sought out, and Emma guessed that George must continue. She donned the beaver hat that had come from the back of her brother's wardrobe—left no doubt because it no longer fit—and walked to the front of the house.

"Tomorrow?" Sir Peter asked in what Emma deemed an anxious manner.

"Tomorrow," Emma agreed gruffly.

There was a man just coming up the steps as Emma opened the door to leave. Without a doubt he was from Bow Street, what with that red vest and all. Emma scurried past him and into the waiting hackney. She was off to Lady Titheridge's before that stranger got a good look at her.

Or so she thought.

She peered from the window, taking note of the people along the street. Could one of these have shot Radley? Did that person by chance speak with a French accent?

Thoughts of spies and thieves and dashing about while waving a sword flitted through her mind. Her Season in London was becoming a far distant thing from what she had anticipated. At any rate, life was scarcely dull anymore.

Chapter 9

PETER turned with curiosity to greet the man the footman showed into the workroom. He'd never met an actual Bow Street Runner, although he had heard numerous stories about them.

This man was a rough-looking character, of medium height and neatly dressed, although not stylish. That he failed to remove his flat beaver hat amused Peter rather than annoyed him. The fellow probably was a former pugilist; he looked the part, with a nose that appeared to have been broken sometime in the past.

"I understand one of your servants was shot while going about his business," Harry Porter said, coming directly to the point after offering his identity.

When Peter gestured to the nearest chair and suggested Mr. Porter be seated, the man sat with obvious reluctance and looked as uneasy as a man totally out of his milieu can look.

"True." Peter perched atop one of the stools, then gave the particulars as he knew them. When finished, he said, "Have a look around, if you will."

The Bow Street Runner wandered about the room, examining all the cases exhibiting the antiquities from Egypt, pausing to study the unwrapped mummy. This object seemed to fascinate him, for he shook his head a number of times before continuing his inspection of the workroom. Then he hooked his thumbs in his red vest and squinted sharp blue eyes at the hole in the window where the bullet had entered.

"As you can see, whoever shot Radley must have done so from that roof over there." Peter pointed to the opposite building. "Since my man was moving about, the villain had to be a crack shot."

"Know anybody who might be wantin' to take this here Radley's life?" The Runner's voice was slightly raspy, as though his windpipe had once been badly injured.

"None," Peter said patiently. "But I am known to have a number of valuable antiquities stored in this room. It might be a Frenchman, hired to acquire several of the objects for their national collection." Briefly, Peter explained what he had been told.

"Or?" the Runner inquired, narrowing his eyes as he studied Peter.

"It could be someone who desires the mummy or the necklace for other reasons," Peter suggested.

The Runner shook his head again. "Wide field, that."

Peter agreed. "Could be a chap who needs money." But he offered this reason without a great deal of conviction. When the thought had first occurred to him, he had dismissed it, for there were far easier ways to snabble a bit of the ready than attempt to sell such well-known items.

Mr. Porter wandered back to study the mummy again. "A market for these, is there? Queer thing to steal."

"There are a few people who believe a mummy possesses special healing properties. They have been used for a long time, but never proven effective. Yet, you know how it is—if someone becomes convinced, that is what he or she must have."

"Hmm," Porter replied, beginning to stroll about again. "I'd like to talk to your butler, this Radley, if I can. Maybe he can tell me something else, seein's as how he was there." Porter gave Peter a quizzical look.

Peter wondered what went on in the fellow's mind when he gazed about. He summoned the footman to take the Runner off to where Radley was recovering from his wound.

Once he was alone again, Peter turned his thoughts back to Emma. He hoped she would show up again tomorrow. He sensed she longed to have George flee, for it was apparent she felt quite uncomfortable in her charade.

As to why he allowed it to continue, he supposed he had several reasons.

For one, if he revealed his awareness of her identity, that would end the fencing lessons—her parents would be properly scandalized. He had come to care for Emma very much, but did not wish her forced to marry him. Rather, he hoped to inspire his dear girl to form a strong attachment, growing to match his own. In Emma he sensed that rare capacity to love and take all that life has to offer with both hands. What a magnificent time they could have together exploring Egypt . . . life. He didn't think she could ever disappoint him.

He had the notion Emma would make a first-rate fencer. The fire he detected beneath her proper exterior when she sparred with him bode well for future pleasure. It promised a good life in every respect.

As well, he had to admit that it would be amusing to thwart all those ambitious mamas and their scheming daughters who hoped to lure him into marriage simply for his fortune. How he detested their obvious attempts. It had driven him to spend more and more time with his collection.

But there was another reason, albeit a curious one. If someone thought that Peter had an ally, that person might be more hesitant to attempt anything serious.

"I suppose I ought to spread it about that I've put that necklace into safekeeping," he mumbled to himself before setting off to see if the Runner had learned anything of interest from Radley. And yet, were he to do such a thing, it might prevent the identity of the would-be thief from ever being known. Of course this was predicated on the necklace being the target of the thief. If, on the other hand, he wanted the mummy, well, the mummy remained.

Radley had been able to add little to Peter's story. The man from Bow Street walked back to the front door with Peter, explaining what he intended to do. It mostly involved haunting places where information of the activities of thieves who dealt in these sort of articles was known.

"If I have a coin or two to slip into the right hands, I can save a deal of time, I can," Porter concluded. He silently accepted the small sack of coins from his employer, who had supposed that a bit of monetary advance would be necessary.

"I shall await your findings with great interest," Peter said before the door closed behind the Runner.

Peter hadn't returned to the workroom before the knocker

sounded again. When the door was opened, his friend Edward, Lord Worcester, entered.

"What is this I hear about someone being shot," he demanded as he strode down the hall to confront his friend.

"Radley was tidying up the workroom—you know I never allow anyone else in there. Not that the maids would enter, what with the mummy there and all," Peter added in a reflective way. "At any rate, someone who had to be a crack shot aimed his gun from across the way over there." Peter had drawn his friend into the workroom and now gestured to the point where he felt sure the gunman had waited for his target to hove into view.

"It might have been you, you know," Edward said fiercely. "I trust you have called in Bow Street?"

"Indeed," Peter acknowledged. "Why do we not leave this somewhat distressing place and saunter down to White's?" Peter had had enough of the matter for the moment. He doubted if anyone would attempt a break-in during broad daylight with the servants on the alert. Besides, with the glaziers at work, he could do nothing of interest here, and they were due within the hour.

"Rather not. I ran into that coxcomb Swinburne there the other day. Must have been a guest of someone, for I know he'd be blackballed were he to be put up for membership," Edward declared in affront, turning again to enter the hallway.

"You'd do that to him? Why?" Peter led his friend into the spacious book-lined library where excellent brandy could be had along with comfortable leather chairs.

"I don't like the attentions he's paying to Amelia. Dratted man offers nothing but Spanish coin. Pours the butter boat over her head something dreadful. She's not such a bad sort, you know. Just because we never see eye to eye don't mean I wish her ill," Edward said in a most defensive manner. He leaned back in his chair and pulled off his gloves. Then he absently slapped them against his thigh, gazing up at the shelves of books while sipping his brandy.

It was clear to Peter that Edward felt more than a brotherly interest in Lady Amelia—regardless of what he claimed. When would he realized it for himself? Peter wondered.

"You've known her for so long, it's a wonder she would not

listen to you when you offer advice," Peter said while trying to keep a straight face at Edward's situation, not to mention his expression of annoyance.

"Amelia? Dratted girl merely says I'm jealous. What a lot of rot that is," Edward grumbled.

"Indeed," Peter replied while refilling Edward's glass.

The two mulled over the problem of Lady Amelia and the coxcombical Mr. Swinburne for several minutes before Peter was able to convince his friend that a drive in the country was just the needed thing.

They went off together, Edward setting aside the matter of the fickle Lady Amelia in favor of the pleasure of Peter's matched grays.

"Oh, dear! What has happened?" Soft gray eyes stared into the looking glass with concern before turning to Braddon for consultation.

Lady Titheridge entered the room just as Emma spoke, swiftly crossing the room to join her. "Good gracious, girl, what have you done to yourself? You are all over little spots—and they are not the least red, but more like tiny bruises. How curious." Her ladyship touched one spot with a cautious finger, watching to see what Emma's reaction might be.

"I cannot say they are very painful, but I look as though I have a ghastly disease of some sort." Emma considered the location of the spots, then concluded, "I expect they are from the fencing. Sir Peter was most merciless in his attacks. Even though his foil has a small button on its tip, it can make a rather annoying jab. Wretched man!"

"But if he believes you to be George, there would be no reason to use great care," Lady Titheridge pointed out.

"Hm," Emma replied thoughtfully. "What am I to do about them?"

"You must wear something close about your throat," Braddon said decisively.

"Perhaps you have a pretty dress with a ruff at the neck?" her ladyship inquired.

"I fear not. I did have one, but outgrew it two years ago." Emma touched several of the spots, grimacing at the sight of them. "They will scarcely look attractive at a party. I shudder to think what a patroness of Almack's will imagine."

"Braddon, what can we do?" Lady Titheridge said by way of ordering.

"A Betsie, my lady. I believe there is one at the bottom of one of the drawers in your chest. Shall I fetch it?"

"Of course," her ladyship said absently. "Now, tell me about the fencing lesson today," she demanded of Emma.

"We practice positions and the mechanics of the movements. I fear I was frightfully clumsy, although he pronounced it a good lesson. He claims that I have the makings of a good fencer, though how he can say that I cannot imagine."

"You are light on your feet and quick to learn, I expect. I believe women are more intelligent than men," Lady Titheridge pronounced to a shocked Emma.

"Well, ma'am, as to that, we are not trusted with our money, nor are we consulted about anything that affects us. We are told whom we shall marry, where we shall live, and that we shall bear children, for it is our duty."

Braddon entered before her ladyship could comment on this particular heretical observation.

The Betsie, derived from the ruff worn by Queen Elizabeth, was composed of seven tiers of pleated sheer muslin. Two stood up, the others fanning out about the neck. The ruff filled in the area above Emma's gown quite admirably and nicely framed her pretty face. When Braddon added a green velvet spencer over the green sprigged muslin dress, no one would guess that Emma hid anything such as numerous tiny bruises on her delicate skin.

Topping the ensemble with a neat green velvet hat to match the spencer was a stroke of genius Braddon declared with absolutely no modesty. The shawl Emma had wrapped lightly about her when she'd left that morning was now draped over her arms. The white on the dark green velvet looked charming, Emma thought.

"Did I not have a lace Betsie?" her ladyship inquired, studying Emma from all angles.

From a small pile of fabric Braddon produced the other, more elaborate ruff, composed of six tiers of fine Brabant lace in the same design.

"This takes care of your evening problems. Even if this style is a year or two old, you must carry it off with aplomb rather than look apologetic. Some society women are like predators; if they scent fear, they will attack you without mercy. You must go with head high and a smile on your lips. Always let them believe you are what you are because of design, not accident."

Emma wondered why her own mama had never thought to counsel her thus.

"Now, we shall go for a ride in the park. I wish a breath of air, and I do not always enjoy the fashionable hour." Her ladyship paused, then added, "It can be so dreadfully tedious." Her smile was a trifle wicked, reminding Emma of her nephew for a moment.

So Emma shortly found herself in Lady Titheridge's landau, driving behind the liveried coachman in the wilds of Hyde Park. It was a lovely June day, and the worries of the Corsican monster and the battle shaping up on the Continent seemed very remote.

They had not gone very far when Emma felt a jab in her ribs. "See who is out and about now," her ladyship whispered.

Coming directly toward them were Sir Peter and Lord Worcester. They both bloomed with a healthy glow in their faces, and Sir Peter, at least, looked as though he was in good spirits. He drew his carriage to a halt just as Lady Titheridge commanded her coachman to stop.

"Good day, dear aunt, Miss Cheney. I am surprised to see you two ladies out so early," Sir Peter said with that roguish twinkle in his unusual green eyes. Emma decided they had the look of dark glade today.

"Naughty boy," her ladyship chided. "It is nearly noon. Emma and I are taking a turn in the fresh air while all those peageese are still abed." She tilted her head, examining her nephew with a narrowed gaze. "I understand that you have had a spot of bother at your house. You do know that if things heat up, you can take refuge at my establishment."

Sir Peter bowed and smiled. "I doubt that it will come to that, but thank you at any rate. Who tattled?"

"Emma's brother told her, and she shared it with me. Emma

and I have become close friends over the past weeks." She turned to wink at Emma, "Haven't we, girl?"

"Indeed," Emma replied, feeling the heat of a blush stain her cheeks.

"May I say that you look especially fine this morning, Miss Cheney?" Sir Peter said with a slight bow from the waist.

"Thank you, sir." Emma couldn't refrain from touching the Betsie, as though to reassure herself that it remained in place to cover her bruises.

"Perhaps you would take a stroll in the park with me this afternoon?" he said with a lazy smile and a warm look directly into her eyes. "Worcester will bring Lady Amelia—that is, if she still speaks to him."

Emma tried to repress a giggle and failed. "Unless my mama has other plans, I should be pleased to accept."

The horses were all getting restless, particularly the fine grays that drew Sir Peter's equipage.

"Run along and mend your fences with Lady Amelia," Lady Titheridge said to Lord Worcester. "She's a fine gel, but mind you, she'll take careful handling. Can't treat her like a horse, y'know. She'll bolt and run off."

Lord Worcester looked faintly scandalized at those words and mutely nodded his reply.

"I think you shocked him," Emma said with a backward glance after the carriages had parted.

"Good. It's about time that someone did. He is in great danger of becoming as pompous as his father," her ladyship replied after ordering the coachman to return Emma to her home.

"I want to see your mama about something, so I shall go in with you."

That suited Emma to a tee as then her dear mama couldn't ask embarrassing questions. By the time Lady Titheridge had left, those problems would have been forgotten.

The ladies entered the Cheney house together. Oldham became puffed up at the presence of the prominent Lady Titheridge. Emma hid a smile at his attitude when he announced her ladyship to Mrs. Cheney, who sat over tea and biscuits with Mrs. Bascomb and Lady Hamley.

The ladies all chatted a bit, then Lady Titheridge turned to

Mrs. Cheney. "And how is your son?" Emma tells me that he is off in Sussex on a digging expedition. I have a great desire to see what one is like. I wonder if you would permit Emma to travel with me so that I might meet your son and see what he does?"

At first Mrs. Cheney was stunned into silence at the astounding notion that anyone, particularly someone as elevated in Society as Lady Titheridge, would have the least interest in what her foolish son did.

"I could bring George his mail and see how he is," Emma coaxed while coping with her surprise at this suggestion. "You never know, Mama, one day George could become famous. Or so says Sir Peter."

"Oh, my," Mrs. Cheney gasped. "I should speak to your father, I suppose." Clearly she was torn between immediately giving permission and the pretense of consulting with her husband when all knew that Mr. Cheney would promptly agree. He did not hold with how his son chose to occupy his time, but thought it was far better than falling into debt or carousing about London.

"Please, Mama," Emma begged quite prettily, although the request had come as much of a shock to her as to her mother.

"When would you go?" Mrs. Cheney inquired, nervously reaching for her vinaigrette.

Mrs. Bascomb and Lady Henley exchanged approving glances and nods.

"Two days after tomorrow, I believe," her ladyship decreed. "We would not wish Emma to miss Almack's, now would we?" She was ever accustomed to getting her way, and most likely the idea that she might not never entered her head. "That ought to give us ample time to prepare for the journey. I shall take my traveling coach, and Emma need bring only her clothing, plus the items for her brother. I imagine he will be wanting a few shirts and the like. I recall my Peter—Sir Peter was named for my husband, you know—was ever wishing for clean shirts when we were off on a jaunt. I suppose we had best remain silent about this trip. I would not wish any trouble while on the road."

Mrs. Cheney was so thrilled to be the recipient of Lady Titheridge's confidences with her bosom friends looking and listening on that she would have agreed to anything at this point. Also, the reminder that Emma had achieved that holy of holies, the assemblies at Almack's, was utter bliss to Mrs. Cheney. She had never dared hope for Emma to aspire to that height.

"That would be most kind of you, I'm sure," Mrs. Cheney replied after resorting to a dainty sniff from her vinaigrette bottle.

After a short time her ladyship bade them farewell.

Emma offered to accompany her to the door and silently walked down the stairs, not speaking until she was certain she could not be heard back in the drawing room.

"That was indeed a surprise, my lady," Emma said in a soft little voice.

"It came to me while we were talking with Peter and Edward that George might take it into his head to return home—for clean shirts, if nothing else. You must persuade him that under no circumstances is he to show his face in London until safe."

"Oh, mercy," Emma whispered. "That thought never occurred to me."

Lady Titheridge gave Emma a playful tap on her arm with her fan. "You must learn to consider all aspects of a situation if you are to be a good conspirator," she whispered back. Then looking enormously pleased with herself, she returned to her landau and drove off in great state.

When Sir Peter called to escort Emma for their afternoon walk in Hyde Park, she found her heart fluttered nervously. She peered over the banister at the tall figure who entered, then followed Oldham to the morning room.

Putting her hand on her heart and taking a deep breath to calm that quaking beat, she walked down the steps until she reached the ground floor. At the door to the morning room she paused, assessing Sir Peter.

Every time they met, she sensed danger lay in wait for her. She could so easily give herself away, and when the wretched man looked down at her with that wicked twinkle in his exotic green eyes, she scarcely knew what she said at all.

"Now I have seen everything," Sir Peter exclaimed with a bow, "a lady who is on time for an appointment."

"It would be very rude to keep a gentleman waiting, I think. *I* do not believe in being rude," Emma replied, trying to avoid clashing with those bewitching eyes and failing.

Firmly taking herself in hand, she tore her gaze away and took several steps toward the hall. "Shall we go?"

"We are to pick up Worcester and Lady Amelia on our way." Sir Peter joined her in the exodus to where the carriage awaited. "Aunt Titheridge kindly lent me her landau so we should not be crowded."

"Oh, I am *so* glad," Emma said with ringing sincerity. The last thing she wanted was to be crushed up against that dratted man.

For some reason this made Sir Peter chuckle, and Emma wondered what she had said that was so amusing.

She edged onto the cushioned seat, taking care to keep her distance. Never must she forget for one second that this man was the most dangerous man in all of London—as far as she was concerned.

"The last I heard, I was not classified among those who bite," Sir Peter murmured while arranging a lap rug over her knees.

"Indeed?" He could have fooled her. Next to him a ferocious lion was a mere house pet.

"It is a lovely day," she offered, wondering if he would find that amusing as well.

"Indeed," he replied, echoing her inflection.

"Well, it is," she said, annoyed he would make fun of her.

"I agreed," he protested. "But after drizzles it is nice to see the sun shining again. Or does the weather not bother you overmuch?" He folded his hands before him. Emma studied his neat gloves rather than meet his gaze.

"Well, I do not develop aches and pains—at least from that." Her hand unconsciously crept up to finger the pretty Betsie frill at her neck which concealed the tiny bruises.

"I rather like that thing around your neck. It somewhat gives you the innocent look of a choirboy. Or cherub, perhaps?" He reached out to flick the pleated muslin with one finger, and Emma gave him a startled look.

"Sir," she demurred. He had made her look into his eyes again, and she had intended to avoid them at all costs. She truly did not trust herself with this man, not that he had done one improper thing, mind you. It was *how* he made her feel.

"You are in a prickly mood today. I wondered what happened."

She most fortunately did not have to reply to that provocative remark as the landau drew up before Lady Amelia's home.

The groom marched up to thwack the door knocker with dispatch. Within short order Lady Amelia and Lord Worcester joined Sir Peter and Emma in the carriage, and the four were off to the park.

"That is a fetching attire, dear Emma," Lady Amelia said with a lift of a brow.

In return Emma gave her a glance that told Amelia all would be explained later regarding the green velvet spencer, hat to match, and the innocent muslin ruff.

" 'Tis a lovely day," Lady Amelia offered with a demure air.

Emma chanced to meet Sir Peter's gaze and couldn't help it. She giggled. That dratted man had her laughing helplessly in moments.

"Well," Lady Amelia said in a huff, "it *is* a lovely day, and I see nothing whatsoever humorous about that." She tilted her adorable nose and made a quiet remark to Lord Worcester.

He was saved from a reply by their arrival in the park.

"Are you certain you would rather stroll than drive?" Lady Amelia asked Emma.

Since Emma had debated whether it was safer to sit at Sir Peter's side in the landau or walk close by him along a path, she was in no condition to make a rational reply.

It all began innocently enough, she thought. They joined the throng of fashionable ladies and gentlemen who were similarly occupied. There were ever so many, and she ought to be as safe here as in church. Or so she believed.

Carriages rolled along parallel to Rotten Row, where the bucks and blades rode to show off their fancy attire and horses and ladies their gorgeous riding habits and splendid mares. Emma cast a critical eye at the scene and decided she was glad they decided to walk.

"You are in deep thought," Sir Peter prompted when she had been silent for a time.

"No, merely not a chatterbox." Besides, if she kept her mouth shut, she couldn't trip over her tongue.

"You know," Sir Peter mused, "it really is amazing how much you resemble your brother. I suppose you hear that frequently." He leaned forward to view her more clearly beneath the brim of her smart green velvet hat.

"No," Emma chirped after swallowing with care. "Not really. He is so rarely at home, you see. And we never go places together, so there is little opportunity for comparison. Although when he was in short coats, there was occasionally some confusion," she admitted. "We are only a year and a half apart in age, you see."

"I do hope George will come for another lesson in fencing. He shows great promise in his parry and thrust. I should like to teach him a few tactics." Sir Peter complacently placed Emma's neatly gloved hand on his arm—bringing her much closer to his side—and proceeded to stroll along the lane, totally ignoring the stares of the fashionable.

"Tactics?" Emma choked on the word. To her the word called to mind intrigue, plotting, and strategy, none of which she wished to engage in with Sir Peter.

"Oh, indeed. It is most necessary to learn tactics. He wants to improve his riposte and certainly learn a better counterattack." Sir Peter guided Emma around a couple who had stopped in the middle of the path.

"Counterattack? You make it sound as though I, er, George would be going into battle—as in a duel or such. I cannot wish George to fight."

Sir Peter appeared not to notice her little blunder, and Emma thought she may have made a successful recovery.

"I would that you give him that message about his lesson, for I never seem to see him about."

"Oh, George is terribly elusive. I scarcely see him myself. Any day now I expect to see him off to Sussex, for he is most anxious to resume his digging."

"I sympathize with his desires," Sir Peter said while assisting Emma over a tree root.

She looked about her and realized they had somehow

strayed off the path and were now in a lovely shaded part of the park. They were also very much alone.

"I think we had best join the others," she said in a tiny voice.

"If you insist," he replied with a sigh. "You will promise me a cotillion at Almack's tomorrow evening?" He reached out his free hand to lightly touch her cheek and looked at her with such yearning in his eyes that Emma felt as though she must melt with the heat of his gaze.

"Indeed," she managed to whisper and then wondered why he laughed.

Chapter 10

"DEAR Amelia," Emma said tentatively, "do have a care regarding Mr. Swinburne."

"But Emma, he is the nicest person," Lady Amelia objected. "His manners are so very refined, and I adore the scent of violets."

Emma shrugged and looked over the assembled throng at Almack's this Wednesday evening. "As long as you view him as no more than an amusing flirt, there is no danger, I suppose." She feared she did not sound convinced in the least.

"Well, he treats me far better than Lord Worcester, you may be sure," Lady Amelia replied with a sniff. Then she confided, "He told me that he has a family on the Isle of Guernsey. Is that not romantic?"

"I cannot imagine why," Emma said, utterly confused at this turn of conversation.

"Think of all those who elope to that isle. I understand that there are boats sailing to Guernsey from Southampton for only five guineas. 'Tis like Scotland; one does not need a license," Lady Amelia explained in the event that Emma had not known about this.

"Sounds ridiculous to me," Emma replied while taking note of Mr. Swinburne as he approached. He again wore his claret coat over the black knee breeches. Emma wondered if he hoped to establish the same sort of following that Mr. Brummell did with his dark blue coat.

Lady Amelia whirled off for a dance on the arm of the stylishly coxcombical Mr. Swinburne, but Emma paid not the least attention now. Someone else claimed her attention.

"Miss Cheney," Sir Peter said from her left, making Emma's poor heart flutter along in a cotillion of its own.

Wordlessly, she accepted his arm and walked at his side, thinking that tomorrow she would be on her way into Sussex. With that thought held fast in her mind, she turned to face her partner.

"So quiet this evening. Is Almack's becoming common-place for you? You seem so abstracted." He swirled her around in a graceful loop, deftly avoiding the others on the floor as they proceeded through the pattern of the dance.

Ashamed that she allowed her worries to overset her to such a degree, Emma smiled and shook her head. "I have a great deal on my mind," she admitted. "I see Lady Amelia is danc-ing with Mr. Swinburne. Did you know he has family on the Isle of Guernsey?"

"He told Lady Amelia that?" Sir Peter said with a frown and a dark glance at the fellow.

"I do hope it was nothing more than idle chitchat."

"Worcester thinks Swinburne offers her nothing but Spanish coin," Sir Peter said abruptly.

"I thought he was tipping the butter boat a bit heavy last evening," Emma admitted, then recalled that she deplored gos-sip and this was little better than that, never mind that she was genuinely concerned for Amelia.

The next time they joined in the pattern of the dance she bravely continued in a different vein, dredging up bits and scraps she thought might amuse him. At last the music con-cluded. She returned to her mama, grateful this part of the evening was over. Sir Peter was utterly too unnerving.

"I see Mr. Swinburne paying court to Lady Amelia," Mrs. Cheney whispered to Emma from behind her fan. "A title and a fat dowry add incentive for a gentleman," she concluded sourly.

"Mama, Lady Amelia is the dearest creature. While she might be a trifle goosish, she has a warm heart." Emma might envy the girl her looks, money, and perhaps her title, but it was impossible not to love her. Her artless charm and delightful enthusiasm captivated one.

Emma glanced over to where the lady in question now pre-pared to depart. Sir Peter offered his arm to escort Lady Amelia to the door and possibly home. Emma knew a sort of sick feeling in her chest at the sight of the lovely Amelia at Sir

Peter's side. Wealth, beauty, charm, plus a title. What chance had Emma with competition like that? Then she wondered where *that* foolish thought came from and turned to her mother.

"I have a trace of a headache. Perhaps we ought to leave. If I am to travel with Lady Titheridge in the morning, I'd not wish to be ill." Even as she spoke, Emma felt the headache become reality.

Observing that the lady in question had not attended this evening, Mrs. Cheney agreed with haste. Shortly, Emma found herself bustled from the rooms and out of the building.

On her way home Emma tried to push the image of Amelia and Sir Peter from her mind. Perhaps he was merely trying to distract Amelia from Mr. Swinburne. Still, Emma knew the ways of Society. She possessed no fortune, nor was she a raving beauty, and certainly possessed no title. What little charm she held seemed paltry by comparison to what Amelia offered.

On that happy note she went to her room. She slept fitfully and was not sorry to leave her bed at an early hour.

Lady Titheridge possessed a venerable but well-cared-for traveling carriage. The faded leather was soft and the seats comfortable. A hamper full of delicacies her ladyship feared unobtainable along the way occupied a space next to Braddon opposite where Emma perched beside Lady Titheridge.

"Had new springs put on," her ladyship announced to a startled Emma. "I believe in keeping up with the times, you know. Some folk turn their noses up at new ideas. Not me," the older lady said with pride.

"To be sure," Emma replied faintly. She retreated into her thoughts for a bit while Lady Titheridge appeared to nod off to sleep. It was to be observed that the carriage ride seemed far smoother than that of the Cheney coach, so perhaps there was something to what her ladyship said regarding the effectiveness of the new springs.

Emma looked out of the window. She had escaped London. No reference had been made last night to George coming to Bruton Street for lesson in fencing, nor had Sir Peter said anything about needing George for anything else. She was free . . . for the moment.

Her heart lightened with that knowledge even as she tucked

that image of Sir Peter escorting Lady Amelia to the dim recesses of her mind. That memory was best ignored.

The journey went well, as a whole. Lady Titheridge was curious about everything. She hunted through her guide book for answers. When she couldn't find them, she asked innumerable questions at every staging inn where they stopped along the road.

At first Emma found her amusing, then she became caught up in the quest for knowledge and also studied the terrain, the villages, and the old houses that they passed. The gently rolling hills were lush and green. Agriculture fared better here than to the north, according to the papers. From what Emma could see, she must agree.

When they passed through Dorking, her ladyship kept sharp eyes to the window and bade Braddon read the guidebook to her while they traversed the streets.

By the time they went through Billinghurst, Emma felt a rising excitement, for she was drawing closer to her dear, though absentminded, brother. They had been close in years past. Now, if he wrote at all, it was but a few words, usually requesting something.

The inns seemed much the same from one town to another. She knew only impatience at having to spend the night, before traveling southward.

Lady Titheridge commanded the best of everything, and Emma confessed to something of an awe at the bowing and scraping bestowed on the lady. And the oddest circumstance of all was that her ladyship never raised her voice, always behaved in a gracious manner, and yet was treated with utmost respect. Mr. Cheney tended to order about with a gruff voice and manner, and he assuredly fared no better if as well.

At last they reached the village mentioned in the communications from George.

Boxgrove was a pretty little place with not a great deal to recommend it—or so it seemed to Emma—although the sight of a charming timbered cottage as they entered and then thatched cottages along the road brought a smile to her face. She glimpsed an impressive church through the trees and wondered if her brother ever remembered to attend.

The innkeeper promptly suggested they might wish to visit

Boxgrove Priory, it being the only outstanding sight for some miles around.

Lady Titheridge besought all information regarding the Benedictine priory established in the early twelfth century. The landlord claimed it was one of the most important medieval buildings in all of Sussex and not to be missed.

"We must see the church, which is all that remains," she informed Emma while they marched up to their rooms. "I feel it is important to view places of distinction. I believe it to be highly illuminating."

Emma murmured an agreement. All she could think of was the need to find her brother and persuade him not to come to London for a time.

What she might offer as an excuse had plagued her for days. At last she sought help.

"What *am* I to tell him, Lady Titheridge? I cannot simply say, 'George, do not come home for a time. Sorry I cannot explain at the moment.'" Emma paced back and forth in the little sitting room that joined her room to her ladyship's.

"That is a bit of a problem. I do not suppose you could tell him the truth?" She gave Emma a hopeful look with this suggestion.

Emma paused in her steps. "It might work, actually. George is such an enthusiast about ancient things, he ought to understand my passion to view the unrolling. He might even approve!"

"What about the fencing?" her ladyship asked.

"Now, that he would not approve. At least, I rather doubt it. In spite of his somewhat irregular mode of living, George can be dreadfully stuffy at times." Emma shared a rueful look with her ladyship and Braddon.

Braddon ventured to voice her opinion—encouraged to do so by Lady Titheridge, who felt no brain ought to be wasted.

"I think perhaps you should find your brother first, see what sort of mood he is in, then choose your path."

"I expect you have the right of it," Emma replied, then leaned against the window surround. "I shall go below and see if our loquacious landlord has heard of George. Usually eccentrics are food for gossip in a small community."

With her ladyship's wholehearted support, Emma made her

way down the stairs and into the hall. Here she encountered the landlord, Mr. Gutsel, without much of a search.

"Do you by chance know of a man named George Cheney? He came to this area to dig for Roman antiquities, and his letters home are mailed from this village." Emma worriedly clasped her hands before her.

"You be a relative?" Mr. Gutsel inquired with a shrewd study of Emma's person.

"I am his sister, and we have been most concerned about George. He is not much for writing, and my mother's health prompted me to discover how he fared."

At that the landlord's expression eased. "He was stayin' here for some time," he admitted. "Then Sir William invited him to lodge with him, being as how it was closer to the field in which your brother was diggin'." The landlord looked as though he was proud that a guest of his inn had transferred to such a residence.

"I see. And Sir William is?" she asked with the hope of learning more.

"Sir William Johnson, baronet and fine gentleman—interested in all manner of agricultural improvements. He's no afternoon farmer. He's drained a bit of pasture, experiments with cattle breeding, and plants crops to feed the Londoners. That was how your brother came to him, heard about the draining and hoped to find something of interest, or so he told me. Odd chap, your brother."

"Indeed," Emma replied while thinking furiously. "I need to see him. May I send a message? Or might I just ride up to the door to call?"

"If her ladyship were to go with you, I'd present myself, I would," Mr. Gutsel said with a sage nod of his head. "Lady Johnson is right fond of company, as is the young lady."

"Young lady?" Emma grew alert. "Sir William has a little girl?"

Mr. Gutsel nodded. "About your age, I'd say. Name of Beatrice." He looked as though the mere mention of her name brought pleasure.

Curious, Emma thanked the man, then hurried up the stairs to where her ladyship rested.

"George is staying with Sir William Johnson, a baronet apparently well-liked and most prosperous. He also has a daughter about my age. Beatrice is her name. I wonder what goes on there?" She exchanged a questioning look with Braddon and her ladyship.

"We shall find out tomorrow," her ladyship replied to Emma's frustration.

"You do not think I might just send along a note to George, asking him to see me here?" Emma begged.

"I suppose you might. In spite of what that landlord says, I am not inclined to present myself at the front door like some ignorant traveler."

In complete agreement a happier Emma shortly whisked herself off to find Lady Titheridge's groom. Once located, she gave him instructions and her hastily penned message. "The landlord or about anyone, I gather, should be able to tell you where to find Sir William's residence."

Once back in her bedroom, she resumed her pacing. Her simple trip was growing more complex by the hour.

It was the dinner hour for Londoners, although late for the country. A fine meal had been promised, to be delivered up to the little sitting room. When Braddon summoned her, Emma listlessly returned, seating herself at the table, with little enthusiasm for the food placed before her.

"He has promised us an excellent pudding, his wife's specialty. If you do not eat, I shall be sorry I brought you down here," her ladyship said sharply at last.

Emma began to consume her meal at once, mortified that she was behaving like a spoiled child. Just because she didn't trust her tongue not to trip her up was no reason to put a damper on the meal.

After the meal and the excellent pudding had been cleared away, Emma sat near the hearth, waiting. "Surely he will come?" she said to Braddon, Lady Titheridge having decided to seek her bed early.

It was close to nine of the clock when George rapped at the door to the sitting room. Braddon opened it before Emma could.

"Hello, Emma. Why are you here?" George said with his customary forthrightness.

"Ah, Mama is worried about you and wished to know how

you go along." At his disbelieving look Emma added with more haste than sense, "And you must stay here for a time, and not return to London until I send you a message saying it will be all right," she blurted out.

Braddon tsk tsked and shook her head at Emma.

"Explain, please," he said stretching himself out on one of the chairs by the hearth.

"Oh, George, I am making micefeet of this. You see, it is this way." And Emma carefully explained the situation. She left nothing out but the fencing lessons. Prudence demanded the omission there. As she had told Lady Titheridge, George could turn up stuffy over the most peculiar things.

"Hmm," he replied thoughtfully. "Can't say as I blame you. Must have been dashed interesting."

"Oh, it was! Quite fascinating! And I have been allowed to draw the necklace and all the other treasures wrapped up with the body," she declared with pride. "You must confess that I am a slightly better artist than you are, so Sir Peter is reaping a benefit there."

"Wish the Romans had thought to bury their dead in that manner," George said, his expression pensive.

"Are you having so little success, then?" Emma inquired with concern.

"Oh, a few coins, enough to keep one going. But not what I'd hoped." He rose from the chair and began to pace back and forth much as Emma had done earlier. "I must find that treasure, now more than ever."

"Does this by chance have anything to do with the fact that Sir William has a daughter, Beatrice?"

"Gutsel tell you about the family? Sir William is a great gun, and Lady Johnson is a nice lady."

"And Beatrice?" Emma prompted, delighted to see her dearest brother in such a state over a young lady.

"She is an angel," George replied with proper reverence. "She understands me."

"I see," Emma said reflectively. "I believe I should like to meet her."

"Oh, Lady Johnson insisted you must come tomorrow." He fumbled in his pocket, then produced a pretty little letter from the lady of the house. He handed it to Emma, saying, "She

would like you and Lady Titheridge to remove from the inn
and lodge with her. It's a big house, Emma, and plenty of
rooms." Then he added artlessly, "And you could get to know
Beatrice better that way."

"I shall tell her ladyship about the proposal come morning.
She has retired for the night, you see," Emma whispered. She
took the letter, placing it on the table near the door to her ladyship's room.

"Just come," George said as close to pleading as he ever
came.

"It is a bargain, then? You remain down here in Sussex until
I send you the word all is clear?" Emma demanded.

"I foresee no problem with that." He moved to the door,
placing his hand on the knob, then paused. "Thing is, I cannot
think of asking for Beatrice with the sum Papa has promised
me. Her father is dreadfully rich. I must find something to validate my claims as a student of antiquity. Since he has no son,
I believe he would set me up, but that isn't enough. I must do
something on my own. Do *you* understand, Emma? God
knows, I doubt Beatrice would comprehend that."

"I believe I do," Emma replied softly. "And do not underes-
timate your Beatrice. Any woman intelligent enough to fall in
love with you must have more than ordinary brains." Emma
moved closer to give her dear brother a comforting pat on his
arm.

George turned rather red in the face, grimaced at his little
sister, then left the room.

"Did you ever?" Emma demanded of Braddon, who had remained silently in the background.

"Indeed," the maid replied, then bustled Emma off to bed.

Come morning, Braddon entered Emma's neat little room
with a pitcher of steaming water. "Her ladyship says to inform
you that she will be pleased to visit with Sir William and Lady
Johnson. She suggests that we leave for the hall shortly after
twelve of the clock. I believe her ladyship would like to spend
this morning viewing the Boxgrove church so praised by the
landlord."

Emma agreed, then hurriedly slipped from her bed to dress
for the day. Nothing much had been unpacked—not that she

had brought so very much with her. Her dear mama had always told Emma to be prepared for anything, so she had brought extra dresses along. Now she was most thankful for that forethought.

"So, we are to meet your George's chosen lady, are we?" Lady Titheridge said with an arch of her brows.

"Is it not the best of things? George has not the least interest to come to London at the moment, so it suits him fine to oblige me on this matter."

"He did not appear to be too shocked?" her ladyship inquired carefully.

"Not in the least. Said he could quite understand." Emma gave her benefactress a happy smile, then tucked into her breakfast with the most enthusiasm she'd known in days.

The somewhat unprepossessing church exterior turned out to contain a number of wonders inside.

Lady Titheridge was in a fine humor while strolling about the interior. "Oh, Emma, do look at this little chapel. What a beautiful thing it is. I have always admired Purbeck marble, and these shafts are splendid, as well as those rich arcades."

Emma nodded, then stared at the ceiling. "That's a lovely painting Ma'am, and quite old, I believe."

"Elegant tracery and lovely colors," her ladyship agreed.

"I believe I like the decoration on that little chapel the best of all," Emma concluded after a tour of the building. "It reminds one of lace, does it not? Such delicate decoration almost looks like a confection from Gunter's." She ran a finger over one of the carved pillars with an admiring look at the little chapel. "It is a pity that the king wouldn't allow poor Lord de la Warr to be buried here after all his trouble and expense of building this chapel." Emma edged toward the door. A bit weary, she hoped Lady Titheridge would tire as well. Besides, Emma longed to be gone.

Her ladyship thought the priory remarkable, but took pity on the impatient Emma. She soon joined her by the door, then hurried her off to the traveling coach.

Braddon had packed their belongings and placed them into the coach. She waited for them in the shade of one of the many trees that grew by the path to the church.

"Ah, the fresh air of the country," her ladyship declared before entering the vehicle.

Emma, eager to meet the woman who might well turn out to be her sister-in-law, waited with barely concealed impatience for Lady Titheridge to settle in the coach.

And at last they were off.

The manor house was lovely, Emma decided in great charity. The drive to the house was splendid, with vast views across the downs. The solid redbrick structure had many sparkling windows that overlooked the farm. A porch with fine Ionic columns covered the entry.

The traveling coach with its crested doors pulled up before this entry. The groom soon had the door open, the steps down, and Lady Titheridge quickly clambered out. Emma hastily followed.

A gentleman opened the front door, and then came across the porch to greet them.

"Greetings to our humble home. Sir William Johnson at your service, my lady." He bowed politely over Lady Titheridge's hand, then looked at Emma. "No need to ask who you are; you look just like your brother. Welcome, Miss Cheney."

He escorted them into the house with great geniality and soon had them settled in the drawing room with his beloved wife.

Seated in a wheeled chair, Lady Johnson looked like a fragile bit of lace. Emma immediately worried that their visit would overtax the lady.

"I know that expression. I may look like the next wind would blow me away, but I am as strong as can be," Lady Johnson declared in a clear, high voice.

"Now, Mama," a girl chided, "you will have them thinking you are shamming." She stepped forward from off to one side of the room, and Emma was pleased to see that George, for once, had been correct in a description of a woman. Beatrice was indeed an angel. Soft, blond hair formed a halo about an oval face from which blue eyes gazed out with amusement.

The greetings were done with a minimum of fuss. The footman entered bearing a tray with a hearty repast, fit for someone who had been tramping through an old church.

"George thought you would wish to view our chief sight this morning. 'Tis a pretty thing, is it not?" Lady Johnson said while pouring another cup of tea for Emma.

"Indeed it is, ma'am," Emma replied politely.

They continued to chat amiably for some time before Lady Johnson turned to her daughter. "Now my dear, show them to their rooms, for I feel sure they wish to change." To Emma she added, "We have so enjoyed having your brother about. Sir William and I were not blessed with a son, and my husband likes to discuss things like farm problems and what-all with a man."

Emma tried to envision her brother talking about breeding cattle and failed. "Yes, ma'am," she dutifully replied.

George had been absent from the welcome, but Emma decided he spent every hour he could hunting for a treasure or some special artifact that would establish him as a sort of scientist and give him that validity he sought.

Beatrice graciously took each of them to lovely rooms, then said to Emma, "Your brother is off south of the house. If you wish to see what he is doing, you might like to walk out there."

Eager to see what she was supposed to have been involved in, Emma changed to more sturdy clothing with Braddon's help, then set off along the lane to the field Beatrice had pointed out to her.

It was a beautiful day. Emma felt as though all was well with the world. What could possibly go wrong now? With George safely in Sussex and she nearly over with her charade, it remained but to wind things up and she would be free.

As to what that freedom might bring her, she couldn't say. She might hope it involved Sir Peter if she were daydreaming as usual. Practicality had reared its ugly head, however. With modest money, no great beauty, and an inclination to peculiar starts, not even the support of his dearest aunt would likely make her an acceptable *parti* for Sir Peter.

At last she saw George. It was a bit of a shock to see him with the workmen, digging up the soil from a pit. Each shovelful would be examined. She saw him eagerly pick out a tiny object, then continue with the process.

"Hullo, George," she cried when close enough.

"Found a coin that is definitely Roman," he replied with a broad grin.

"Does that validate your efforts?" she asked with hope.

"Not much, but it offers inducement to continue."

Emma watched him dig for a bit, then sat down on a nearby rock. She studied the terrain, taking note of the humps and ridges, the lines of trees in the distance.

"Was this a swamp before Sir William drained the land?"

"It was," came a tired reply.

"Well, I think you might dig over there"—she pointed in the direction she meant—"along that ridge at the edge of the field. Seems to me that if this has been a field, it must have been plowed. How would a chest of treasure or anything special remain hidden?"

George looked at her with that patient, resigned expression brothers give to sisters who come out with stupid suggestions.

"Well, excuse me," she said in annoyance. "I was only trying to be helpful. I best return to the house."

Just as she was about to rise, she spotted Beatrice striding along in a graceful walk. Emma waited until the girl drew near, then rose.

"George, there is a man to see you."

"And who might that be? Very few people know where I am." He wrinkled his brow in consternation, for it was plain he did not wish to leave his site.

"He said he is Sir Peter Dancy."

Emma sat down with a thud. Had she actually thought that things were going well?

Chapter 11

EMMA looked at George and cried, "Now what shall we do?" She paced back and forth, then turned to glare at her brother as though he were the reason for all her troubles. "I truly do *not* wish him to find out everything at this point."

Beatrice looked puzzled, and possibly a bit hurt at not knowing what had caused such a dramatic reaction to what seemed like rather ordinary news.

Taking matters in hand, George kindly explained things to his beloved in the most succinct way. Then the three found rocks upon which to sit while pondering the problem.

"Are you certain he thinks you are your brother?" Beatrice asked skeptically. "I mean, you two resemble each other to an amazing degree, but there *is* a difference."

"He claims he is nearsighted." Emma favored the others with a wry grin. "I swear that is what the man said. I may buy him a pair of spectacles when this is all over."

"Well, I fail to understand why you simply do not tell him all," Beatrice said, her confusion clear in her voice.

"I would never be allowed to study the mummy and the other things if I were myself. And besides, I fear my parents would force him to marry me if they found out about what has been going on, and that would be dreadful." Emma propped her chin on her hands and stared off into the distance. The memory of Sir Peter with Lady Amelia popped up from where it had been stored.

"I see," Beatrice said in a voice that said she did not see at all. "But he is quite handsome and has lovely manners. And Lady Titheridge introduced him as her heir. Would it be so disagreeable to marry him?" she offered hesitantly. It was very difficult for any young single woman to understand how another young single woman could refuse a situation that was so tempting.

"Not if he desires someone else." Emma gave her a speaking look that told volumes more than Emma suspected.

"Oh," replied an enlightened Beatrice. With a glance at George she added, "I see what you mean."

"That does not solve the dilemma, however," George said. He had become more alert when Beatrice pronounced Sir Peter handsome. George looked as though he had been pondering that bit of information for the few minutes while the ladies talked.

"It would be impossible to switch," Beatrice offered. "My parents would wonder greatly, and my dearest mama would most likely say something at the worst possible moment."

"True," George agreed, with an apologetic glance at his dear love.

"If you could send him out here where the digging is going on, perhaps I could fool him. I could borrow something of George's to wear." Emma looked at her brother, then added, "I do not know why the dratted man has to show up here at this moment!"

Beatrice thought for a bit, then said, "I shall send her ladyship's maid out with clothing for you. She will know what you need. In the meanwhile I will try to keep Sir Peter amused until Braddon sends word that all is ready. It will be up to you to convince Sir Peter."

George looked very unhappy at this proposal, but said nothing.

"I suppose your lovely mother will suggest Sir Peter stay here," Emma said with dawning consternation.

"Oh, dear. I fear she already has. She adores company as it is so difficult for her to travel. I know this is hard for you, but mother is loving every minute of the visits." Beatrice rose from her perch and offered her hands to Emma. "We will do what we can. Perhaps we can convince everyone later on that George has been called away for some reason. Then we can smuggle you both up the back stairs to your rooms. Emma can become herself for dinner. George will have to eat in his room, I fear."

At this George rose to his feet, looking as though he would protest the arrangement.

Beatrice crossed to his side to give him such a melting smile that Emma was certain George would eat anything, anywhere she suggested.

"Capital," George said with more enthusiasm than he had shown before.

Emma watched as Beatrice hurried back toward the house. Then she turned to her brother. "I like that girl."

"I told you she was an angel."

"You know," Emma said, changing the subject lest she become involved in a discussion of Beatrice's sterling qualities, "it is a good thing I was out *here* when he came."

"You really wouldn't wish to marry the man? Beatrice said he is handsome." George studied his sister with the keen eye of a scientist, as though he sought to know her very thoughts. It was probably the first time in his life he had seriously given consideration to her affairs. He seemed to find her more perplexing than the elusive Roman treasure trove.

"He is," Emma admitted. "But I suspect he may have an interest in Lady Amelia Littleton. I could be wrong, only he showed her particular attention last Wednesday at Almack's. That is an ominous sign." Emma sat down on her rock, propping her chin on her hand once again.

George didn't seem too cut up over this knowledge, and Emma guessed he was happy to find out that Sir Peter-of-the-handsome-face might have other interests.

When Braddon came marching across the field with an armload of clothing, Emma resigned herself to making the change once again.

"Here you are, miss," the abigail said when she strode up to the rock.

Emma walked to a shack not too far away where she changed with Braddon's help. The maid carefully hung up Emma's gown, adjuring her to dress properly before she attempted to return to the house.

George shook his head when he first saw the other George. "And he believed you were me? Ha!" he said with no attempt at elegance of speech in the least.

"Yes, and I cannot think why," Emma agreed.

Braddon studied the pair before her and smiled. "It is surprising how much you two do resemble each other. Just remember to keep your voice low," she admonished Emma, then left.

"What would Papa say," Emma said with a grimace while she brushed down her pantaloons.

"Not to mention Mama," George added. "I had best go while I can. I'll tell the diggers to leave. That way, there will be less to gossip about."

Emma watched him stride away to the digging site, where the other men had kept working. After a few words the shovels were set aside, and they all sauntered toward a few outbuildings some distance away. Emma prayed they would all have a few pints of ale and forget there was anyone else out here.

Deciding she had best make a pretense of digging for a Roman treasure hoard, she jumped down into the hole and picked up the hand trowel that she had seen George using.

A gentle wind stirred the long grasses interspersed with oxeye daisies, fragrant red clover, and the bright yellow plumes of Lady's Bedstraw that grew along the edge of the field. A sniff of the fresh country air brought the sunny June afternoon alive with bucolic charm. Somewhere in the world there was trouble and war. Here all was at peace. If there were clouds on the horizon, Emma ignored them.

She could see cattle grazing in the next field, some of Sir William's special breed, no doubt. It was a scene that should have been idyllic, reducing her to fanciful daydreams.

Instead, Emma turned to her digging with a sinking heart, knowing that Sir Peter would shortly come striding across the fields to confront her. How could she possibly convince him of her charade in the bright light of day?

Then her trowel struck metal. Forgetting all about her dilemma for the moment, Emma began to dig frantically in the soil with her fingers after tossing the trowel aside. Bit by bit she uncovered a mass of coins, a small hoard to be sure, but definitely *old* coins. She picked up one, rubbed it off on her coat, and wanted to shout with joy. It bore the likeness of a noble Roman, and if it wasn't an *old* Roman she'd eat every one of the coins. She began to separate them and found upon brushing the dirt off that a number appeared to be gold!

That proved too much. She lifted up her face to the sky and cheered, "Hurrah!" and performed a little dance of joy for her dearest brother.

Peter paused in his tracks at the sight of the slender figure halfway down in the digging not far from the edge of the field. Dressed in her brother's clothing, she had a smear of dirt on one cheek. Her curls tumbled about her pretty face in mad abandon, and she was now jumping up and down in utter delight. It was a sight that warmed his heart. Emma had definitely been bitten by the quest for treasure.

"What ho?" he called out to her, hurrying forth to where she had been digging in the dirt.

She stopped her exuberant display of joy and turned to face him with a wary look. "Hullo. What a surprise. What brings you down here?"

"You."

She looked perfectly horrified for just a moment until a polite mask came over her face.

"Did you find something? I could not help but notice a bit of elation there as I walked up," Peter said with customary British understatement.

"That I did," she admitted with obvious reluctance. "I believe these to be of Roman origin and in excellent condition. There are even a number of gold coins in the hoard. Ought to set the antiquarian community on their ears," she concluded with rising enthusiasm.

"Think there might be more?" Peter crouched down by the dig to examine the hoard of coins. They were magnificent in quality and number from what he could tell.

"Perhaps. If these had been buried prior to a battle, the one who left them was most likely killed. I doubt anyone could simply *forget* such a cache. It is conceivable that other items were also buried and left unfound," she concluded, her hope ringing clear in her voice.

Peter stared down into her eager face, her gray eyes glowing with happiness and wonder. He suddenly realized he loved this little scamp, smear of dirt and all. It had struck him like a clap of thunder when he glimpsed what it would be like to have her at his side while excavating.

But she pretended to be her brother, and therein was the

problem. There were too many reasons he couldn't reveal that he knew her identity. For one, she might be furious that he had played along with her charade, believing he ridiculed her. He wanted her joy and exuberance quite undiminished and all for himself. And as to her parents, well, he still suspected they would demand marriage, whether Emma declared love for him or not. He found he wished the best of life, and that meant Emma willingly in his arms.

He looked up at the sky where dark clouds gathered, prophetic of rain. The late afternoon sun had dipped behind them, and the landscape dimmed in luster.

"Perhaps we had better head for the house. It looks to rain before long." He rose and stood waiting to see what she would do next.

With reluctance Emma scrambled from the hole where she had made such a momentous find. Sir Peter was correct, it looked to rain and she didn't want any more evidence—such as a dripping wet body—that she wasn't George.

"Hurry on back to the house; do not wait for me," she begged. "I will take these coins over to my shed and work with them for a bit. I'll see you later," Emma announced, then strode off across the field toward the little shack where her clothes were, without waiting to see what he did. She needed to get changed and back to the house before it poured.

"Indeed," Sir Peter called out. "I shall leave the announcement of your find for you to offer when you come."

The words floated across the field to reach Emma as she hurried toward the little shack.

When she reached it, she half turned to see with great relief that he now walked rapidly toward the house, not so much as looking behind him.

Once inside, she dumped the coins into the basin full of water that she ought to have been using to wash her face and hands, no doubt. A glimmer of gold shown up at her, and she hugged herself with pure delight.

A sharp rap came at the door, and then her brother slipped into the shack. "What happened? I chanced to look out and saw you dancing about like a red Indian."

Emma just grinned and pointed to the basin. "See for yourself," she said with pride.

George crossed the shack in a few strides and stared down at the contents of the basin with disbelieving eyes. "A bit more digging and I'd have found that," he said with a rueful grimace at his sister. He poked at the coins, pushing them about to detect the number of gold ones.

"But it *is* yours! And you certainly would have uncovered the coins in mere minutes had I not interrupted you. I would wager anything that there is more to be found. Perhaps there was a battle. You know how people tend to bury things when they fear that someone might steal their wealth. Why, there could easily be another pile of coins even greater in value than these. Oh, look at the gold, George," she said with glee. "Gold!"

When he turned his gaze from the basin of coins and looked down at her, Emma couldn't help but offer him a hug of exhilaration. "You will find more, I just know it."

"I think it is a pity that Sir Peter is so nearsighted. He could do worse than marry you, I believe." He grinned at her with a brother's mockery.

"What a brute you are to say such a dreadful thing to me," Emma chided him in feigned anger. "Take your coins and leave; I need to get dressed before it rains and I turn into a most pathetic creature."

He picked up the basin and its precious contents, then made to depart.

Emma said quickly, "Where do you intend to go now?"

"I know an antiquarian who lives not far from here. I believe I will dry off these coins and see what he makes of them."

"Good luck," she said softly with a heartfelt smile.

He went out the door, allowing it to drift shut behind him. Emma hurriedly slipped from George's clothing, then donned her own with more haste than care.

Once outside she could see the clouds had turned a threatening gray. If she made it to the house before the downpour, it would be a miracle. She ran, stumbling across the field until she breathlessly reached the side door Beatrice had told her about.

She had no more than put a foot inside the house than the rain began to come down in torrents. Closing the door, she climbed up the tightly winding stairs until she reached the second floor. Her room was blessedly close to this end of the hall, and she slipped inside with fervent thanks that she had met no one on her mad dash.

Within several minutes Braddon entered after a discreet knock. "Ah, you are not wet, but not unscathed, I see."

Emma turned to face the looking glass and laughed when she saw the dirt-streaked face reflected.

"What a terrible sight. Do help me dress after I clean up. How go things belowstairs?" Emma scrambled from her soiled dress, then sought the basin of tepid water awaiting her use. Fragrant rose-scented soap reminded her of the field of sun-warmed grass and wildflowers and the happy scene she had just left.

"Miss Beatrice entertains the ladies with pretty songs and her harp. Sir William has dragged Sir Peter to the billiard room for a game or two. I believe you are quite safe."

Emma dried her face, then turned to Braddon with her happiness shining from her eyes. "I found a hoard of old coins, some of them gold. I do hope this will help George to win Beatrice."

Braddon nodded, a surprised expression settling on her face. "Indeed."

"Her ladyship has not given me away, has she?"

"Never, miss. I believe she finds it all highly diverting." Braddon ran a comb through Emma's curls, checked her face, then handed her a pair of gloves.

Feeling that she was now properly attired, Emma explained that she had left George's clothes in the shack.

"I shall fetch them later. Not to worry, miss."

With exceedingly mixed emotions, Emma wound her way down the stairs to the drawing room. Delicate notes from a harp floated out to greet her.

When she paused in the doorway, she barely restrained a gasp. Beatrice sat near the window. Although the light was dim, it brought a shining gold to her hair. Her voice rang out with pleasing clarity in a popular song of the day while she plucked at the strings of her harp. Small wonder George thought her an angel.

When she saw Emma, she brought the music to a close and rose from the harp to greet her adored George's sister.

"Did your brother make it in from the field before the rain?" Lady Johnson asked politely.

"Actually, he made it to the house for a few moments before he left again. He has found a wonderful hoard of coins, a few of them gold," Emma announced, generously ascribing the finding to him. "They look terribly old and appear to have a Roman-looking profile on them. He intends to seek confirmation of their antiquity from an authority he knows who lives nearby."

"Did he truly?" Beatrice cried with pleasure. "And there are gold coins as well? Papa will be most impressed, I believe." She clapped her hands with delight.

"Impressed with what, my dear?" Sir William asked in his genial manner, entering the room at that minute.

"Papa, it is so exciting. George has made a discovery in the old swamp. A hoard of coins . . . and some of them are gold!"

"It is my belief that he will most likely find more in that area, particularly if these were hidden to escape detection from enemies," Emma declared, edging away from the window to a more shadowy part of the room. Sir Peter had joined Sir William and had given her a very peculiar look.

"Where is the fellow? I should like to congratulate him. I'll confess I thought his expectations a lot of nonsense, but now . . . " Sir William turned to where Emma stood, his look inquiring.

Emma explained about George and his plans to call on the antiquarian authority.

Lady Titheridge urged Sir William to join their little group by the fire—so comfortable on a rainy day.

Emma remained in her shadowy corner, ostensibly examining a painting.

"So," a familiar voice began, "George made a remarkable find."

"Indeed. I am so happy for him." She continued to study the painting, hoping to discourage Sir Peter from conversation.

"And you were there at the time to see his good fortune?" Sir Peter said in a suspiciously bland manner.

Emma darted an alarmed glance at him, then shook her

head. "I learned of it from George when he paused to change before leaving," she replied while continuing to study the painting of a pair of rather insipid spaniels.

"He is fortunate to have such a sister . . . who rejoices for his good luck," he added.

She turned a startled gaze on him.

"Well, I wish George the very best. It is easy to see that the possibility of a Roman treasure trove is not the only thing that lures him to remain here." She gestured toward Beatrice, who waited upon her fragile-looking mother with loving patience.

"Ah, yes, the other reason. She is very lovely." He bestowed an appreciative look on the blond miss.

Emma wondered when he had developed this roving eye. From what Lady Titheridge had revealed, Sir Peter had been somewhat of a recluse, seldom going into Society and certainly paying little attention to the young women making their come-outs. Without any doubt he did not miss a one now, she thought gloomily.

"Will George be joining us soon?"

Emma studied that bland, innocent expression and wished with all her heart she knew what went on in Sir Peter's mind. "I cannot say. I imagine it depends upon whether or not he is able to see the antiquarian. And he may elect to remain there until the rain is over," she offered with inspiration. "I fancy that when someone like that is able to talk to another who is fascinated with the same topic, they may lose track of time."

"True," he replied with a sage nod. "I also tend to become absorbed in my Egyptian things. Have you ever had an interest in antiquities?" He propped himself against the wall, almost coming between Emma and the painted spaniels and uncomfortably close.

"Oh, indeed. I find it all quite fascinating," Emma said truthfully, backing away a step or two. "A young lady is limited to reading about it, I fear."

"What about Lady Hester Stanhope? She certainly has led a most adventurous life so far."

"I . . . I do not wish to scandalize," Emma said thoughtfully. "Were I to venture abroad, it must be with a husband, I believe. But I should like to travel some day."

"Rome? Egypt? The Orient?" Sir Peter prompted.

"Rome, certainly," she said with a judicious tilt of her head. "Egypt, yes," she added with a nod. "However, the Orient is too far away," she concluded decisively.

"Interesting."

"I should like to view your Egyptian collection some day," she said, plunging into dangerous waters.

He smiled, a slow smile full of charm and enticement. "We must arrange to have your mother bring you over one day."

"Mother?" she replied with alarm. "I think not. She would faint at the sight of the mummy," Emma replied, not realizing what she revealed at that remark.

Sir Peter gave her a bland look, then countered, "My aunt would most likely do the honors, then. We shall arrange it when you return to London."

"I came here to see how George goes on, you know," Emma said, trying to convince Sir Peter, although she wasn't quite certain why she must.

"I know," he replied gently.

"And now I wish to become acquainted with Beatrice and her charming family. I sense we all might be related one of these days," Emma explained earnestly.

"It is possible," he replied in that same gentle manner.

"Well," she said with the manner of one who has concluded business, "how do things go with you? Does the man from Bow Street believe he can nab the culprit who tried to steal from your collection?"

"He does," Sir Peter replied, a definite twinkle in his interesting green eyes.

That twinkle unnerved Emma for some reason. She didn't think he laughed at her; he was too polite for that. But something lurked in his mind, and she wished she knew what it was.

"Are you pleased with the fellow who guards your home at night? I gather you must be or you would never have left London," she mused, thus answering her own question.

"He is a sterling chap if you can describe a man who looks as though he has cauliflowers for ears and a nose that is all askew in that term. But he has possession of his faculties and is burly enough to discourage the most daring of souls."

"I hope so. I'd not like to think of the mummy going to be smashed up for medicine, or something equally horrid."

He wrinkled his brow and Emma felt her heart sink to her toes. She ought not have known about that particular bit of information. It hadn't been mentioned to her in his hearing.

"Ah, George told me about it," she hurriedly inserted.

His brow cleared, and he smiled at her again.

"Dinner is served, my lady," the servant announced, and Emma breathed a sigh of relief.

Sir Peter wheeled in Lady Johnson while Lady Titheridge accepted the arm offered by Sir William. Emma found herself being seated next to Sir Peter and gave Beatrice an inquiring look.

Beatrice gave a tiny shrug back, so it was not her doing.

Emma slipped her gloves off and laid them across her lap. The food was offered to her, and she accepted generous helpings. After being outside much of the afternoon and tramping about the church all morning, she was starving.

"Country air gives one a healthy appetite," Sir Peter commented quietly to her.

"Indeed," she replied. Then she caught sight of her hands. While *they* were clean, there was telltale dirt beneath a few of her nails, something no well-bred lady would ever permit. What could she do? Were she on the other side of the table it wouldn't matter in the least.

However . . . she sat next to Sir Peter, and if he happened to observe the dirt, might he not wonder how she acquired it while wandering about a church? As far as he knew, she had not been in the field today, but had taken a nap after arrival.

She tried as best she could to keep her nails out of view until she remembered that Sir Peter was nearsighted. At that recollection she relaxed and began to eat normally.

"You had a busy morning?" he inquired politely.

"Oh, yes," she replied, recalling the pretty interior of the Priory.

"Did a bit of investigating, did you?"

She gave him the blankest of looks, not understanding what he meant in the least.

He almost smiled, then gave a pointed look at her hands.

"That is exceedingly bad of you to notice," she said with a

forced smile. He had found her out. Yet perhaps she might salvage all somehow. She thought frantically, then said, "I wanted a cutting of a geranium, and I fear I must have picked up a bit of dirt. I cannot think how it escaped the soap and water. I guess I was in a bit of a hurry." She was babbling, she knew it, and it made her sound as guilty as could be.

"I see," he said in reply.

Emma wondered what it was he saw and how he managed to see it.

When the ladies went to retire to the drawing room, Emma discovered that things were done differently in this household, mainly for the sake of Lady Johnson. They all left the table at once, the men deciding to enjoy their port by the comfort of the fire with their charming ladies, as Sir William graciously phrased it.

Emma quickly pulled on her gloves and strolled to a window where she could make out the distant fields in the dusk. Sir Peter joined her, his glass of port in hand.

"Do join us by the fire, you two," Lady Titheridge commanded from her chair. "We decided to play a game of crambo."

Emma slipped away from Sir Peter like an eel, taking a seat next to Beatrice with deceptive speed. From this point of safety she spent the remainder of the evening, praying she might elude that provoking man until time for bed.

She hoped he intended to leave on the morrow, even as a part of her rejoiced in seeing that handsome face. Was ever a girl in such a dilemma as this?

Chapter 12

WHEN Emma entered the breakfast room the next morning, she found Sir Peter seated at the table. Her hand crept up to fiddle with the pretty pleated muslin ruff she wore around her neck. She had taken such a liking to it that even though the bruises had faded some, she continued to wear it over her dresses. Now it served to occupy her nervous fingers. What would he say after last evening?

"Good morning, Miss Cheney," he said pleasantly, looking spruce and fit. There was not the least sign that *he* had found it difficult to fall asleep.

"Indeed," she murmured in a voice deliberately a little higher than normal.

He gave her an assessing gaze, then continued, "You really do look remarkably like your brother. I suppose everyone tells you that. Enough to be twins. Amazing." He sipped his coffee while watching her over the rim.

Beatrice, who had entered directly behind Emma, smiled as she walked to the sideboard to fix a plate for her morning meal. She said, "It truly *is* remarkable how much they resemble each other. As you said, they could easily be twins. Emma is a trifle shorter, but only just. Even their voices are a bit alike. Perhaps that is what makes me so drawn to Emma," she said with a mischievous twinkle in her pretty blue eyes.

Sir Peter appeared confused at this agreement with his evaluation. He looked from Beatrice to Emma and back.

More relaxed after Beatrice's assistance, Emma joined her at the sideboard to select a modest repast. When she sat opposite Sir Peter at the table, she felt better able to withstand any searching looks he cast her way.

"Has George come down as yet?" Sir Peter inquired of Emma.

"Actually, I believe he is still asleep. It was very late when he returned here last night, from what Braddon told me. He did send me a note, however." Emma stopped speaking to sip at her tea.

"And? Do not leave us in suspense," Sir Peter scolded.

"I believe he intends to make a hasty trip to London. Something to do with the coins he has found, I think," she concluded vaguely.

"Oh, I do hope he finds out they are worth a fortune," Beatrice said softly to Emma.

"Does he intend to sell them?" Sir Peter asked idly, even though such a question was somewhat improper. But then, he did not appear to allow propriety to stand in his way when he wanted something.

"I could not say," Emma replied with a demure glance from beneath half-closed eyes.

"Well, if your brother is to hare off to London, I may as well follow him. He's dashed elusive, I must say." Sir Peter finished the last of his coffee, then announced his intention to return to London shortly, with a brief stop to visit a friend along the way. He promised to seek out Sir William before he departed, to say good-bye and to thank him for his hospitality.

Once Sir Peter had left the room and Emma could hear his steps receding up the staircase, she gave a sigh of relief.

"I quite agree," Beatrice replied with a fond smile at Emma.

"I have never in my life tried to deceive anyone before. This has become so terribly complicated I wonder if I shall ever straighten it out," Emma said with a grimace. She rose from the table, leaving a partially eaten meal behind her.

Beatrice gave Emma a troubled look, then followed.

The young ladies lurked about the drawing room so as to know when Sir Peter came down. At last they heard a clattering on the stairs that could only be a gentleman in a hurry.

Emma glided to the hall to catch sight of his portmanteau and other gear by the front door. Sir Peter had disappeared toward the study where Sir William often spent his time when not out of doors. She heard a low murmur of voices, then saw

Sir Peter striding back along the hall toward where she stood. Before she could retreat, he caught sight of her.

"Ah, there you are. I hoped to say good-bye before I left." He reached out to take one of Emma's hands, and she was thankful she had carefully scraped her nails clean last night. She had even persuaded Braddon to find a slip of a geranium for her in case he inquired about it later.

"When do you plan to return to the City?" He gazed at her with such an intensity that Emma almost forgot to speak.

"Ah, I am not certain. Perhaps in a day or two. Your aunt announced that she never travels on Sunday. So that would be next Monday, I suppose."

Emma sought to remove her hand from his clasp and failed. His touch did such peculiar things to her. Standing so close to him made her long to throw herself on his manly chest and sob out her sorry tale of woe. Would he forgive her for her deception? Some men wouldn't like being hoaxed. She knew he had strong emotions, for he had reacted to the attempted robbery and the shooting of his butler in a very intense manner. What would he say to her in the event the truth be known?

"I shall look forward to seeing you when you return. Tell George I wish him the very best." Sir Peter dropped her hand, and half turned to leave, then he paused. "Oh, and do tell George that I hope he can give me a hand once again. The man from Bow Street wants to set up a trap for the thief. We feel George would be a great help to us in that. And I would like to give your brother another lesson in fencing. He has a natural aptitude for the sport. The next lesson will be in tactics." His eyes seemed to dance at the word, compelling Emma to wonder at his thoughts.

Too unnerved to answer, she merely nodded.

Coming to her rescue, Beatrice stepped forth and bade Sir Peter a pleasant farewell. "I shall remind Emma to give him those messages in case she forgets," Beatrice concluded.

Sir Peter gave her a smile that would have had most women swooning with delight. Since Beatrice had an interest in George, she was immune, but Emma took note of that smile and coveted it for herself.

Then he turned again to her and his smile intensified. "Until later, Emma," he murmured in that deep rich voice that sent tremors to her heart. In moments he was gone.

"Mercy," Beatrice said, fanning her face with her handkerchief, "you two are enough to start a fire without a tinder box."

"Nonsense," Emma declared stoutly. "He smiles like that at Lady Amelia Littleton as well. I saw him while at Almack's last week."

"You have been to Almack's?" Beatrice cried excitedly. "Oh, do tell me all about it. What did they wear? And was the Princess Esterhazy there? Is she as interesting as they say? And are the refreshments truly as deplorable as I have been told?" Beatrice drew Emma along to a pretty sofa by the window that looked out on the ripening fields of grain, with the cattle grazing in a distant meadow.

Her lively interest in a topic Emma could eagerly explain brought the two girls together for a comfortable coze. About an hour later George looked in on the scene and grinned.

"I'm off to the field," he announced. "I trust the other guest has departed? I may safely go out?"

"Indeed, you may," Beatrice replied with a fond look.

"I told him you intended to make a quick trip to London about your find. He thinks you will see him there," Emma said, prudently omitting the business about the fencing lesson. George didn't need to know everything.

Beatrice gave Emma a puzzled glance, but did not interpose any comment.

"How long do you intend to remain here?" George said, mostly out of curiosity and not of concern.

"We most likely will return Monday," Emma said with a little frown.

"As a good Christian, Lady Titheridge does not travel on Sunday," Beatrice added.

"In the meanwhile I shall have a chance to watch you at your dig," Emma declared with great satisfaction, crossing the room to join him near the door.

"I am glad you had a crack at digging, Emma," her brother told her.

Emma grinned and gave him an affectionate pat on his arm. "Well, I do know how much you long to make a find, and I'm sorry that you didn't uncover those coins, but it was great fun, I must admit."

"We have yet to hear what your authority said about the coins," Beatrice reminded him.

"Oh, the chap declared them to be genuine Roman coins of considerable antiquity. He thinks the fellow depicted is the Emperor Honorius. He lived from A.D. three ninety-three to four twenty-three. Impressive, is it not?" George said with pride.

"And the gold coins are quite valuable?" Emma said breathlessly.

"Oh, indeed they are. I believe I can finance quite a dig using those as collateral." The look he sent to his dear Beatrice quite excluded Emma and the rest of the world.

Emma gave him a disappointed frown. "I expected something different, somehow."

"Oh, never fear, I shall be able to ask for my dearest before long. You see, I believe you, little sister. I think there will be more treasure trove out there. That is why I am gone as of this minute." With that he turned away, then disappeared out of the front door.

Emma strolled back to the window and could see him cutting across the lawn in the direction of his dig in the drained swamp.

"When may we go out there?" she murmured to Beatrice.

"Oh, I believe we ought to wait." At Emma's disappointed expression, Beatrice relented and continued, "At least until we find our hats and gloves, and possibly a parasol. The sun promises to be warm today."

Emma beamed her pleasure. "What do we tarry here for then?"

Before long the two girls, dressed in sprigged muslin—Emma sporting the pretty ruff at her neck—strolled across the lawn in the same direction George had gone. They most properly wore gloves, straw hats tied beneath their chins, and carried colorful parasols to guard their skin against the danger of the sun.

"It is such a relief for me to put aside my troubles for a time. And I hadn't seen George in an age. I shall report to Mama that he is fine. I shall also hint that there is more than one reason for him to linger here."

"Your mama . . ." Beatrice said hesitantly as they approached the field where George was already at work. "Is she likely to be upset at an alliance between her son and my family?"

"Mercy no," Emma replied with heartfelt sincerity. "Mama will be in alt, you wait and see. She has always carried a special feeling for George, and this will please her no end."

If Emma knew a pang of envy for the special regard her brother received from their mother, she didn't reveal it by the flutter of an eyelash.

"Come," she sang out, "let us hurry along. We wouldn't want George to find his treasure before we arrive!"

Across the fields Peter drove toward London with much to consider.

At Dorking he took a detour north of the town to visit an old acquaintance of his, David Percy, Lord Leighton. He had but recently returned from his lengthy honeymoon. However, Peter wished to visit with his bride, the former Elizabeth Dancy, who was also Peter's cousin. Perhaps she might be forthcoming with a bit of cousinly advice.

The more he thought about it, the more he worried. It was not going to be easy to handle Emma Cheney once she found out about *his* deception. Hers was wicked enough, but he ought to have let her know that he was aware of it long before this. It seemed that the longer the charade continued, the more complicated matters became.

He was welcomed into his cousin's house with warm regard. He took note of her devotion to her husband, plus her interesting condition and realized why the couple had not come up to London for the Season.

When asked—in a most subtle way, mind you—the reason for this surprise visit, Peter breathed a sigh and began, "Well, I need a bit of advice, Elizabeth."

"If you ask my advice, you should forget the entire matter," Beatrice counseled while they awaited the arrival of Lady Titheridge's traveling coach. "I cannot imagine appearing in public, wearing a gentleman's breeches! And fencing!" She paused for a thoughtful moment, then said, "What is it like?"

"Actually," Emma replied with equal reflection, "the

breeches are exceedingly comfortable. They permit far more freedom of movement than our gowns. As to the fencing, well," she admitted, "it is rather fun, all things considered."

"Even though it causes you to wear a ruff all the time?" Beatrice asked while eyeing the pretty bit of pleated muslin.

"It shall become an eccentricity of mine, I fancy," Emma replied with a hint of a smile.

Beatrice exchanged a look with her, then said, "I shall miss you and think of you bearding the dragon in his lair, fending off the épée, having all manner of fascinating exploits. I believe it may become rather dull when you must become just you again."

"I can scarcely wait," Emma replied with a rueful shake of her head.

Lady Titheridge bustled down the stairs, urging Emma to follow her and ordering Braddon to carry the things considered necessary for a journey back to London.

The parting was swift and brief, for all of them had become close in those few days and thought it sad to separate. Amid promises to visit again and good wishes for an agreeable trip, the trio left Sir William's home with some regret.

"At least you know that George is safe and happy," her ladyship said when they had reached the main road that led to London.

"And," Emma added, "that he will not be returning to the City anytime soon."

"You had best hint to your parents that an acceptable marriage is in the offing there. I believe they would prefer to be forewarned, as it were," Lady Titheridge advised.

"I shall, you may be certain." Emma paused, then continued, "Did you ever find out why dear Lady Johnson must sit in that wheeled chair?" Emma inquired of her ladyship.

"A nasty fall some years back. That is why they never had any more children. Sir William appears to be an extremely thoughtful man," Lady Titheridge concluded in a musing tone.

Emma agreed and leaned back against her seat to consider what she must do when back at her home. The first matter of business was Sir Peter, of course. And she needed to send off another embroidery pattern to the magazine. Odd, she hadn't thought to even look at the latest issue to view her design.

They arrived late in the afternoon of the following day. Mrs. Cheney fluttered about, her vinaigrette in one hand, a handkerchief in the other.

"And dearest George? I trust you found him well? Such a flying trip, I declare."

Emma sat her mother down and poured out a considerably edited tale suitable for her ears. Mention of the exchange of identities was omitted, but she did mention the appearance of Sir Peter, for the dratted man might just say something to Mama and the fat would be in the fire.

"And Mama, George found a hoard of Roman coins, some of which were gold," Emma concluded, again generously ascribing the find to her brother. "He feels certain he will find more, and that will enable him to marry Beatrice."

Mrs. Cheney had looked rather unhappy when she had learned of George's interest. "You like this girl?"

"When George described her as an angel, he couldn't have found a better word. And Mama, Beatrice is the only child of an exceedingly wealthy farmer. Actually, Sir William is more than a farmer; he breeds special cattle and practices all manner of advanced farming methods. He is viewed with great esteem in that area."

Mrs. Cheney began to smile. "The girl sounds most acceptable."

Emma decided her mama would just have to meet Beatrice and fall under her charm.

"Sir Peter left a note for you. I believe it is on the hall table," Mrs. Cheney said absently, her mind clearly with her precious son.

Emma tried not to dash to the hall and succeeded admirably. Breaking open the seal, she scanned the missive hastily, then read it a second time. She returned to the drawing room to address her parent.

"He wishes me to go for a drive with him tomorrow afternoon. May I?" Emma studied her mother, wondering what schemes floated through her mind. She might not mind in the least to have George the heir of a baronet, even if it was to a profitable farm.

"What? Of course," Mrs. Cheney replied in the same absence of attention as before.

Giving up on her mother, Emma hurried to her room, locking the door behind her. She picked up a whip that was about the size of the épée and began to practice the lunges, parry and thrust, she had learned in her lessons. She wasn't sure she had remembered the timing correctly, but figured Sir Peter would be happier to scold her about something.

Why did he wish to take her driving? Or was she searching for motives when none were necessary. Perhaps he merely wished to keep on the good side of the Cheney family and George by showering her with a bit of attention.

A knock on the door tore her from her musings.

"Flowers for you, miss," Fanny announced through the crack.

Emma quickly unlocked the door and flung it open. There in Fanny's hands was a bouquet of June roses and other summer flowers. It was a romantic cluster that reminded her of the afternoon she had spent in the digs with Sir Peter thinking she was George.

Ignoring the inquisitive look on Fanny's face, Emma found the card tucked well into the bouquet. "Sir Peter," she softly exclaimed.

Once she learned who the sender was, the maid disappeared to spread the word belowstairs.

Emma drifted across the room to sit by the window in her favorite chair. Leaning back, she floated off into a daydream in which she had *not* practiced to deceive, nor had all the other dreadful things occurred. Rather, Sir Peter had seen her at Almack's, sought her out because he found her silly cap of dark curls and ordinary gray eyes of interest, and he didn't mind her height in the least.

The following afternoon Emma was dressed in her prettiest green-and-white carriage dress with the dark green spencer over it. She paced back and forth in her room, smoothing her gloves over nervous fingers.

"What if he invites me to drive only to tell me that he knows me to perform a charade?" she asked her looking glass. "I do not know if I could weather a storm like that."

"Sir Peter be downstairs," Fanny announced from the doorway. It was a trifle early for a Society drive, but Emma was too eager to leave to care. Not that it mattered to her one way or the other, anyway.

Emma thanked the girl, then walked down the two flights of stairs, emotions warring within.

"Good day, Sir Peter," she said, annoyed that a squeak appeared in her voice.

"Ready?" If he noticed that Mrs. Cheney hadn't bothered to appear, he failed to show it. Mrs. Bascomb and Lady Hamley could be heard in conference with Mrs. Cheney up in the drawing room. Emma suspected they were pouring over the history of the Johnson family to determine the lovely Beatrice's worthiness.

The day could not possibly have been lovelier. Few clouds marred the sky, and once they reached Hyde Park, the combined scent of freshly scythed grass and spring flowers brought a smile to Emma's face. She was a silly peagoose. Sir Peter would not have sent her flowers were he to expose her charade. She relaxed to enjoy the drive and the summer sunshine.

"The flowers were lovely, Sir Peter," she said once they had cleared the gate into the park.

"They reminded me of an afternoon down in Sussex," he replied without looking at her.

Emma suspected she paled at those words. Did he know? Would he accuse her? She clasped her hands together as though that might ward off the worst.

"I thought you might enjoy a memory of your visit at Sir William's home as well. You seemed to enjoy the country," he added with a friendly glance at her.

Emma visibly relaxed. "I did, and the flowers immediately brought it to mind. It was most kind of you."

"Do you see what I see?" he murmured to Emma as they approached another vehicle coming toward them.

"Good grief, Lady Amelia and Mr. Swinburne. I had not thought she would go so far."

"The chap is barely acceptable. I have it on good authority that were he to seek entry into White's, he would be blackballed," he said in an undertone.

"No!" Emma exclaimed under her breath. "George told me

that Mr. Swinburne was in Dun Territory the last he had heard."

"True, I have heard the same. Have you any influence with her at all?"

Emma was prevented from replying to this when they drew side by side with Mr. Swinburne's vehicle. It was a fancy phaeton—the very latest design—and looked to have just arrived from the carriage maker's shop.

"Swinburne," Sir Peter acknowledged with a faint nod.

"Lady Amelia," Emma said most properly, "I have not seen you in days. I have such exciting news to share. Do tell me that we may have a lovely chat soon."

Lady Amelia looked confused and turned to Mr. Swinburne for help of a sort.

"I believe you said you have tomorrow morning free, did you not?" the dandy declared. He picked a piece of nonexistent lint from his sleeve, then bestowed an icy smile on Emma.

She narrowed her gaze in return, then concentrated upon Amelia instead.

"Tomorrow morning . . . late?" Amelia said far more hesitantly than was her wont.

Emma agreed and the two carriages parted.

"There is something strange there or I miss my guess," Emma declared to Sir Peter. "How *can* she turn to that odious toad for guidance like that?"

"I seem to recall his presence in your drawing room," Sir Peter said with that bland manner he had used before.

"That was my mama's doing, and before he found out that my dowry is a mere pittance compared to Amelia's." Emma gave a little flounce and settled in an indignant mound of muslin.

"You truly care about Lady Amelia, don't you?"

"Indeed. She may be a raving beauty, titled, and have packets of money, but she also has a warm heart and a sensitive nature that in the past has been a delight. I do not like to see her played for a fool."

"Well said," he replied with obvious approval.

Which left Emma wondering what his feelings might be for the beautiful Amelia. It was difficult for Emma to see how any gentleman could prefer herself to such an admirable young woman as Amelia.

The remainder of the drive passed in quiet reflection for Emma, while Sir Peter wore that confused expression again if she had but turned her head to see it.

At Almack's that evening Emma found the place abuzz with rumors. Some said that Napoleon must have defeated Lord Wellington and that the army had suffered terrible casualties. Others talked about the reports that hundreds of English had fled Brussels. A man who had caught the first boat taking on the escapees had dashed to London, so to be the first with his news.

A feeling of gloom battled with the hope that somehow the great Wellington would succeed.

Needless to say, the dancers were affected. Lady Amelia was not to be seen, so Emma sat quietly conversing with her mama and Lady Titheridge, who thought the entire affair badly managed.

"Had I the running of the government and the war, I'd have shot Napoleon long ago. Utter nonsense to coddle the tyrant only to allow him to escape from Elba. Fools!" she declared with a nod of her turbaned and bejeweled head.

Emma lost interest in the war when she espied Sir Peter strolling along with friends, deep in conversation. When he saw her, he broke off and came in their direction.

"Miss Cheney, will you do me the honor of this dance?" Sir Peter said, bowing before her after greeting his aunt and Mrs. Cheney with due deference.

"I should be delighted, Sir Peter," Emma said, wondering if he was disappointed that Amelia was not in attendance.

She watched him, trying to think of something clever to say. At last, having abandoned being witty, she said, "How goes the protection of your collection? Does the fellow with the cauliflower ears and broken nose still keep the thief at bay?"

He looked down at her with a faint smile. "That he does. And Harry Porter does an admirable job of snooping about London for clues. He thinks he is on to something, but has yet to report what it might be."

Emma shuddered briefly, for the thought of a thief with a

gun who was willing to shoot at anyone who came into view frightened her.

"None of this, please," he said in admonition. "I believe there is enough gloom here for the entire nation." He looked about him, shaking his head in dismay.

"Do you believe Wellington has lost the battle and the war against the Monster from Corsica, as the newspapers call him?" Emma gave Sir Peter a worried look with a tender glance at her fragile mother. That poor lady always feared the very worst and believed the French were about to set foot on English shores at any day.

"England shall prevail, never fear," he replied as though repeating a phrase often said. Then, to obviously change the subject, he continued in a very different direction. "Has your brother come to London as yet? I wish he would call in the morning. Does he rise early? Could you tell him I'd appreciate talking with him about the collection? And remind him that his next lesson is to be on tactics."

Emma swallowed with difficulty and nodded, almost afraid to say a word. At last, when her silence became too much, she said, "I'll speak to him when I return to the house. I imagine he will come for a time, although he does have an appointment in the late morning," she concluded, thinking of Lady Amelia.

"Of course."

And she wondered precisely what he meant by that. His look seemed far too knowing.

Chapter 13

"HOW do I look?" Emma asked Braddon. "I must be able to remove this coat so as to fence," she reminded the maid.

"You will do excellently," the maid assured. "Now you had best be off, for it will only be a brief lesson so you may dash home to meet with Lady Amelia."

Emma had revealed her appointment with the puzzling Amelia and her fears for her. With scarcely a backward glance, Emma ran lightly down the stairs, thinking again how vastly more convenient pantaloons were instead of her confining skirts.

Once at Bruton Street, Emma entered the house with a wary step. Never certain what to expect from Sir Peter, she walked back to the workroom, where she found him studying the contents of one of the cases.

"Good morning," Emma said, trying to duplicate George's voice and intonations. "Afraid I cannot stay very long, for I have an appointment late this morning. May I be of assistance in something?"

"Your sister mentioned you were to be occupied later on," Sir Peter murmured. "Dashed pretty girl, your sister." He concentrated on the case contents, tilting his head first one way, then the other, as though trying to decide if the arrangement was just right.

Emma prayed that she would not blush at this bit of an encomium from Sir Peter. She mumbled something totally unintelligible in reply, then bent over the case to look at what was within.

"What? You have brought home the necklace? I thought

you intended to keep it safe!" Emma cried in alarm, almost forgetting her George voice in her shock.

"Well, if I hope to nab the crook, I had best have adequate bait," he said, sounding most reasonable.

While Emma could see the sense of this, she thought he might have substituted a fake and said so.

"A counterfeit? And where could I find a jeweller I could trust to make such a thing? He'd likely palm off the false one and abscond with the real. You know there is a ready market for the piece," he concluded, finally looking up to meet her troubled gaze.

"I do not see how the French can afford to buy much of anything. From what I have seen in the newspapers, Napoleon has about bankrupted the country," Emma pointed out.

"There is always someone with money" was his vague reply. "Well, what do you think about the arrangements?"

Emma slowly turned around, absorbing every detail of the room. The glaziers had neatly replaced the broken window. One or two of Emma's sketches hung on the wall over each case, with explanations regarding those items.

"It looks much like a museum," Emma said at last.

"Good," he said with relish. "I have invited a few chaps over to view the results. Do you want to join us?" The invitation was casually put forth, tossed off as Sir Peter walked toward the door, obviously expecting George to follow him.

"When is it to be?" Emma countered in a strained voice. As deeply as she was involved at this point, she really dare not attend any function where someone might have better eyesight! As long as she kept this business to just the two of them, she felt she had a chance to escape unscathed.

"This afternoon. The invitations went out yesterday, but I thought I'd be seeing you this morning so waited to ask you now."

"Too bad, old fellow. I would like to be here, but I'll be occupied all afternoon," she replied. Emma did not bother to explain; she could not think of a thing that George might take part in that could not be set aside if he so chose.

"Pity," Sir Peter tossed over his shoulder. "Well, we had best get on with our lesson, for it will be a brief one. Shame you had a morning appointment. Your sister has one too—with Lady Amelia."

"Um," Emma murmured, deciding her best defense would be vague replies and ambiguous comments.

He selected the foils, then handed Emma her mask. While she tied it securely over her face, she watched him do the same. Then they picked up their épées and walked to the center of the mat, which he referred to as a *piste*.

"Tactics," Sir Peter began, "involve the application of swordplay to differing situations or perhaps different types of opponents."

"But," Emma objected, "I have no intention of becoming involved in a match or the like, and certainly not a duel."

"True, you may not plan that, but it is well to be able to defend yourself if necessary," he advised.

And so they began. Emma flexed her legs and arms, prepared for another grueling session. He might say the lesson would be brief, but she suspected he would make up for that by the intensity.

Why she did not simply refuse his offer to teach her she did not know. Perhaps it had something to do with her truly wanting to learn the masculine sport that challenged her to such an extent. And, she confessed, she rather enjoyed being with him.

When she brought up her sword in the salute, she almost wished she might face him as herself. It would be so good to get the best of him, though she admitted it would be beyond her ability. But practice improved one, and one might always have hope of the impossible, particularly with someone who insisted he was nearsighted.

"Too slow, too slow," Sir Peter scolded when Emma's timing was off and he was able to complete his attack of her. He seemed to fly through the air with a swiftness that took her breath. She rapidly ran backward from him when it seemed he would collide with her. He paused, almost touching her, looking at her with a peculiar expression in those green eyes. An odd sort of tension hung in the air between them.

Emma wondered what he was thinking. If she were herself, what would he do? His eyes held what almost seemed to be a longing in them. Or was she merely imagining things? That could never be if he believed her to be George! She put that thought from her mind and concentrated upon her lesson.

He swiftly backed away, turning from her for a moment before he again faced her. Standing with his épée balanced in one hand, his other hand on the tip, he glared at her. "You must not only defend yourself, you must be prepared to counterattack."

As she had thought, he seemed to enjoy admonishing her. She made no reply, but listened and watched while he demonstrated the correct cadence.

"It is necessary to seize the advantage of any momentary lapse your opponent may make," he pointed out with perfect sense. "Now, again."

Practice continued on the footwork, the thrust and parry, the riposte, until Emma longed to collapse on the mat. Perhaps she ought to allow him to stab her. At least she would have good reason to fall down.

He glanced at the clock that sat on the table below the case where he stored the swords. "It is growing late. I suppose I had best let you go. If you are tardy for your appointment, I may find your counterattack too fierce." He chuckled at his *bon mot* and accepted Emma's sword along with her mask. "I enjoy our sessions," he said. "I trust you find them agreeable as well?"

"Indeed," she said with more truth than he knew. Emma felt herself lucky he kept that button on the tip of his épée, or she probably would be off her toes—forever.

While he stowed the equipment away, careful as always, Emma hastily pulled her coat back on and edged toward the door.

"Sorry I must leave so soon. You know how it is," she said with less than perfect truth. She then added, "the lessons interest me."

"You are improving. I'll wager you have done a bit of practice in your off hours. Am I right?" Sir Peter clapped Emma on the back with a hearty slap that nearly unbalanced her. She just barely managed not to stagger from the blow.

"Indeed," she managed to croak in reply while wondering if

she would not only have those wretched bruises but a stiff shoulder from this lesson.

At the doorway she stopped to thank him again, and he waved her appreciation aside.

"Your sketches are more than compensation to me. In fact, I intend to pay you for them." He smiled, that perfectly charming, beguiling smile that lit up the depths of his eyes in a way that turned Emma's knees to jelly.

"Not necessary," Emma replied gruffly. How could she accept the money—even if she *could* use it? She was so besotted with the man that she could not possibly accept compensation for doing something for him.

"I shall find a way to satisfy the situation. Perhaps you would like to be in on the final chase for the jewel thief? Ought to be a bit of excitement, I daresay," he said in a coaxing way.

Emma ran a nervous tongue over her lower lip and nodded, "Oh, jolly fun, to be sure. However, I might be gone by then, you know. I am thinking of returning to Sussex quite soon."

"I understand," Sir Peter said with a knowing wink. "Beatrice is a beautiful girl. You would do well to marry her before some other chap steps in. You know how it is, while the cat's away, the mice will play."

Emma could not believe her ears. How could he joke about such a thing.

She fled from the house within minutes and rode back to Lady Titheridge's in confusion.

Peter leaned back against the door and permitted the laughter that had longed to escape to be freed. Dear Emma scarcely knew which way to turn. As he had said to Radley, she was confused and he intended to keep her that way.

Once he released his pent-up merriment, he strolled back to the workroom, whistling a popular tune. He studied the arranged precautions again, then turned to greet Harry Porter when he entered the room.

"Shall we cover the details one more time, sir?" the Runner inquired with proper deference.

"Let's do," Peter said with a decisive snap that had been absent while he was with Emma Cheney.

Upon her return home, Emma informed Oldham regarding her expected guest, then quickly ran up to her room. She checked her appearance to see that every curl was as it ought to be and that her Betsie covered any telltale bruises. Fortunately, this dress possessed a higher neck than most she owned.

"Lady Amelia has come," Fanny announced from the door. Behind her Amelia peeped into the room.

"I thought perhaps it might be better were we to have a comfortable coze up here," Emma said to a hesitant Amelia. After requesting Fanny bring them tea and biscuits, Emma drew her friend along to the window. Emma settled Amelia so she faced the window while Emma carefully put her back to the light. She intended to watch every expression on her friend's pretty face. First she told Amelia all about the trip south and George's lovely find of coins.

"And now, my dearest Amelia," Emma began when Fanny had brought the pot of tea with thin slices of buttered bread and tiny ginger biscuits, "tell me what is going on."

She had not really intended to be so direct. She ought to apply her lessons in tactics here, but the sight of the pale worried face had made her forget her motive.

"Nothing, Emma, nothing at all." Amelia absently shredded her sheer cambric handkerchief into bits while her forehead was pleated into worry lines. "I . . . er . . . I" She halted, unable to say what was on her mind.

"I see. Ginger biscuit?" Emma offered. She poured out a cup of steaming tea, sat back, then watched Amelia while not saying a word, hoping the silence might draw her friend into speech.

"Well," Amelia began hesitantly. "No. I promised, and I never break my word," the anxious girl concluded softly.

"I would never wish you to do that," Emma replied, wondering precisely what it was that bothered Amelia. Emma figured the odds were that whatever it was had something to do with Mr. Swinburne. He had appeared to have some manner of hold over Amelia when they had met in the park.

Rather than pursue the issue Emma longed to investigate, she turned the conversation to the weather and likelihood of rain on Wednesday evening. Not that any of those who were privileged to attend Almack's would allow a trifle like a rainstorm to interfere with their being present at the prestigious assemblies.

From there Emma launched into the favored topic of the latest style on gowns. It was but a jump to the silks from France that still managed to be smuggled into England by those more interested in a bit of money than were troubled by aiding the enemy.

"Do you think England is truly in danger?" Amelia whispered as though someone might hear.

"Sir Peter made me feel most hopeful that everything will turn out right," Emma replied earnestly.

Pink color flooded Amelia's face, and she breathed a sigh of relief. "Oh, I do hope so. It is so dangerous for the ships out at sea with the French at war with us forever. Just think of the poor people in Guernsey."

Emma was confused at Amelia's concern over shipping, but made no comment. Nothing could induce Amelia to return to the topic of her worries, nor would she be drawn to the subject of Mr. Swinburne.

But Emma felt uneasy at best and anxious at the worst when she bade good-bye to her friend.

"Welcome to my collection, gentlemen," Sir Peter said with his usual quiet charm and *bon ton* that afternoon.

Edward remained in the background, taking quiet note of each man present and how they reacted to the items on display.

Reginald Swinburne slowly strolled along the cases, inspecting the contents of each until he reached the one containing the necklace.

"Splendid bit of trumpery," he declared, lowering his quizzing glass when turning to face Peter. He dangled his glass from his hand, swinging it to and fro on its chain while gazing about the room.

"Trumpery?" Edward retorted. "I say, old chap, scarcely

that. It's a priceless piece, and I daresay there isn't another like it to be found anywhere."

"Now, Worcester, not all people appreciate the rare and beautiful. Do not be so hard on the fellow." Peter could see that Edward's indignation was not feigned, and he hoped to defuse the situation before his good friend spoiled the whole show by a flush hit to Swinburne's nose.

"I pride myself that I am as much a connoisseur as anyone around," Swinburne said with a trace of pomposity.

"Is that so?" Edward said with dangerous quiet.

"If I may say so, your collection is by and large an excellent one, although I do wonder about the necklace," Swinburne proclaimed with a air of sagacity. "It simply is most unlikely that the jewels and stones could be genuine. There are little tricks to imitation, you know."

"No, really. Do tell me—I have always wondered about that," Peter said with admirable restraint.

He led Swinburne close to the area of the room where Harry Porter lounged in a shadow. The Bow Street Runner was discreetly attired in gentlemen's clothing and blended into the background extremely well.

Peter gave Harry Porter the nod and a faint wink. The signal was returned while Peter drew Swinburne into a chat.

The men present gathered around for some of Peter's excellent port, sherry, and brandy—or anything else one might think of—and discussed the idea Swinburne presented. Quite a number of them objected to his notion of a fake being placed on the mummy during the wrapping.

"I still say," said Major Jenkins, retired, in his hearty voice that had once reached from one end of a parade ground to the other, "that is the gen-you-ine item. Saw many a gewgaw like that when I was stationed in Egypt. Why, the beggars would dig them up every now and again." He winked his assurance that *he* knew the truth of the matter and knew it well. He twirled the ends of his magnificent mustache with an air of bravado and strutted up and down the aisle while looking daggers at Mr. Swinburne.

Peter winced at the mere thought of such beauty being desecrated by shabby treatment and careless handling.

Augustus, Lord Fintersham, agreed with Major Jenkins.

"Why, when we chaps went abroad of a morning, there were stacks of those mummies here and there about Cairo. I believe they used them for firewood. No reason to bother fabricating one necklace when there were likely a good many about," he reasoned. "No, I feel certain this is the genuine thing."

Others continued the debate, coming to the conclusion that Swinburne was wrong and that Sir Peter was on to the real article. Major Jenkins appeared to enjoy his vindication, for his smile at Sir Peter before leaving was one of superior smugness.

Eventually—the subject being debated sufficiently—the men straggled off to their clubs, the afternoon calls, and rides in the park. The rumors regarding the conditions in France were contradicted hourly, and Peter wondered if his plan would fall into ruin because of circumstances. It would be most frustrating to be so close and then fail.

Neither Amelia nor Mr. Swinburne attended Almack's that Wednesday evening, an omission that bothered Emma a trifle. Lady Amelia adored the assemblies, with the scheming and preening of the girls making their come-outs, not to mention the manipulations of their dear mamas. June brought the flowers of the marriage mart of the *ton* into full bloom.

But Emma had little time in which to discover any reason, for her dance card filled rapidly. She wondered why, then decided that the partiality shown her by Sir Peter intrigued the others.

"I see you are taking to London very well, Miss Cheney," Mr. Brummell said when he approached her during a lull between dances.

"Perhaps for the moment," Emma admitted. She plied her fan more than customary, for the rooms were stuffy and the dances energetic.

"The people mill about with more than usual gossip and gaiety this evening, I believe," he said, looking around them.

Aware that she was receiving a great number of curious looks from those who followed the fashionable Mr. Brummell with avid eyes and ears, Emma also looked about the room and nodded.

"It is as though a restlessness seizes them, that they wait for word from Wellington and occupy their hours beforehand to keep from speculating on the worst," she said.

"How astute you are for one so young," he replied, looking down at her with his quizzing glass in hand before him.

"Not to mention female," she said in surprise, laughing at his expression of chagrined amusement.

"I did not say that," he complained, then chuckled softly at her.

Emma merely smiled and, when he strolled on to visit with another, found herself besieged by gentlemen curious to see what had held the celebrated Brummell by her side, not to mention made him chuckle.

But Lady Amelia still did not come. Even when eleven of the clock arrived, she had not yet appeared. Emma thought it most strange.

"Well, you wear the ruff again. I cannot decide if you intend to set your own style or revitalize our esteemed queen's fashion," Sir Peter said. He took Emma's hand in his, leading her to the floor for a Scottish reel.

"I like the ruff, and you do not have this dance," she said with spirit. She did not have to check her card, for Sir Peter's name was not there. The lines had been filled before he arrived, and she secretly had been enormously pleased at this.

"Fobbed the lad off. Told him I'd slice him to bits if he dared to claim your hand for the dance," Sir Peter said just loudly enough for her to hear while they danced through to the bottom of the line.

Emma gave Sir Peter a scandalized look. "I do hope you are joking, sir. I should hate to think you really said such silliness."

"Does it bother you that I wish to partner you?" He bestowed one of those rakish looks on her that always set her pulse racing, before she drew up to the position opposite him in the line.

Bother was scarcely the word she might use to describe her emotions when confronted with Sir Peter. Apprehension, vexation, indignation, not to mention a serious case of the chills. At least, she attributed the tremors and flutters to a sort of chill. She refused to admit what she knew hid in her heart.

A curious increase in the level of conversation caught her attention. Heads turned, people drew together.

"Something has happened," Emma mouthed, hoping Sir Peter would understand her.

He nodded in reply, and as the dance drew to a swift and gay flourish, he guided her along with him to a gentleman who was a member of the cabinet.

"It has been reported that the Honorable Major Percy has arrived at the War Office with a message from Wellington. Nothing is known about the contents of his dispatches," the cabinet member said quietly to Sir Peter. "The news was brought to me and smuggled up by means of a bribe." He grimaced with the reminder of the strict refusal by the esteemed patronesses for admittance to anyone who presented himself after the hour of eleven.

"I imagine you want to join Bathurst immediately," Sir Peter replied.

The gentleman nodded. "Although Bathurst will be off to report to Prinney regardless, I'd like to know what has happened. This demmed business of not knowing is driving me as mad as the rest of these poor souls." He gestured to the people who milled about the rooms, then began to edge himself through the restive crowd and soon was lost to view.

"I wonder when we will know the truth of the matter," Emma said while they strolled to the room where the insipid refreshments were offered.

"Do you wish to leave now?" Sir Peter asked with insight.

"I have the most peculiar feeling regarding Amelia," Emma said after agreeing. "She would never miss an evening at Almack's, and she was as fine as fivepence when I last saw her, unless you count her uneasiness. I tried to find out what troubled her, and I fear I only made her wary. She did say something to the effect that she always kept her promises."

"And that is odd?"

"It is when you consider she seemed to wish to confide to me what was bothering her."

Mrs. Cheney ws found only too glad to leave early. She also felt the disquiet that permeated the rooms. "I declare," she said in a soft voice, "I would rather be home under the covers of my bed."

Sir Peter joined them on the ride, inviting himself and accepting Mrs. Cheney's appreciation with calm assurance.

Emma shrugged at her dearest mama's transparent hopes and turned her thoughts to her friend Amelia.

"Would you like to find out if Lady Amelia has taken ill?"

"Oh, yes," Emma said gratefully.

They paused before the Littleton home, but found no one there.

"I believe the earl and his countess were to dine at Mansion House this evening. Could no one tell you anything about Amelia?"

"Not a word. She is not to home."

Emma frowned, mulling over some of the peculiar remarks Amelia had uttered in the past week. When they arrived at the Cheney residence, the trio entered the house, and Mrs. Cheney went off to consult with Oldham regarding her husband and refreshments.

Emma stayed in the entry hall, toying with her silver mesh reticule, wondering again about the look she had seen in Sir Peter's eyes this morning. What would he do if alone with her? But then, if she were so silly as to fall in love with an utterly impossible man, she could jolly well speculate and it would serve her right if he waltzed off with someone else.

"Do you have fears for Lady Amelia?"

"Oh, I do, indeed. Remember when we met Amelia in the park? She was with Mr. Swinburne. Did you not think she acted as though he had some manner of hold over her? Or am I being fanciful?"

"You believe he might elope with her?"

Emma gasped at the bold words that when spoken, were ominous. "I do. That odious dandy needs her plump dowry. Regardless of the airs he puffs about, I suspect he needs money quite badly, and soon."

"Do you think I should go after them?" When Emma nodded emphaticaly, he added, "Would your brother come along?"

Emma had been wishing to follow Amelia, for little things were beginning to return, dredged up from her memory. The notion of going off as her brother offered her the chance, for it was unlikely that she could travel as herself.

"While I shall remain here, I believe George would relish the chance to puncture the pretensions of that detestable Reginald Swinburne. I shall give him the message. Where can he meet you?"

Sir Peter considered this a moment, then said, "I will return to Bruton Street to change and be back here as quickly as possible. If George could be waiting for me, we can leave London immediately. I suppose they would flee to Scotland?"

"I do not think so," Emma said thoughtfully. "Amelia mentioned that Swinburne had relatives on the Isle of Guernsey, and you know they do not require the calling of banns there. She also seemed to be concerned about danger to shipping, which could also refer to the boats that sail to the island. She even knew that it costs only five shillings to take the boat from Southampton to Guernsey. Is it not possible they went in that direction?"

"He might convince her that he takes her to his family," Sir Peter said with an agreeing nod.

"I will find George," Emma said, edging toward the stairs while wondering how she would manage the change of clothing without Braddon's help.

Sir Peter agreed, then clapped on his hat while leaving the house in a hurry.

"Dear me," Mrs. Cheney complained when she returned to the entry hall. "He certainly left in a rush. I had thought we might have a bit of tea or sherry."

"He had an errand, Mama. And I must go up to bed, for I am dreadfully tired," Emma said, wishing she might confide in her mother, but afraid to explain, for it would unleash all manner of problems.

Leaving her mother murmuring to herself while pattering along the hall to the morning room, Emma lifted her skirts and hurried up the stairs to her room. She must change and be ready to go at once. The worst thing in the world would be for Amelia to marry Swinburne.

But Emma found the challenge of becoming George once again and charging off in the company of the man whom she adored to be immensely agreeable. Together they would find their quarry.

Chapter 14

EMMA waited until it grew silent below, then slipped down the darkened stairs to the entry. Oldham was attending her mother, and so she could leave the house with no one the wiser. The carefully worded note left on her dressing table would explain enough when she was far away.

Her departure went far better than she had dared to hope. Wrapped in a cloak with a soft brim hat pulled down about her face, she doubted her own mother would know her.

Her ears strained for the sound of a carriage, and as soon as she heard the clip-clop of the horses' approach, she stepped to the side of the street. He was driving a barouche, a vehicle popular with the sporting gentlemen. Emma supposed that he liked to travel in a fast, safe carriage out to the racecourses, although she couldn't recall his mentioning going to races.

When the barouche pulled up before the Cheney house, Sir Peter urged her inside. He sat up front where the driver usually sat. No groom was present to assist Emma. But then, George would have managed for himself, and so she did, flinging the door open with surprising ease.

Emma hopped up and inside, then almost gasped when she saw Lord Worcester had joined them. She hadn't counted upon this complication. Lord Worcester was not nearsighted in the least. However, he seemed to pay her no attention, urging Sir Peter to great speed.

"Swinburne has a good deal of time on us, best take the fastest route out of town," Lord Worcester called out.

Sir Peter merely nodded, guiding the horses with skill through the thoroughfares toward Westminster Bridge and the road that led south and east to Southampton—and with any luck, the pair of runaways.

They clattered along the darkened streets, avoiding merry-makers on their way home from parties and carriages and chairs returning from balls and routs. Here and there a house gleamed with lights from every window, evidence of a party within. Otherwise, an occasional flambeau outside a front door or candles shining through a window offered small illumination for the travelers.

Worcester turned to Emma and said, "Do you have any idea as to when they might have left? Did Emma have the least clue?"

Taking note that Worcester had not identified her as Emma, no doubt due to the lack of light, Emma replied, "Amelia called on my sister this morning. Emma said she appeared nervous and most ill at ease. But . . . it might have been anytime after that."

"We paused to question her maid," Lord Worcester explained. "Amelia did not leave there until this evening, supposedly to attend a masquerade. She took a bandbox, which presumably held her costume. Claimed she was to change at your house with Emma."

"And darling Emma was at Almack's this evening. I danced with her," Sir Peter called back from where he perched.

Emma took note of his use of the word *darling* and hugged it to her heart.

The carriage was open to the front, although the hood curved over where they sat, offering protection from the chill of the evening and the wind, which had risen some.

Wrapping George's cloak about her for greater warmth, Emma subsided into the corner of the barouche and hoped Lord Worcester continued to stare straight ahead.

"I had not expected Amelia to do such a bird-brained thing," Lord Worcester complained.

"Why do you quarrel with her forever and anon?" Emma wondered aloud. Then, recalling that George might not know this, she added, "Emma says you two have a go at it every time you are together."

"I have always been in the habit of doing so since we were tots. It was only when I saw that odious Swinburne paying court to her with his perfumed violets and scented note paper and that blasted violet poodle that I realized I could never permit her to marry the wretch."

"Violet poodle?" Emma exclaimed in amazement. She hadn't seen this apparition.

"He insists the dog adds to his consequence, and he adores violets, demmed twiddlepoop. It is his own innovation and sets him apart from all others—or so he claims." Lord Worcester sighed, slumping back into his corner of the commodious vehicle with a decidedly blue-deviled expression, from what little Emma could see in the dim light of the lamps that had been clipped to the frame on either side of the driver.

The carriage had been modified so as to drive through the night, and Emma prayed that they would have no accident along the way. Too many stories had reached her ears of nighttime terrors on the road.

They clattered through the Pimlico Gate while scarcely slowing down, then dashed across the Westminster Bridge, which was quiet this time of night. Once over the bridge Sir Peter urged the horses to run flat out.

The lights from Vauxhall glimmered through the trees and shown into the sky. Memories of her evening there with Sir Peter returned to bring a wistful smile to her lips. Maybe, just maybe, she might escape from this predicament and at least have a stab at her heart's desire.

Loving Sir Peter, as she confessed she did, she *must* have hope. She could not live without some shred of confidence that all would turn out well in the end.

The bridge and Vauxhall, along with her memories, behind them, Sir Peter again urged the horses to greater speed. Once through the Kennington Gate, London was far distant. There was nothing much to see, for although the clouds were thin and scattered, the moon wasn't full.

Emma was certain they clipped along at a good speed—at least ten miles per hour now they were in the country. She suspected a cloud of dust rose in the air behind them, for even the better roads were not free of this nuisance.

Rather than sit in silence, Emma decided to attempt conversation. Perhaps if she might find out something of Lord Worcester's feelings for Amelia, she might be able to help the pair.

"You care for Amelia, do you not?" Emma ventured into forbidden territory, that of another's most personal feelings.

"You might say that," he admitted reluctantly.

"I doubt she believes that to be the case . . . from what Emma has said," Emma added hastily. It was very difficult to remember that she was not herself.

"As to that,—" He stopped, possibly reflecting on his past words and actions, "Well, my concern for her ought to tell her something." He sounded so indignant that Emma stifled a laugh with difficulty.

"Somehow, I believe a young lady likes to be told of a gentleman's feelings on the subject. I know Emma would," she said.

"Indeed? You must be very close to your sister in that case," came the dry rejoinder.

"We are surprisingly close," Emma agreed, thinking that if Lord Worcester but knew the truth, he would be vastly amused.

"I still say the chit is daft in the head for running off with Swinburne when she could have me."

Emma wanted to hit the lofty gentleman right over his conceited head. "Since I doubt if Amelia has acquired the ability to read minds, you may have to relent and tell her of your affection in so many words. Besides, from what Emma said, 'tis possible she did not go willingly. She was most worried about the dangers from the French fleet, for you know how close the Isle of Guernsey is to French shores. When Emma met her in the park while driving out with Sir Peter, she noticed that Swinburne appeared to have some sort of control over Amelia, for she looked to him regarding a simple meeting with Emma."

"By Jove!" Edward exclaimed. That bit of information set him to thinking, leaving Emma once again to silence.

It was about then that trouble began. A coach approached from the opposite direction. Emma peered around Sir Peter, thinking that the oncoming vehicle, whose lights swayed in an alarming manner, seemed exceedingly erratic and the horses out of control.

"Hold on tight," Sir Peter called back at them.

It was clear to Emma that he would try to keep as far to one side of the road as possible, hoping to scrape past the wayward vehicle as best he could. She closed her eyes, unwilling to watch. Yet, if she were to be tossed into the ditch, she had best be prepared, so she reluctantly opened them again.

"Here it comes," Lord Worcester shouted in alarm.

Sir Peter veered to the left as far as he could without going completely off the road. For a few moments it seemed that they would make it. The other carriage sailed past them, the drunken driver waving his hat in merry glee.

Then the barouche hit a stone, the vehicle wavered, and over they went as neat as pie. Not a splinter, nor a break—just plopped on their side. When Emma had learned the barouche was a safe vehicle, she hadn't envisioned testing the knowledge. All that was likely to result from the accident was scraped paint and perhaps a dent or two and one smashed lantern. How fortunate that they landed on an upward slanting slope with thick grass to cushion the upset.

"This is a fine kettle of fish," Lord Worcester grumbled.

Having tumbled to the floor rather than upon Lord Worcester, Emma scrambled over the side of the carriage to join Sir Peter, who stood staring at the carriage with a most resigned expression.

"You all right?" he bothered to inquire while checking the barouche, carrying one of the lanterns so he could see.

"Fine," Emma said in a husky voice just a trifle lower than normal. "What can I do to help?"

"We have to right the dratted thing ourselves, or we could be stranded here for hours."

"Right-o," Lord Worcester replied. "Good thing this is a light vehicle."

"Light?" she whispered. Staring at the barouche, Emma tried to think how much use she would be; her muscles were hardly up to a gentleman's, particularly one who sparred at Jackson's. In her estimation the carriage looked as heavy as lead.

Sir Peter gave her an amused look, then joined Worcester by the side of the carriage where they discussed the best approach to righting the vehicle.

Whether or not they did, Emma had a sinking feeling that this was a prelude to an unsuccessful trip. By the time they managed to reach Southampton, Amelia would most likely be long gone. Unless . . . the little minx truly did not wish to go and she managed a diversion or two along the way.

"I am dreadfully hungry, Mr. Swinburne," Amelia complained.

"We stopped for tea at the last inn," Reginald Swinburne replied, clearly vexed with his chosen bride.

"Be that as it may, I am hungry and when I am hungry I can become horridly ill. I do not wish to cause a problem, but it is utterly wretched to be ill in a carriage," she cried, ending with a most affecting sob. She pulled her handkerchief from her reticule to dab at her nose, then her mouth, and hoped she looked as pale and wan as the looking glass had revealed after she had applied a generous amount of rice powder to her face.

"Very well," came the reply through undoubtedly gritted teeth. He pulled into the inn that stood at the edge of Basingstoke, then turned with an impatient look at Amelia.

"Thank you," she said demurely. Amelia accepted the assistance of the groom who came dashing up to help, then tottered into the inn on Swinburne's arm.

"Tea, I believe, and perhaps a nice slice of roast beef with potatoes and the tiniest wedge of pigeon pie followed by a dainty sliver of poppy seed cake ought to do me for a little." She wasn't certain she could eat all that, but she would give it her best.

"Good grief," Mr. Swinburne muttered. "I had no idea you possessed such an expensive appetite."

"I brought all my pin money as you suggested, dear Reginald. I shall pay for my own food," she declared with the air of a martyr.

"I have sufficient blunt for now," he snapped. Then realizing that this was perhaps not the best way to treat the woman he intended to marry, he amended, "I did not have time to procure funds from my bank before we left. When we reach Guernsey, there will be not the least problem."

Amelia gave him a skeptical look. From what she suspected, he most likely was in Dun Territory and owed everyone. How could she have allowed herself to be so taken in by this violet-scented rogue now escaped her. He might be a dandy and appear as though he wouldn't bother to harm a flea, but underneath he was something else.

It was all Edward's fault. Had he not driven her utterly mad with his stupidly obtuse refusal to see her other than the little girl next door—and a pest, at that—she would never have given Reginald Swinburne more than an amused glance. She had played her part well, until even dearest Emma had been convinced and cautioned her against Swinburne.

How she wished she had taken that advice. She never dreamed that Reginald Swinburne possessed the spirit to kidnap her—for that is what it amounted to, as she went against her inclinations—and flee to Southampton. She held little hope that Emma had taken the hints dropped to her. Emma had seemed most preoccupied for some time now, most likely with thoughts about Sir Peter Dancy.

Oh, if Edward only had half of Sir Peter's sensitivity and astuteness, she would have been married for at least a year by now. Wretched man!

The food arrived and Amelia gave a dismayed look at the quantity before her. The only good thing about it was that it would take time to consume and time was about the only thing in her favor at this point.

"All right now, while George pulls on the strap over there, you and I will push from this side, agreed?" Sir Peter pointed to the strap attached to the roof of the right side of the vehicle. The other end of strap wound around one of Emma's hands; she prayed that she would be able to do what had been asked of her. While tall, she wasn't sure of her strength.

"Sounds as though it might work," Worcester admitted.

"Let's go then, or we will never make it to Southampton by tomorrow, much less in time to stop Swinburne."

Sir Peter and Worcester positioned themselves against the lower side of the barouche, taking hold of the roof. With much straining of muscles and a good deal of pulling on Emma's part, they managed to lift it part of the way. But that was all.

"Pity we can't use the horses," Emma murmured.

"I suppose we could, although I don't know the beasts all that well," Sir Peter said of the horses received at the last staging inn.

The animals were taken around, the straps attached to the harness, then Sir Peter led them along, watching with wary eyes as to their response. They proved to be easy-tempered and agreeable to a bit of work other than pulling a carriage. Within a remarkably short time the barouche had been righted.

"Well," Worcester declared with surprise, "it's a good thing we had George with us, or we'd be still trying to push the dratted thing up."

"George never fails to amaze me," Sir Peter added, while sorting out the bits and pieces attached to the horses, and connecting the proper lines to the barouche.

Emma watched from a distance, well shadowed from any light. She studied Sir Peter's face, strongly lit by the lantern. While tired, he revealed strength of character and a certain integrity that she admired greatly. But then, was there anything she didn't find to like in the man—with perhaps the exception of his insistence that George learn to fence? And even that was not so bad anymore.

"I have always wanted to see Winchester Cathedral," Lady Amelia declared as the carriage bounced along the road into the city. "I read there is a charming little river here, and now I shan't see it or anything," she wailed. "I believe I need another cup of tea."

"Not again!" Swinburne declared, obviously dismayed. "It is but twelve miles from here to Southampton. Could you not wait another hour or so."

"You'll not easily find horses to travel that fast," she said firmly. "I should like a cup of tea. Else I shall be ill."

Swinburne pulled into the yard of the next inn, resigned to a long delay. It was then he discovered that one of the wheels had a serious crack and urgently required changing. It seemed to cap the trip for him, and he swore violently with total disregard for Amelia's tender ears.

The barouche rattled along High Street and beneath the imposing Southampton Bargate about ten hours or so after departing from London. Had they not had the delay, Sir Peter might have made the trip in about eight hours, given speedy changes of horses and not bothering with meals.

A tired Emma searched along the street, looking for something that might offer help or perhaps a glimpse of Amelia or Swinburne. At the Royal George Inn on Lower High Street they drew to a halt. She felt pity for the poor horses, who had most nobly performed for the equally tired Sir Peter.

"This looks like a good place in which to inquire." Lord Worcester jumped from the carriage as soon as it had come to a halt.

All along their route it was Worcester who had rushed into the inns to inquire if the pair had been seen and when. At discovering that they had fallen prey to a damaged carriage, and that Amelia had insisted upon a meal, thus causing a delay, he had taken heart.

"Couldn't possibly have made the boat to Guernsey this morning, I'll wager," he said with growing confidence as he disappeared into the inn.

Sir Peter handed over the barouche and horses to the ostler who hurried forth from the stable area. He strolled back to stand by Emma, who was blinking in the morning sun and wishing for a cozy, warm bed in which she might drift off to sleep. Now if Lord Worcester paid her not the least attention until she could find a shadowy corner, she just might scrape through this.

"We have come to the end of the line," he observed.

"I hope they did *not* make the boat to Guernsey. If she went reluctantly, she may have found reasons for delay—like the meals along the way. Emma said she can be perverse when she wants."

"Emma seems to confide a great number of things to you. Remarkable." Sir Peter pointed to the door of the inn and suggested they go inside.

More than willing to escape the revealing light of early morning, Emma needed no nudging. She marched inside the inn with promptness that brought a pleased smile to Sir Peter's face.

Inside the inn Emma immediately spotted Swinburne slouched in a chair on the far side of the common room close to the fireplace. He looked more than disgruntled; he looked utterly furious and extremely haggard, not to mention ready to throttle someone. The sight of the dandy in apparel that was less than pristine and hair that appeared downright tatty made Emma grin. She suspected that Amelia had given him a trying time of it.

"Where is she, Swinburne?" Lord Worcester challenged in a voice that not only sounded menacing but even gave Emma the chills. Worcester made Swinburne's name sound like something particularly nasty.

The dandy jumped to his feet, overturning the chair in his haste. The fatigue pushed aside, he now looked ready to flee if such a thing were possible.

"She is upstairs asleep, thank God," he cried in defense. "At least she can't eat while abed."

Worcester gave the dandy a confused look.

At her side Sir Peter murmured, "Perhaps you could persuade a maid to show you where Amelia's room is located. If we could but spirit her out the back door, we could leave Swinburne here to suffer his just deserts."

Not pausing to wonder why he didn't do the job himself, or why he asked her rather than encourage Lord Worcester to seek his childhood friend and love, Emma merely nodded and slipped from the room.

The maid took one look at Emma and almost refused.

"I'm in disguise, for you know no lady may travel alone," Emma whispered. "We are here to rescue a dear friend from a forced marriage."

Tickled to be permitted to foil the endeavor made by the obnoxious man in the common room, the maid beckoned Emma to follow her up the stairs. Once at the top they quietly made their way to a door at the end of the neat hall.

At a nod from the maid Emma used her natural voice to call to Amelia.

The door crashed open, and Amelia flung herself into Emma's sympathetic arms. Then Amelia froze and stepped back before bursting into giggles.

"Whatever are you doing in those clothes, Emma Cheney?"

"Chasing after you," Emma replied while urging Amelia back into her room.

Carefully shutting the door behind her, Emma walked to the window to peer out to the back of the inn. Sir Peter's barouche, looking a trifle battered but still serviceable, had been set to with fresh horses and waited at the ready.

"Do you wish to marry Mr. Swinburne?" Emma said when she turned around to face her dear friend.

"Not in the least," Amelia snapped. "That dreadful dandy! I merely wished to bring Edward to his senses. Only nothing worked out as I planned." She sank down on the edge of a pretty bed and stared at Emma with a vexed expression. "Edward is so obtuse he could be a block of stone."

"He needed to be taught a lesson and how important you are to him," Emma replied with caution. She did not want to reveal Edward's show of egotism.

Amelia brightened. "Do you think he really cares for me? Truly?"

"I do. He has been nearly demented all the way from London." Emma gave a tired sigh and a longing look at the bed. It was undoubtedly soft and comfortable, and her bones nearly ached with fatigue.

"Well, how do I escape this inn? Now that it hasn't been perfectly acceptable. The food is excellent."

"Mr. Swinburne said something about your appetite." Emma gave Amelia a curious look.

Amelia giggled. "I was perfectly dreadful all the trip. I made him stop for tea or a meal at every town we passed through. I feel certain I exhausted his patience, not to mention his purse by the time we reached here. We missed the boat, and that made him furious."

"We had best slip down the back stairs and settle in Sir Peter's barouche." Emma picked up the bandbox in her role as George, then paused by the door. "Say nothing about my masquerade to anyone, even when we are just the four of us." She didn't bother to explain why, and Amelia didn't ask, concentrating on the matter at hand.

They made a silent escape from the inn, then climbed into the barouche. Once settled, Emma sent a groom to the common room with a message to Sir Peter.

She sat drowsing against the side of the barouche when the clatter of horses alerted her to the arrival of another carriage. Curiosity compelled her to peek around the corner of the hood and she began to laugh.

"Whatever is it now," Amelia demanded.

"It wanted only this," Emma said with a tired giggle. "That, unless I am very much mistaken, is Lady Titheridge's traveling coach!"

Amelia scrambled around Emma to peer at the newest arrival. The door to the carriage opened, and a groom rushed forward to assist the person within.

"Well," her ladyship declared upon descending from her carriage and catching sight of Emma and Amelia peeking at her, "you had best transfer to my coach, and we shall leave at once. How fortunate we found you, Lady Amelia. It would be a dreadful scandal if word of this seeped out to the *ton*. I propose we visit my country house for a day or so before returning to Town. That should silence any tabby who dares to meow."

Emma and Amelia exchanged wordless looks that spoke volumes. Not waiting for a second summons, Emma hurried from the barouche, then helped Amelia to descend. She urged her into the traveling coach, then followed as quickly as possible, shrinking into the corner with the intention of going to sleep as soon as may be.

"Shall I tell all to Lady Titheridge?" Amelia asked in a rather small voice.

"I rather expect she knows most of it, but you might give her the details of your trip here. She does enjoy a good laugh," Emma said musingly.

Half asleep by the time Lady Titheridge returned, Emma watched through lowered lids while her ladyship settled onto the opposite seat next to Amelia.

"It is all settled," she announced complacently. "The boys will come along later. Mr. Swinburne is off to the Isle of Guernsey for an indefinite stay." To Emma she added, "George has been called to Sussex. But never fear, I have a selection of gowns for you in the boot."

"I wish I knew what was going on," Lady Amelia complained. "Nobody tells me anything."

"Peagoose," Emma replied affectionately. "Not to worry about a thing. In fact, the less you know, the better. Rather, you should concentrate on what you intend to say to Edward when you confront him at Lady Titheridge's."

The traveling coach moved out from the inn yard and along the Lower High Street until they were once again on the London Road—going away from Southampton.

"Indeed, I will," Lady Amelia declared. Turning to Lady Titheridge, she began to explain. "You see, Edward has treated me like a child since we were in short coats. Of course I *was* one when we first played together, but I am not a child now," she said with an indignant nod.

Her ladyship exchanged looks with Emma and winked.

"At any rate, I thought to encourage Mr. Swinburne with the hope that it would make Edward jealous. I did not count on Mr. Swinburne needing money and kidnaping me so I would have to marry the wretch. It is all Edward's fault."

"It is?" her ladyship dutifully inquired.

"If he had asked me to wed him a year ago, this need not have happened at all, and so I shall tell him the first chance I have!"

"Oh, I am so pleased that Peter sent me that message to follow him. I would not have missed this for the world," Lady Titheridge murmured to Emma.

Emma nodded her agreement, although most muted, and promptly dozed off.

Chapter 15

"YOU slept the entire way to Under Petersbridge and right up to this house," Amelia complained when Emma woke with a start. It did not matter that Amelia had dozed most of the trip; Emma had slept all the way.

The carriage was motionless, no more jouncing over roads nor pauses for a change of horses. It was that very stillness that had awakened an exhausted Emma. Judging by the sun, it was rising noon. The door of the carriage stood open, and Amelia waited to exit with impatience.

"Well, I had been up all night, not to mention helped right the barouche after we were forced to the side of the road and overturned." Emma shuddered at the memory of that upset and what might have happened.

"Overturned! You never said a word about that," Amelia said with an accusing look. "Nor have you completely explained about your odd attire. I must say, those pantaloons are most shocking."

"It was all terribly involved. And explanations take too long," Emma said, still not quite awake and yawning hugely. She much preferred a good night's sleep in her own bed, or at least one where she was not disturbed.

Lady Titheridge had paused patiently before her door and now beckoned to the girls. "Come, you must have a bite to eat, then a bath, and after that you may rest again if you please."

Amelia gave Emma a look that said she would demand details later on, then turned to leave.

They climbed down the traveling coach and stretched as much as was proper for young ladies. Emma gazed appreciatively at the pretty manor house of warm red brick with mullioned windows and a large oak door with the typical Tudor arch.

A lovely garden full of pinks, wallflowers, and Canterbury bells bloomed to either side of the brick walk. A wisteria vine now past its bloom clung to a far wall with a pretty cascade of delicate greenery.

Over the entry door initials had been incised many years before. It read, "C.T. & J.T. 1692." Emma rather liked that little touch. The first owners of this home must have felt great pride in it one hundred and twenty-three years ago. It was a house of immense charm and seemed most welcoming to a weary traveler.

"Hurry, hurry," insisted her ladyship. "You want to change from your clothing before the boys arrive."

Emma grinned at the thought of Sir Peter being called a boy. Anyone less to be considered a boy she could not imagine. But it would never do for them to see her in her garb as George . . . at least Lord Worcester. It was bad enough that Amelia might blurt out something at an inauspicious moment. She ran ahead to present the matter to her ladyship.

Lady Titheridge convinced Amelia that Emma had donned a man's clothing so she might pursue Amelia with Sir Peter and Edward and not fear censure. Amelia understood that threat immediately. Emma trailed her friend into the house while wondering how this would all work out without a disaster of some sort.

The muted gray slate floor was clean and crisp in appearance, and the soft brown of the oak paneling offered intricate carving and interesting shadows. A long-case clock off to one side chimed the hour of twelve.

Lady Titheridge again fussed at them, urging the girls up the staircase with its carved newels, pierced balustrading, and rich carving. There was an air of dignity and spaciousness in the entry and stairs that greatly appealed to Emma.

"Peter inherits this one day. He said that of all our houses, it is his favorite," Lady Titheridge informed Emma in passing while they hurried up to the second floor.

"I can well see why," Emma replied, wondering who might reside here with Sir Peter come the day he gained this lovely home as his.

A bath in a copper slipper tub revived Emma. The sight of her appearance in the looking glass, dressed in a charming green-blue sarcenet gown edged with fine lace did wonders for her disposition. Braddon threaded a pretty matching ribbon through her curls, offered a dash of lavender scent, then stood back to survey her results.

"You will do. I doubt if Lord Worcester will see his companion of the road in this pretty young lady." She shared a look of knowing with Emma.

Emma glanced at the looking glass and admitted she looked considerably different.

When she joined Lady Titheridge, she curtsied deeply, then offered her appreciation for the use of the lovely gown.

"You ought not do so much, my lady, but I do thank you. It could have been most awkward to appear in George's clothing before Lord Worcester. I will take great care of the gown. Had you sought out my dresses at home, my mother would have been most alarmed."

"Sensible girl," her ladyship said with approval. "But the dress is yours. I have not had such a diverting time in an age. Bless dear Peter for believing an old lady like me would be able to keep up with you young people."

"You are not the least old. I suspect you are younger in heart than any of us," Emma said with a laugh.

There was the sound of a door slamming shut, then boots crossing the entry tile. Emma gave Lady Titheridge a warning glance, then turned to face the entryway.

In moments Sir Peter and Lord Worcester stood in the doorway. Both men looked weary, yet satisfied about something.

"Hullo," Sir Peter said in greeting with a smile for Emma. "We finally arrived. Had to see that Swinburne boarded the boat to Guernsey."

"Did you actually see the boat leave?" Lady Amelia said from behind them.

"No," Lord Worcester admitted. "But he boarded and they were ready to pull anchor when we took off."

"I do not trust that man in the least," she snapped. "And as for Mr. Swinburne . . . Edward, if you had possessed one ounce of brains, I would not have been subjected to his odious attentions at all!" She glared at her beloved, then whirled about and left the house for the garden in what could only be described as a huff.

"Better go after her," Sir Peter advised. "Don't want her thinking up any other harebrained scheme to win you."

"You are off the mark there. She hates me," Edward replied with a gloomy face. He turned and headed in the direction his irate little love had gone.

"Ah, the path of true love is never smooth," Lady Titheridge said with a delighted smile.

"I was glad you found us in time. What happened to George?" Sir Peter inquired of his aunt while searching the room as though expecting to see George pop up from behind a chair.

"Well, he had to leave for Sussex," her ladyship said blandly. "A message came for him, and Emma thought to come along with it. Seems the workmen had found something interesting, and George felt obliged to hurry back."

"Indeed? how curiously interesting." He turned again to Emma, giving her a highly speculative look.

"I do hope it is something momentous," Emma said, followed by a delighted smile. "I know he wishes to marry Miss Johnson, and George may be patient when it comes to digging up Roman ruins, but not for his dear Beatrice."

"That is as it ought to be," Lady Titheridge said with a sidelong glance at Sir Peter. "A gentleman who waits too long to declare himself may find he is too late . . . missed the ship, as it were."

"Well, I think Worcester may make up for that lapse, dear aunt." Sir Peter settled onto the largest, most comfortable-looking chair in the room, seeming on the verge of falling asleep if given a few moments of peace.

"And you are so certain that I refer to Edward?" her ladyship said archly.

"Who else?" he said, followed by that sleepy grin that Emma could not fail to note and appreciate.

Ignoring her ladyship's implications that were so vague they meant nothing to her, Emma sought a place to rest. She settled securely on a chair near the window where she could watch Sir Peter and even note the happenings in the garden if she leaned forward a trifle.

"What happens next?" Lady Titheridge said, bent on discovering what her provoking nephew intended to do.

"I believe I shall embark on a nap, then a meal, then return to London in that order. With Swinburne out of the way, I can dismiss the man from Bow Street and that former pugilist as well."

"You are so certain that Swinburne was behind the attempted robbery?" Emma said with a frown.

Sir Peter nodded. "I had Harry Porter inquire into his background. Seems as though Swinburne has relatives in Guernsey with French connections. And Swinburne is in dire need of funds. Ergo, he must be the one."

"I hope so. What a dreadful man he is, to use Amelia so badly." Emma shared a look with her ladyship that said a great deal concerning the problems that faced a young woman who possessed a goodly portion.

"She has escaped with less difficulty than might be expected or that she possibly deserved," Sir Peter declared, barely suppressing a yawn.

"I only hope that you have the right of it, and that with Swinburne out of the way you may know peace," Lady Titheridge said shrewdly, apparently not having a great deal of faith in her nephew's calculations of the moment.

He yawned hugely behind a hastily raised hand, then rose from the chair. "Another minute and you will have to walk around a sleeping body." He strolled from the room and tramped up the stairs and out of sight.

Emma rose to stand by the window, contemplating the mental image of Sir Peter's sleeping body until she realized the impropriety of her thoughts.

"Oh, dear," Lady Titheridge said at once.

Emma wondered if her ladyship read minds.

With her gesture at the garden to the rear of the house, Emma looked up to view the spat between Lady Amelia Littleton and Edward, Lord Worcester. It appeared to be a battle royal.

"I do not feel inclined to interfere with those two," Lady Titheridge stated decisively. "Anyone who steps between combatants is likely to find his own nose bloodied." At Emma's startled glance, her ladyship added, "My late husband was fond of saying that, which is why he always stayed out of wars and the like. He had no intention of dying in a duel."

"If I may inquire, how did his lordship go aloft?" Emma asked, feeling that with her ladyship it would not be an impertinence.

"He caught a dreadful cold and would not go to bed. Died four days later. Which only goes to prove, I suppose, that when your time has come, no matter what you would do, you go." Lady Titheridge wandered off from the room. Emma could hear her footsteps fading away down the hall.

Emma reflected on this bit of philosophy while watching the altercation in the garden. Suddenly realizing that she ought not even be observing so intimate a matter as a quarrel between two who truly did love one another—in spite of contrary opinions—she also left the room.

Out in the garden Amelia faced Edward with fiery resolution. "Shall we agree to disagree about this, Edward?" She stood face-to-face with him, her hands clenched at her sides, hidden in the folds of primrose yellow muslin.

"Now that sounds like a first-rate idea," he agreed. "I vow you have had me flummoxed."

"I wished you to see me as other than the little girl next door," Amelia said, taking a tentative step toward him.

"You succeeded admirably," he admitted with a grin. "I find myself quite attracted to my little neighbor."

"Oh, I fear I do love you, you know, for all my sins. I fought it and tried not to love you, for you must be the most utter wretch in the country, but 'tis no use. I still love you," she said suddenly, sounding utterly exasperated with herself, "and all you can do is treat me like an infant."

"I say!" Edward replied, much struck with this admission. "Upon examination, I believe I care for you as well, little one." He bent to kiss her, and she gave him a smile that should have warned him.

"I am *not* an infant," she insisted quietly. Then Lady Amelia Littleton wrapped her loving arms about Edward, Lord Worcester, and proceeded to demonstrate just how grown up she had become.

*   *   *

Emma discovered Lady Titheridge in the morning room, going over some mail. "May I be of any help, my lady?" Emma asked politely.

"Actually, I was wondering if George might be able to return to London should we need him." Lady Titheridge gave Emma a cautionary look.

"Need him?" Emma echoed. "What do you expect to happen? And how in the world could I, that is, George, help?" She groped for a chair, seating herself with care while anxiously watching Lady Titheridge.

Her ladyship crossed to check that the hallway was empty, then turned to face Emma. "I am not so convinced that Swinburne is the culprit. Oh"—she waved her hand dismissively— "he kidnapped that little peagoose for money, but I wonder if the dandy would actually steal the Egyptian jewels. *That* is a messy business, and requires bold marksmanship. Now tell me, does Reginald Swinburne seem to you the sort of person who could perform such a daring deed?"

"Not in the least," Emma replied truthfully. "I have been mulling it over and reached the same conclusion."

"So, we are agreed that you will be on call should you be needed. I confess that I worry about my nephew. I am dreadfully fond of the boy, and he has no heirs to succeed him. I would see him married and settled down with at least half a dozen children about his knees. To do that he has to be alive and find him a wife."

Emma could feel the heat in her cheeks and prayed that she did not blush a fiery red as sometimes happened. She might wish that she had a place in Sir Peter's future, but it was rather silly to daydream about it as she had been doing.

"I am sure he will oblige you before too long. He seems a dutiful nephew," Emma replied in a colorless voice.

"I am counting upon that," her ladyship said.

Before Emma could discover what might be contained in that obscure remark, Amelia and Edward appeared in the doorway, looking at once meek and triumphant, if such a thing were possible.

"Edward and I have seen the light," Amelia announced with an evangelistic fervor.

"What she means is that we mended our fences and are to be married," Lord Worcester explained with a wry look at his treasure. "Since our parents are best of friends, I misdoubt there will be the slightest complaint in that quarter."

"Good." Lady Titheridge studied the pair, then said, "I think you both should rest, then we shall have a meal before going on to London. The news of your betrothal will allay any gossip." At their astonished expressions Lady Titheridge continued, "I know, we are all tired, but Peter desires to return to London immediately, and I believe we should all go with him. It should not be dangerous," she concluded in a hesitant voice, as though she was certain it might be the opposite.

"Amelia and I could follow later," Lord Worceser said hesitantly, placing a protective arm about his little termagant.

"Oh, no," Amelia declared. "If Lady Titheridge thinks there might be trouble, I, for one," and she glared at her Edward, "intend to be along. Besides, I do not wish to be thought coming."

Her downcast and demure expression brought a chuckle to all in the room.

"Why do we not all take a nice nap before it is time to leave? I have no doubt Sir Peter will wish to hurry once he awakens."

Immediately seeing the reason of this, Amelia went up the stairs with Emma. Just outside her room she paused. "This has turned out very well for me, dearest Emma. I only hope it goes as well for you."

Pretending not to understand her point, Emma merely nodded and slipped inside her door.

Several hours later the group straggled into the dining room to survey the repast that had been set out for them.

"I say," Lord Worcester said in wonder, "I had not realized how hungry I was."

"I cannot eat more than a morsel," Amelia declared, looking at the food with mild revulsion. "I have consumed enough to last me a week."

Emma smiled, then said, "You were exceedingly clever to pretend hunger. It saved you from disaster."

Amelia tossed a smug glance at Edward, then sipped tea and munched a ginger biscuit.

Sir Peter changed the topic, and the others fell to their meal with hearty appetites.

Only slightly more than another hour had past when the traveling coach drew up before the house again. Emma was sorry to leave, for there was great charm here. She had admired the view from her bedroom window before coming down to join the others. She would liked to have spent days exploring the pretty gardens and the stream that wandered along the property.

"You do realize that it will be late before we arrive in London. Can anyone think of a plausible reason for this particular group to be absent from the city for two days?" Lady Titheridge asked as they sipped coffee and tea following their meal. "In the event that someone is so inquisitive as to ask, that is."

"Indeed," Emma chimed in, "we cannot allow a hint to escape that Mr. Swinburne absconded Town with Amelia at his side." She looked to Sir Peter for a solution, as he seemed to be the one who thought up most things.

"Why does everyone look at me?" he complained. "We have a near six-hour journey ahead of us. May I suggest we put our minds to good use while on the way?"

That effectively broke up the meal, and they straggled out to where the traveling coach and the barouche awaited them.

"Ladies into the traveling coach," Sir Peter said and gestured. "Worcester and I will attempt to set a record in the barouche," he concluded.

Since Emma had already determined that to be the best plan, she gave him an impatient look, then hopped into the carriage with no further words exchanged.

"I hope they have no problems. I wonder if we might not have done better to spend another night. Although I expect your parents would be frantic by that time, even if the boys took notes to them explaining where you are."

"Parents have a way of worrying about the most simple things," Amelia observed. "I imagine when they learn that Edward and I intend to marry they will forget to quiz me about my stay. I told them I was with you, Emma."

"Good grief!" Emma replied, thinking of her note that said the reverse.

The hours passed faster than expected, for Amelia chattered about her forthcoming marriage until one by one they drifted asleep. Even the necessary pauses to change horses failed to do more than rouse them slightly.

It was nearly midnight when Emma crept into her house by way of the little door to the scullery. No one was about, and she succeeded reaching her room with little ado.

Morning proved quite a different matter.

Never the most suspicious of women, Mrs. Cheney entered Emma's room early the next morning—that is to say, about a quarter to twelve—waving Emma's note in the air.

"And what was this all about, missy?" she demanded. "I have been fraught with worry. There was a celebration of the great victory last evening, and you were nowhere in evidence."

"Napoleon has been defeated?" Emma exclaimed, sliding from her bed to give her a mother a hug. "Tell me all you know, for we did not learn anything on our traveling. Lady Titheridge begged Amelia and I to assist her. The poor dear has no children and declared she needed our help. Do you know we made a flying trip to her ladyship's pretty home just outside Under Petersbridge? It is so lovely, Mama."

Fascinated by this information and hoping to obtain the details of the home to share with Mrs. Bascomb and Lady Hamley, Mrs. Cheney plumped herself on Emma's favorite chair, demanding to know all. First, she informed Emma that while details were few, there had been a battle at a little town called Waterloo, and the great Wellington had indeed defeated the nasty Napoleon. A small illumination took place on some government buildings, or so she had heard. Mrs. Cheney and her husband had remained at home, disliking crowds.

Later Emma realized that her dearest mama never did ask what it was that Emma was required for, and that was a very good thing. Between the news of the great victory and the fascination with details of Lady Titheridge's manor house, the explanation had been neglected.

When Emma presented herself at Lady Titheridge's for tea that afternoon, she immediately inquired for news of Sir Peter.

"The boys broke the record, although I confess I did not know there had been one. They arrived a full hour before us!" her ladyship exclaimed with pride.

Not terribly impressed that the "boys" had risked their necks to be in London in such a rush, Emma shook her head, "No, I mean about the jewels. Sir Peter takes a most casual attitude toward them."

"Everything is quite fine, and I am not the least *unconcerned*, Miss Cheney," Sir Peter said, his voice distinctly chilly.

She whirled about to face the doorway, dismayed to be found saying words that might be construed as criticism. "I did not mean that you do not care about them. *I* fear that it was not Mr. Swinburne, and that someone else is responsible for the attempts." Emma clasped her hands in consternation at the formidable look that had settled on Sir Peter's face. At this rate, she would not have the most remote chance of attaching his interest.

"Dear Aunt," Sir Peter said with a bow in her direction, "do not fill this young head with mischief."

"She did not have to . . . I felt that way before she said a word," Emma said indignantly. "But I will confess that your problems were nearly driven from my head with the news from France. Is it not wonderful? Peace at last."

"Indeed!" Sir Peter raised his quizzing glass, which had the effect of giving Emma a case of the giggles.

They discussed the end of the war and the effect on the country for a few minutes, then Sir Peter raised his glass again to view Emma after she had declared that the French would no longer be a threat to his collection—they had no money.

"You odious man, put that dreadful thing away and tell us how you found things," Emma said when she could speak again.

"Harry Porter agrees with me. We believe there is nothing more to worry about, unless this chap takes a notion to sell the necklace elsewhere. Porter has been paid off, the pugilist dismissed, and I can once again concentrate on the display and collection. I wish your brother could be handy. I could use a few more drawings." He paced the floor of the drawing room, rubbing his chin in an absent, reflective manner.

"Emma is most talented with drawing," Lady Titheridge inserted. "I suspect it runs in the family."

The young lady in question found it difficult not to laugh at this preposterous statement, for George's ability was most rudimentary. Beatrice had proven to be a blessing with her sketching talent.

"Emma? Would it not raise a few eyebrows were she to enter a bachelor establishment?" he frowned at his aunt, then looked at Emma as though to study her reaction. Even if he had considered it before, he would not risk harming her name just to satisfy his wish of the moment. Having her come as George was entirely different.

Lady Titheridge sighed in acknowledgment of this truth. "Of course you are right. I fear you will have to manage on your own. Unless, of course, George should come to London for some reason."

"We have not had a letter from him in the past few days," Emma said. "I could write to him, find out his intentions."

"Would you?" Sir Peter said with relief. "I would welcome perhaps one more day of work, if he might spare me the time. I like his style, and it would be a nice touch to have all drawings done by the same artist."

They chatted for a brief time, then Sir Peter excused himself.

He had set the cat among the pigeons with his request, he reflected while running lightly down the stairs and out to where his carriage awaited. It was quite reprehensible of him to want Emma to *again* come to his home, but he really did want those remaining drawings, and how else to arrange it? He hoped that his scheming aunt would take matters in hand. She could usually be counted upon to see things his way.

Back at Bruton Street Radley opened the door for him before he had reached the top step.

"Well . . . is all in readiness, do you think?" he inquired of his butler and often conspirator when he wanted something out of the ordinary.

"Indeed, it is, sir," Radley confirmed. "How long do you think it will be before our artist appears?"

"I predict *he* will show up on my doorstep by tomorrow at the latest with some tale about finding a treasure."

"My, my," Radley said, all admiration.

*   *   *

"Good grief," Emma declared after Sir Peter had departed. She turned from the window where she had watched his carriage disappear from view around the corner in the direction of Berkeley Square. What are we to do?"

"That is simple," her ladyship countered. "George will have to make a flying trip to London for the purpose of assessing the value of the treasure he has uncovered. I hope he has dug up something of worth," she added as an afterthought.

"Do you realize how complicated this has become?" Emma demanded. "I vow, if I ever manage to squeak through this with my skin intact, it will be a miracle."

"How soon shall you have George pay a visit to Bruton Street?"

"It cannot be until tomorrow morning. I can only hope for a letter in the mail, else I will have to compose something to satisfy dear mama. I cannot like this deceit, dear ma'am." Emma gave Lady Titheridge a rueful look.

"I know. I feel dreadful about it myself," Lady Titheridge said in a cheerful voice.

Emma left shortly after that, worrying and wondering how in the world she might manage one more appearance at Bruton Street without detection. One of these days there was apt to come a person who was neither nearsighted nor absentminded nor totally absorbed in something else.

The following morning Emma presented herself at Lady Titheridge's establishment at an early hour. Her face wreathed in a broad smile, she hurried up the stairs to the room where she usually turned into George.

"Good news, I trust," her ladyship said as she entered, wrapped in her dressing gown.

"Oh, indeed there is. A letter *did* come from George, and he wrote that he has truly found a treasure! There are bracelets, necklaces, coins, all of unsurpassing beauty and value. He does intend to come to London soon, but has promised to stay with a friend who is one of the Antiquarian Society. Sir William travels with him, as does a respectable guard. There is no chance he will encounter Sir Peter. None at all."

"Good. You had best be on your way then. This should be

the last time you will need to act a charade. And since the defeat of the French, I am persuaded there is not the least thing to worry about."

Emma gave her ladyship a cautious look, then crossed her fingers.

Chapter 16

EMMA stared at the front door of the house on Bruton Street with more than a few misgivings. This would absolutely, positively be the last time she would come here in her disguise. No matter what.

When Radley ushered her along the hall to the workroom, she cast him a disbelieving look. Not so much as a raised eyebrow at Emma's appearance. He must be one of those marvelous butlers who neither saw nor heard anything unless he was supposed to, in which case Sir Peter was only to be envied.

Sir Peter stood on the far side of the room, studying a bronze statuette that Emma had not seen before. She passed a case containing a collection of scarabs to join him.

"I found this at the bottom of one of the boxes that contained the things brought from Egypt. It was wrapped in old clothes and papers, and I nearly threw the lot out."

Emma reached to gently touch the exquisite likeness of a woman, presumably a goddess of some sort. It was small, not more than eighteen inches tall. With her arms outstretched, she looked welcoming and almost tender in her expression. "Lovely, truly lovely," Emma said reverently.

"I intend to go to Egypt as soon as may be, now that hostilities have ceased. I want to learn more about the things my father brought here. These drawings ought to be of enormous help to me." Sir Peter gestured to the neatly matted representations Emma had created of the major finds.

Her heart sinking to her toes, Emma merely nodded sagely and murmured her agreement. How she longed to travel with Sir Peter and see the places where these exotic objects had originated. There was little chance of that occurring.

"I don't suppose you would like to join me? No," he said, answering his own question, "I imagine you will be off to Rome one of these days to explore that area. On your honeymoon, most likely. Lucky chap. However, I have similar plans. I intend to take my lady with me to Egypt," he announced with a sparkle in his eyes.

The announcement hit Emma with all the impact of an immense dray loaded to the hilt and pierced her heart like the épée Sir Peter had her use for practice—with the button off.

She tried to think of any particular woman with whom Sir Peter had been linked and could only come up with Richenda de Lacey. Anyone less likely to enjoy a trip to Egypt Emma could not imagine. Richenda was born to be pampered and could not survive such hardships as Emma had read about.

"I had not realized you were contemplating matrimony," Emma said in a frozen little voice. "May I be among the first to wish you happy?"

"You may," Sir Peter murmured, turning again to study the statuette.

"Actually, I shall be married quite soon," Emma countered, happy for her brother and Beatrice. "I had a spot of luck and dug up a treasure worthy of an emperor. I fancy it will make a bit of a stir in the antiquarian community." Emma was past caring whether Sir Peter ran into George at one of the meetings. She wished to be done with her promised help, then retreat.

But, oh, how she longed to spear Sir Peter with his blasted épée. He had teased her, kissed her, brought all manner of yearnings to her heart, and now she was to be dumped aside, abandoned like the wrappings from the statuette. But then, Richenda de Lacey had a plump dowry that would be useful in a trek to the realm of the pharaohs.

"My, that is a fierce expression," Sir Peter commented when he raised his face from his contemplation of the little bronze goddess.

"Indeed?" Smoothing her countenance into one of polite inquiry, Emma merely glanced at him, then took out her pencils and pad. She set to work, perched on one of the high stools. How she wished she might keep coming here to draw for Sir Peter, unrealistic though her desire might be. If her quiet hours in this wondrous room of treasures might go on, she would be most happy. With a bit of effort she managed to put aside the declaration of Sir Peter's impending marriage and concentrate on the drawings.

"She is a lovely thing, is she not?" Sir Peter said quietly over Emma's shoulder while she worked at a sketch of the goddess.

"Richenda? I suppose so. She is deemed a Diamond of the First Water by most." Once the words were said, Emma realized she had betrayed herself.

"How did *she* enter this conversation?"

Sir Peter seemed genuinely puzzled, and a tiny hope rose within Emma. "Well, Emma mentioned that you seemed most taken with the girl."

"No," Sir Peter replied vaguely. "I have another in mind."

"She does not know of your intent?" Emma said, unable to keep the surprise from her voice or face.

"She will before too long." Sir Peter produced other items he wished drawn, then sauntered from the room.

That man deserved to be rejected for his enormous conceit. Fancy planning to wed a girl and not telling her about it!

Emma worked at top speed, her hurt and anger lending impetus to her fingers. By noon she placed her beautifully colored drawings in a neat pile. Not seeing Sir Peter around, she intended to slip from the house with nothing more said. In fact, she decided that she had already said more than enough.

Still, she wondered who the woman was that Sir Peter intended to marry—if and when he remembered to ask the poor dear.

Radley bustled forth to greet Emma when she ventured into the hall. Any hope she had of slipping out without having to face Sir Peter again was abandoned when Radley spoke.

"Sir Peter wishes you to join him in the fencing room, Mr. Cheney. Will you follow me?" It was quite clear that denial was unthinkable.

Emma knew the way, but fell in behind Radley without a word. Indeed, she felt quite at a loss to understand why Sir Peter would want to see her, unless he merely wished to thank her for her efforts. Deciding that had to be the case, she braced herself for their final scene. After this she would go home and never, never don a disguise again as long as she lived. Charades were simply too dangerous to her peace of mind.

"Sir?" Radley said when he stepped into the room.

"Thank you, Radley. Done with the drawings, Cheney? I appreciate the superb work you do." Sir Peter turned around to face Emma, and she observed his garb with a sinking heart.

It was not possible that the dratted man wished to practice again! Apparently he did. He wore a short, neat-looking sort of jacket that buttoned up along one side. Emma felt at a disadvantage in her shirt with the ruffle along the opening below her neck. Her waistcoat and knee breeches seemed frivolous compared to his knit pantaloons that clung to that masculine form far too faithfully and offered a greater freedom of movement. Still, her garb had the advantage of concealment, and she needed that.

"I had not anticipated another bout of fencing, old fellow," Emma said gruffly. He made no reply.

She accepted the mask from him with a sense of fatality, then took the épée he handed her and walked to the *piste* with a sense of impending doom hanging over her head.

After saluting him, she began to perform the various positions, lunges, and parries that she had practiced in the privacy of her room. In her anger she was more aggressive than usual, perhaps wishing that she might sneak under his defense.

"You are improving your technique," he said, not seeming the least breathless from his exertions. He neared her side and looked down at her, his eyes glittering from behind the mask. Then, that look gone, he leaped back with one of his graceful maneuvers.

"Indeed," Emma snapped back, lunging at him in the hope of catching him off his guard. She succeeded for a moment, then he pushed her foil aside with ease.

Emma was puzzled when he said, "Enough." He returned the implements and masks to their places, then joined Emma in the stride to the front door. She hastily donned George's coat while they walked, thinking her exit was accomplished with unseemly speed.

"You will do well enough," he said, rather mysteriously to Emma's thinking.

"Is everything set for this evening, sir?" Radley said when Emma and Sir Peter joined him in the entry hall.

Looking at her nemesis, Emma wondered what was to happen this evening, although it certainly had nothing to do with her.

"Yes, all is in readiness." He turned again to Emma. "By the way, George, I took your sister's advice and planted a few hints of additional treasure in the various clubs and with the greatest gossips. Since Emma is convinced that a thief still lurks about London, I have set a trap for him. Harry Porter indicated he might stop by here later on, toward dark. Would you be so kind as to join us?" He thought a moment, then added, "I know you are occupied with your newly found treasure, but I could use your skill with the épée."

She was utterly speechless. Could he actually desire her help? But she was a mere woman, even if he thought she was George. Yet, he said she would do well enough and now he claimed to desire her skills.

Echoing her thought, she said, "You desire *me*?"

"I certainly do," Sir Peter replied with gratifying promptness. If Emma did not know of his interest in a particular woman, she might have wondered a trifle at that enthusiastic answer to George's query.

She considered what her mama planned for the evening and at last nodded her agreement. In spite of her vow to never don this disguise again, she had to know what happened and how better than to be in on the action? "What time?"

Sir Peter exchanged a look with his butler, who appeared to have a great deal more to say about things than Oldham did.

"Twilight lasts quite long this time of year," Radley said with a considering frown.

"I suggest you plan to arrive here about nine of the clock," Sir Peter said while Radley opened the front door for Emma to depart.

"Nine," she repeated, then headed for the hackney that awaited her as usual. She was all kinds of fool, she knew that, but she had to be with Sir Peter this evening.

Behind her the door shut with a firm click. Peter whistled softly while his butler shook his head at him.

"It should be a lark," Peter said with amusement.

"You ought not draw the young lady into this, sir," Radley gently scolded.

"Nothing will happen. I will have a last evening with good old George and that will be that."

Radley did not appear convinced.

"What? Are you to go to my nephew's house in the evening? Is that not dangerous? While no one is about early in the morning, with every passing hour you risk detection." Lady Titheridge voiced her concern while pacing back and forth in the little bedroom where Emma hurriedly changed into her dress.

"Can you not see?" Emma begged. "I simply have to know what happens. I am convinced that if there is someone who intends to steal the treasure, it will be soon and why not tonight?"

"The moon will be hidden by clouds, 'tis true," her ladyship mused after a glance out of the window. "And were one in pressing need of money, the sooner one struck, the better. But what about the swordplay? Do not tell me that Peter expects George to lurk about the house with sword in hand!"

"That I cannot say," Emma replied, taking one last peek in the looking glass before leaving the house to assure herself that she no longer resembled George, but looked herself.

"Well, do be careful. I shall be gone this evening, but Braddon will assist you in your disguise. For one final time," her ladyship concluded with a minatory look at Emma.

"He promised it would not be dangerous."

"I believe men are quite free with their promises at times. Do not believe a word of it, my dear."

Emma paused by the door, then with her head bent, said, "He mentioned that he intends to marry shortly and take his bride with him to Egypt. He did not reveal her name, but it is not Richenda de Lacey. I asked, for she is the only woman I can think of with whom he has been involved as of late."

"Except for yourself," Lady Titheridge said quietly.

Emma digested that remark while marching down the staircase to the front door and all the way home. There could be no conclusion, for she refused to accept that Sir Peter would possibly find her as possible marriage material—no matter that she loved him most desperately and would agree, even were he to be tardy in his request.

The day passed slowly. Serving tea to Mrs. Bascomb and Lady Hamley was tedious in the extreme. She had fetched Dr. Vernal's Tonic Pills for her dear mama when she was appraised of George's great news. Fortunately that was the topic for the afternoon, and Emma could listen with one ear while contemplating the upcoming evening with something between dread and anticipation.

"I would hope that Sir William and his family will come to London before too long," Mrs. Cheney said to Emma, penetrating her abstraction.

"I rather doubt that, for Lady Johnson is confined to her chair, as you may recall. She adores company and will love to have you and papa come to visit, I daresay."

The prospect of a trip south to Sussex occupied the remainder of the call until it was time for those dear ladies to depart, having exhausted every aspect of the subject.

"I would have you put on your pretty cream sarcenet this evening," Mrs. Cheney admonished Emma. "It is feminine, and those curls are neither here nor there if you catch my meaning. I cannot see why some gentleman has not sought out your papa for your hand. You have done well at the balls and assemblies, and not every girl acquires vouchers to Almack's. 'Tis a puzzle," she concluded before wandering up to her room for a quiet rest.

Emma watched her dear mama leave. Turning aside, the young woman faced reality. Not only would she have to cope with the sight of Sir Peter fawning over some other woman, she had to accept the fact that *she* must marry someone. Every girl must, or face a life of service as a companion or unpaid servant in the household of some relative. Unless she found someone she might tolerate, Emma would most likely end up helping out George and Beatrice.

However, Sir Peter wanted her by his side this evening. Emma resolved to do her best—whatever that might be.

The cream sarcenet was a success, judging by the reaction of her many partners that evening. Even Mr. Brummell praised her attire, and that must be appreciated. He came early for a change. Emma kept checking the clock on the far mantel as to the time.

"One would think you wish to be elsewhere," Mr. Brummell chided, to her embarrassment.

"La, sir, I merely look to the hour."

She looked in vain for Sir Peter to show his handsome face. Perhaps he was off to see that lady he claimed he was to marry.

"There you are," said a familiar voice some minutes later. "I have hunted everywhere for you."

She turned to face Sir Peter with a resigned sigh and an inward leap of her heart. "Did you try the dance floor? I have just finished a country dance, and that quite occupied my time and concentration."

"You look very lovely this evening. I like that dress. No Betsie tonight?" he inquired with a pointed look at her exposed neckline.

Her hand fluttered to cover her skin, for it seemed his gaze burned with intensity. "No, I do not wish to become tedious."

"Dance with me, my dear." The strains of a minuet floated out from the little orchestra led by Colnet, the conductor at Almack's who frequently played for private parties.

She could not refuse; polite Society would frown on such. She wanted to touch his hand and be at his side through the patterns of the elaborate dance, worse luck. If Amelia was a ninnyhammer, Emma was far more foolish.

She met his gaze over raised hands as they advanced and retreated in the pattern of the minuet. There was something seductive about the dance, a thing she had never noticed in the past. Was it perhaps her yearnings toward Sir Peter that prompted this emotion? She steeled herself to think of something else entirely until such time as she might leave his side and flee. What a blessing that it was so easy to persuade Mama to go home early.

At the conclusion of the provocative dance Emma curtsied gracefully, then thanked Sir Peter when he brought her back to her mother's side. She had to leave. She could not bear to see who he elected to dance with next. Besides, it was nearly nine of the clock, time to depart.

Emma dropped on the chair at her mother's side, professing concern. "Are you all right? You look dreadfully pale."

"Oh, mercy," exclaimed the susceptible Mrs. Cheney. "And I do not have Dr. Vernal's Tonic Pills along with me tonight. I believe I best go home. I am sorry, love, but I cannot take a chance with my poor health." She arose in a flutter of her fan, reticule, handkerchief, then leaned on Emma's arm to say good night to their hostess.

After one brief glance at the clock to note that the hands marked eight and thirty of the clock, Emma kept her gaze narrowly confined to the floor in front of them, the people they must pass. Not until they were safely down the stairs and out into the carriage did she relax. How she would manage to survive the remainder of this dreadful evening was beyond her.

She patiently fussed over her mother before leaving her in Hocknell's capable hands. The maid knew precisely how to soothe her mistress.

Emma wrapped a cloak about her and slipped from the house with no one the wiser.

Braddon urged speed once Emma arrived. "One does not know when a thief will decide to strike," she counseled while checking Emma's face and hair.

Giving the maid a swift hug for her excellent care, Emma then slipped from that house to dash over to Bruton Street. Radley allowed her entry, then silently ushered her to the workroom.

One candle burned on the far wall. Emma searched the shadows for Sir Peter, wondering how long he had stayed at the ball.

"I am pleased to see you could make it. I feared you would be deep in conversation with Sir William and forget all about the promise for this evening." Sir Peter came out of the shadows in the hall, dressed all in black.

"I do not forget promises," Emma replied indignantly.

"Good. I will remember that," he said softly. "Now, here is your sword. Do not use it unless necessary, but then aim to wound seriously, yet not kill. We must know—in the event there is a plot to steal the Egyptian treasures—who is behind it."

Emma accepted the sword, placing it on one of the glass-topped cases while she removed her coat. Looking down at her cambric shirt, she grimaced. "I stand out like a beacon."

Sir Peter disappeared, then returned with a black shirt in hand. "Here, pull this over your head. It ought to cover you nicely. Oh," he added, "I let it be known that I planned an evening of merrymaking—the ball, then the clubs."

"A night on the town," she whispered back, disconcerted to find his ear so close to her mouth.

Emma pulled on the black shirt as requested, then silently waited.

There in the warm darkness Emma glanced at the man she loved. What an utter rogue he was, although he could not possibly know the feelings he aroused in her. She dare not reveal them either way. As George it was unthinkable. As Emma it was prohibited. A proper young lady simply did not throw herself at the gentleman she desired.

So she sat in the deepening darkness, silently studying his face, what she could see of it, until she could see nothing but the faintest glimmer of his skin.

Then she heard it—a noise. Her indrawn breath was matched by Sir Peter. He placed a cautioning hand on her arm.

"I truly had not believed Emma. Apologize to her for me," he whispered.

He did not plan to see her again, Emma decided. Obviously, he intended to whisk his intended bride away from London and off to Egypt with no further ado.

The sound of breaking glass was heard, then muttered imprecations flowed through the air, turning it somewhat blue. Emma longed to cover her ears, but dared not move an inch. Which feeling was made more difficult by the proximity of Sir Peter. He had shifted until his thigh nudged hers. It must be accidental. In his effort to avoid detection, he most likely had hunkered down behind the display case.

A light flickered, then took hold as a candle flamed to life. Emma peeped around the case, hoping to see the man.

When he half turned, she nearly cried out. It was none other than Mr. Swinburne! A very changed Swinburne. Gone were the dandy's exquisite clothes and airs. Rather, he wore dark garb similar to that which Sir Peter had donned.

Sir Peter began to creep from behind one case to another.

He might have succeeded in achieving his goal but for his sword. It scraped across the floor just as he neared the villain, sounding like an explosion in the near silence of the room.

Swinburne whirled about from where he had been at work on the first of the cases. "Who's there?" He stared into the darkness, looking about with alert eyes.

Sir Peter waited. Emma carefully edged to the opposite direction from the one Sir Peter had taken. She took care to keep her sword up and away from any surface where it might accidentally make contact.

"I heard something." He froze in place, searching the shadows of the room.

"Meow."

"A blasted cat," Swinburne muttered in a voice unlike the one paraded before the ladies of the *ton*. Emma almost giggled at the imitation of a cat until she saw the animal jump up on one of the cases. It surveyed the intruder, then began to stalk him.

The cat knocked over one of the tools Swinburne had brought with him, and that noise startled both the cat and the thief. "Scat," he raged at the hapless animal.

The cat jumped down to disappear from sight.

Emma had lost track of Sir Peter and flinched when she heard the sound of tinkling glass as the first of the cases was smashed open.

Continuing to edge to the other side of Swinburne, Emma strained for some sign that Sir Peter was still in the room. She heard a whispered swish like that of a foot being slid on the floor.

"Cat?" Swinburne snarled. "Leave be. Go while you can."

His voice made Emma tremble with its hint of viciousness.

All at once the room exploded. In the flickering light of the candle Emma saw Sir Peter jump Swinburne, knocking him to the floor. She crept forward, sword still in hand. There was a great deal of thrashing about, curses yelled and muttered, threats shouted.

A lamp, then another lit the scene as Radley and Porter dashed into the room with Argand lamps in hand.

It was horrible. Swinburne had his arm about Sir Peter's neck and looked to be choking him to death. With a face turning paler and bluer by the moment, Sir Peter appeared defeated.

Emma rose from her place of concealment, sword at the ready. "You villain," she growled. "You complete knave, you scoundrel!"

He was clearly startled that a third person was in the room, one who crept up on him from behind, while the others advanced from the door.

"You were supposed to be out on the Town," he snarled at Sir Peter.

Giving a mighty lurch, Sir Peter freed himself from the awful clutch. However, he had to gasp for breath as he rolled away from Swinburne and could not attack.

Emma recalled the words Sir Peter had shouted at her in one of their sessions. "Seize the advantage of any momentary lapse your opponent may make," he had called out. Swinburne concentrated upon Sir Peter, evidently taking Emma to be of no account or worry.

She inched her way closer until she was within striking distance. Gradually shifting into a lunge position, she leaped forward and plunged her sword into Swinburne's shoulder.

The man screamed with pain, whirling about to see who had dared to strike him thus.

Emma held tightly to her sword, ready to strike again.

Sir Peter yelled, "Good show!" He staggered to his feet, then charged at Swinburne from the opposite side.

The villain moved in Emma's direction. She found herself unable to strike again and pushed rudely against the wall. She could feebly defend herself, but not advance. What a nuisance to be such a weak female at a time like this, she fumed.

"Prepare to surrender," Sir Peter called to Swinburne.

"Not on your life," the villain snapped. He grabbed the statuette of the goddess, and before Emma realized what he intended, he brought it down on her head.

The last thing she knew was a sinking sensation, with Swinburne leaping over her head and Sir Peter yelling something that sounded utterly dreadful.

*   *   *

When she came to, she tried to sit up, but could not. Her head ached, though that did not worry her. She was trapped, held in someone's arms—masculine arms covered in dark cloth.

"Who . . . what happened?" she whispered, aware that she sounded very groggy.

"Thank heavens," came a fervent prayer from none other than Sir Peter. He drew Emma close to him and cradled her most comfortingly in his arms. She found herself being stroked and petted and liked the sensations very much. Gentle kisses rained across her forehead and face between softly murmured words of reassurance and affection. The scent of costmary and lavender mingled with spice to tease her nose. His hands performed marvelously delightful caresses on her sensitive back and shoulders.

"Poor darling" and "precious treasure" were music to her ears after all she'd been through. She had for so long yearned to be clasped snugly against his manly chest, and now she nestled against him, savoring every sensation. The fine cambric shirt could not prevent the warmth of his body from offering her a sense of well-being in spite of her aching head.

She lifted a tentative hand to stroke his dear face. How she had wished to do such a thing. His beard rasped against her fingers, sending a frightfully intimate sensation through her.

And to have him gazing at her as though she were a chest of priceless jewels made her heart soar. Even in the dim light she could see the fiercely adoring look in those remarkable green eyes.

And then it hit her.

Gentlemen did not cradle and caress one another in her book. She struggled to rise and was prevented by being clasped more tightly, to her growing dismay.

"If anything had happened to you, I don't think I could bear it," Sir Peter said in a distraught voice. He tilted up her face and proceeded to kiss her until she thought she would swoon. If being caressed and cuddled until distraction was delightful, being kissed by Sir Peter Dancy was nigh unto extraordinary.

Then her senses battled to the fore, and she pulled away, although it really was most difficult when the rest of her clamored for another of those most remarkable kisses.

"You ought not do this, you know," she scolded. Her voice sounded odd and raspy, not unlike George's.

"Oh, it is quite proper. I intend to take you away with me. Seize the advantage and all that," he said in the most tender of manners, stroking her curls away from her brow before dropping a tiny kiss on her forehead.

"You cannot!" declared a scandalized Emma, struggling to rise against all the desires that had surfaced, urging the contrary.

"I feel certain your parents will agree, once I tell them the details," he said, caressing her cheek, soothing the hair over the bump on her head with gentle concern.

"But you think I am George," she wailed in distress.

"George? He's staying with Sir William," came the calm reply. Then Emma coped with another kiss more precious than the first.

When she could speak once again, rational thought finally won out. "You *know* I am not George?" she said with bewilderment and yet relief. "And you are not furious with me for deceiving you?" Her mind strove to grasp the new realities.

"My adored Emma, I have known who you were from the very first when you swiped George's invitation to the unrolling and came for a viewing of the mummy. You may sound a bit like him, even resemble him slightly, but believe me, George's legs cannot begin to compare to yours. I am not the least nearsighted, you see." He tilted his head in a considering way. "You shall wear the princess's necklace at our wedding. I think you would look wonderful in it."

At this an indignant Emma struggled to sit up and succeeded. Ignoring the bit about the necklace and a wedding, she punched Sir Peter as hard as she could and shouted, "You knew? And to think of all I went through. Oh!" She might have continued in this vein for some time, for she was highly incensed, but Sir Peter had other ideas.

He reached for her again and proceeded to settle the duel in a most satisfying manner.

And within moments Emma subsided into his arms, content to agree—for the time being.

Standing on guard by the doorway after having seen Harry Porter off with the villain, Radley beamed a smile of approval at the pair over by the Egyptian goddess now restored to an honored place in an exhibit case.

And as for the goddess, she smiled on all with her tender regard.